HORNS

HORNS

Jamison Roberts

sabre
press

The following story is based on true events. Names, characters, events, locales, and incidents are either the products of the author's imagination or used in a fictitious manner. Any resemblance to actual persons, living or dead, or actual events is purely coincidental.

While this exact scenario hasn't happened as of yet, who's to say it won't happen tomorrow or the next day? Who's to say it's not happening right now?

Published by Sabre Press

Tulsa, OK

ISBN: 978-1-7353068-1-0

For Mom:
My sounding board and the ultimate beta reader.

1

It was almost time. Galvanized by a swell of mounting enthusiasm, Mallory Rockwell battled to keep her emotions in check as she crept across the deserted road. A pair of ancient fieldstone walls loomed ahead, gleaming silver in the pale moonlight on either side of a gravel drive; one side stood intact, the other shattered with time—only a shell of its former glory. Built into the remains of the truncated right-hand wall, a stone pillar held the legend CRACKER FARM. Though partially hidden by an encroaching hedge, the words etched into the pillar's craggy face were as clear as they had been when they were carved more than a hundred years before. The wall to the left hugged a corner of the pasture, flanking the gravel drive for a bit before seeming to morph into a slatted wooden cattle fence. And there—a third of the way up the drive—were a dozen cattle pens marking their destination.

Her breathing came in ragged gasps and her hands trembled while her heart hammered, as if trying to bust through her sternum. She had no doubts about what she was going to do. Why would she? She was moments away from the one-in-a-million idea that might—no, *would* propel her skyrocketing to fame. And it was all hers.

"Mallory," Bethany huffed, struggling to keep up, though it wasn't the equipment the girl bore weighing her down, "this isn't a good idea."

Mallory sighed at her friend's stunning lack of vision. Bethany had even wanted them to set up in her living room— as if such a basic setting would do. There was no inspiration, no spark. She wasn't just mindlessly recreating some popular trend here, wasn't impulsively imitating someone else's idea. This was her idea, her vision, and she'd put a lot of thought into it. It couldn't look like she was just halfheartedly going through the motions. For this video, she needed to make a splash.

"It's perfect, don't you see?" She glanced back. "It's a bull, just like the lyrics. Just wait, it'll be amazing. By this time tomorrow, I'll be famous." Mallory sped up, hardly able to contain herself any longer; she had to bring her idea to life.

And what an idea. The song had just dropped; the two of them had been listening to the deliciously naughty new pop anthem, idly gazing over the pastures from Bethany's second-story window when inspiration hit. The plan had materialized almost fully formed in her mind, bringing with it a wave of goosebumps she could almost still feel crawling across her skin. A farm. A bull. It was just so clever. Any farm might have worked, but Bethany's house just so happened to sit on the edge of the development alongside a real live dairy farm; it was literally right across the street. It was fate. It was—*what was that word?*—serendipitous.

Mallory had wanted to get started as soon as the idea came to her, but, to her dismay, she hadn't been able to set it up right away. The wait for Bethany to arrange a sleepover had been nearly unbearable. All the while, she was afraid someone was going to steal her idea right out from under her. In the handful of days, she was so inconsiderately forced to delay filming, she'd scoured the web, waiting for the dreaded video to drop. Waiting for someone to take her idea and claim her glory. Astonishingly, nothing remotely similar to her vision had appeared.

She swept her palms across the rear of her jeans, wiping away the worst of the dampness as her tummy churned. Here she was, mere minutes from securing her dream. And she dared not put it off any longer. Even now, a horde of other creators would be rushing to put their spin on the new song. Each hoping theirs would inspire a new trend, to compel everyone to emulate their idea. And hers was the best; she just felt it. She just knew she would wake up tomorrow with thousands of views. Maybe tens of thousands.

"No," Bethany whined, barely audible over the muffled scrape of gravel beneath their feet. "I meant; we shouldn't be doing this."

Mallory merely sighed in response to her best friend's apprehension. She might have slowed down, but every fiber of her being urged her forward—it was all she could do to not let her coiled energy take over. It wasn't like this was the first voice of opposition from her friend, nor, she feared, would it be the last. She did feel somewhat guilty about springing the idea for the night's adventure on the girl only minutes ago. She'd assumed, rightly it seemed, that Bethany wouldn't be too keen on the idea, but she was an important aspect of her plan—well, her house was.

Mallory glanced back. Besides, the squat, lean girl was her friend. Her BFF. And Bethany was a good friend, despite occasionally being a buzzkill. She just didn't understand. And how could she? The poor girl's parents hadn't allowed her any presence on social media until a couple of weeks ago—after she'd turned thirteen. That kind of overprotectiveness blew her mind. Due to that excess caution, Bethany was woefully lacking in followers, and Mallory felt it was her duty to help the girl, her friend, by featuring her in some of her latest videos. And it had worked; together, in those few short weeks, Bethany's fledgling accounts swelled to well over a hundred followers. And that was just the beginning. It didn't hurt that Bethany was cute as a button: naturally sun-kissed skin, gleaming chestnut eyes, and just the hint of an underbite.

Gentle lowing drifted through the still night air, recapturing Mallory's straying attention, returning it to the animals ahead. Cattle. She couldn't believe it. Suddenly, she saw these lumbering beasts as more than a source of noise and smell. She couldn't even guess the number of times she'd complained to her parents, yet no matter what argument she brought forth, they seemed to be under the impression that since they'd known about the farm's presence when they moved in there wasn't much they could do. If she had to be stuck in hicksville with all these cows, she might as well use them to her advantage.

Mallory huffed.

She still couldn't even begin to comprehend why her parents insisted on living out in the middle of nowhere. Didn't they have any ambition? How could she become a successful influencer if she was stuck all the way out here? Didn't her parents see that? Didn't they want her to be successful? Sure, they'd supplied her with all the equipment she'd needed, but it wasn't enough. If they would just move to L.A., she was sure to get in with one of the established squads and absorb even more followers through collaborations and shout-outs. She'd tried to tell her parents as much, urging them to move, but they'd merely laughed off her pleas. The nerve. She'd simply resolved to work that much harder to realize her dream. Even if she had to do it by herself. *Especially* if she had to do it by herself.

"I don't want to get caught trespassing." Where before Bethany's apprehension had done no more than chip away at Mallory's enthusiasm, those sudden disquieting words—the girl's first salient concern—cleaved a wide fissure into her resolve.

A new chill swept through her as she tore her gaze from the scatter of milling animals and shot a fretful glance around. Ahead, the weathered two-story farmhouse sat nestled into the crook of the drive, dark save for the bands of glistening moonlight and a single porch light. Behind, a patchy hedge wall lined the street; the overgrown vegetation ought to provide some protection from what few drivers passed by at this ungodly hour. So far, they hadn't been seen, and while she didn't think it likely the farmer would appear so late, it was a possibility. They'd have to be careful.

When her eyes found Bethany again, she couldn't decide if her friend's ghastly pallor resulted from dread or just the pale moonlight bathing her features.

"Oh, it'll be alright. There's nothing to worry about," Mallory soothed, as much to comfort herself as her friend. Bethany was right about one thing; it wouldn't do to be caught trespassing. Not yet, anyway. After the video was completed and posted, it would only be a matter of time before it went viral. Then she'd be famous. Surely, they wouldn't discipline her too harshly. And even if they did; what of it? They couldn't take her success away, so it didn't matter. They were just minutes away.

Blessed silence reigned for mere moments before Bethany tried again. "The song isn't even about an animal."

"Oh, come on," Mallory sighed, "it's just a song!" Bethany's objections were really starting to needle her.

"It's just so dirty!"

"You didn't even know what it meant until I told you," Mallory said. "Besides, that's what makes it so fun, the double meaning."

"But—"

"Hush now," Mallory sighed, turning away, "I want to get this done." After that, the only sounds in the night were the gentle lowing of cattle and the slight crunch of gravel as they crept along the fence line.

Before long, they came to the first of the cattle pens, and she spotted the perfect prop. An enormous ebony-smeared bull—a biological ink blot—loomed on the far side of the enclosure, rooting through a pile of hay. With horns, it had to be a bull, right? Close enough. Still … Mallory tilted her head to the side— the equipment hanging below the animal clearly marked it as a bull. Weighing at least a ton, with wide shoulders and thick hindquarters, the massive ink-splattered bovine would be perfect.

Heart fluttering, struggling to contain the adrenaline coursing through her, Mallory swept her damp palms across her back pockets again. It was happening.

"Can't we at least film on this side of the fence?" Bethany begged.

Mallory stopped for a moment to consider. The size of the animal had suddenly given her pause—they didn't look this big flashing by along the highway—but as her gaze swept over the fence's thick wooden slats, then drifted to the beefy animal on the other side of the pen; she shook her head. It wouldn't do.

"No, that would look terrible. The bull needs to be clear in the shot behind me." She turned to her friend. "Alright, give me—"

"I don't know how safe—"

"Stop!" Mallory held up a hand, unwilling to rehash that conversation. How could a cow be dangerous? It was ridiculous. "Start filming. I want you to shoot some behind-the-scenes footage."

She wanted every moment captured for posterity. This could—*would* lead to her big break. She just knew. It was just so clever. She wouldn't be restrained by such a pathetic following any longer (only a few thousand, and many of them creepy old guys—that couldn't be helped). This would propel her into the big time. If she were very lucky, it might even be the first step to being like Charli—

"Mallory, please! I'm telling you, it's danger—"

"Enough," Mallory hissed.

"… ous," Bethany finished weakly.

"Are you going to help me or not?" Mallory let enough of her building exasperation bleed into her tone to finally silence her friend. Bethany slumped, nodding as she dug a GoPro from her pocket. She could just be impossible sometimes.

"Ready?"

"Yeah," Bethany whimpered as the camera chimed.

Three quick steps, weathered slats creaking under her weight, and Mallory was over the fence. Her pretty new boots, a gift from Daddy, squelched into the mud on the other side, sinking into the viscous material and invoking a loud snort from the bull. Her head whipped around. Eyeing the bull wearily, she tried to gauge his reaction. He'd stopped eating, but he was still on the far side of the pen, languidly turning his massive head to face her, his large dark eyes locked upon her baby blues.

"Are you getting this?" she whispered. Bethany just nodded. She seemed even paler in the moonlight. "Pass me the light."

"Do you think th—"

"Bethany," she commanded, "the light."

Bethany kept the camera obediently trained on her as she tentatively passed the ring light over the fence—for that, at least, Mallory was thankful. When she grasped the cold metal stand, goosebumps shot across her body, and her stomach fluttered. She was almost there. She extended the light's stand and jammed the tripod base into the mud. God, she hoped it was mud. Eww. Mallory shook at the thought; it almost made her want to pack up. If only she had …

With a quick adjustment to the stand's flip locks, she extended the ring light to the right height. She mounted her cell phone onto a clip in the center of the ring, then flipped a switch. As light flooded the night, the bull let out another loud snort behind her. A glance revealed that he'd turned to the side. His entire flank showed brilliantly. The profile view of the grand animal would translate wonderfully in the video. It was almost like he wanted to be filmed, wanted to be a star. Like her. Well, she would oblige him. She'd have to find out his name, give him the credit he deserved. It was only right. *I'm so close,* she thought as she adjusted the ring light's temperature to complement the cool moonlight.

Electricity arced down Mallory's spine, leaving her skin prickling and the hair across her arms standing on end as she hurried through the last few steps: scrolling through the app, selecting the sound to add, then queuing the music and priming the timer. She paused to study herself on the screen. She wore a faded pair of hip-hugging Wranglers—marred by stylish rips on the knees—with purple cowboy boots peeking out from underneath, and an old, lilac graphic tee knotted around her belly to show a thick swath of midriff. She dared not show too much skin for fear of her parents pressuring her to remove her content. It was as if they couldn't grasp the correlation between skin and views.

Subtly shaking her head, her gaze dropped to the corner of the screen. The bull's large dark eyes were locked on her as he loomed behind her, still presenting his flank. He seemed to be in no danger of charging—a big animal like that; how fast could he really move, anyway?

Her eyes returned to the red bar across the bottom of the screen. Before tapping it, she glanced over to Bethany. "How do I look?" she asked.

While Bethany was still dutifully filming, her gaze was locked on the bull, worry written across her pale face. Mallory let out an exaggerated sigh.

"I don't kn—"

"Bethany!" she said. "How do I look?"

The girl's eyes darted to her, ran up and down her profile, then flicked back to the bull. "Yeah, you look good," she murmured.

Well, that was reassuring! She didn't want to have to do this again. Her eyes fell to the ground; who knew what she was slogging through right now? Her new boots had surely been ruined, congealing mud and whatever else staining them. Well, it would be worth it. Once she made it big, she could afford any shoes she wanted—not that she had to do more than ask. She had Daddy wrapped tightly around her finger.

A movement drew her eye to the bull looming in the background, pawing at the earth and lowering its head. *Perfect!* At least it wouldn't be standing there like a side of beef.

The chorus rose around her: bulls snorted and groaned in the adjoining pens, blending with the more distant lowing from the pastures beyond the line of outbuildings. She broke into a smile at the thought; that would sound great under the music. She would have to play with the levels before publishing the video to get the right sound.

The bull snorted behind her, and Bethany let out a stifled squeak. Mallory's smile faded, and she ground her teeth; the girl's anxiety was really beginning to irritate her. She'd thought Bethany would be the perfect assistant for this video—she'd been so enthusiastic with the others. Mallory shook her head. It didn't matter, anyway; she'd get this thing shot and be famous.

She took a moment to calm herself, shutting her eyes and visualizing her first few moves—she'd come up with her own choreography inspired by some old videos she'd discovered online. After making sure Bethany was still filming, Mallory took in her image once again, then flicked her gaze to the edge of the screen where the bull was languidly spinning to face her in the background. *Oh, how perfect!*

Her heart fluttered in her chest. She was just fifteen seconds away from realizing her dreams.

Mallory tapped the glowing red icon on the bottom of the screen and took two quick steps back, lining herself up in the frame. A radiant smile washed across her face; she didn't even have to force it, as she watched the countdown fall to two, then one. Tinny music drifted from the speakers, somewhat drowned out by the bull's snorting as the recording began and she started her routine. Had he gotten louder? It didn't matter, she could lower his volume in post.

She moved with the music: stepping left and right, swaying her hips, and swinging her arms. Her smile brightened as the lyrics approached the chorus and she prepared for her *coup de grâce*, hopping into position—feet spread shoulder width apart, knees out and bent, one arm fell to grasp an invisible rope while the other drifted over her head, then she thrust her chest out and let her free hand wave as she rolled her hips to the catchy lines …

"… *just relax, sit back, and watch me ride my bull* …"

Then everything went wrong.

Bethany's scream merged with the bull's angry bellow, shattering the moment and causing Mallory to jump, thus ruining the perfect take. For a split second, fury flared within her as she shifted to confront her companion. What was her problem?

But the mask of sheer panic etched across Bethany's pale face, along with her frantic gestures, robbed any words from Mallory's lips.

Mallory gasped and whirled around. *No! No!*

The bull was closing, head down, back tensed, trotting in her direction. More than trotting, he was picking up speed. She stood frozen for a moment, whatever enthusiasm remained within her finally crumbling away. It couldn't be.

"Run!" Bethany's frantic cry shattered the stillness of the night, startling her into action. Mallory swung around and flew to the edge of the enclosure. A handful of bounding steps brought her to the fence, then she vaulted onto the first rung, all while the thudding hoofbeats closed.

Mallory was shifting her weight to scale the next rung when her smooth muck-caked boot slipped. Her foot plunged to the ground as she fell into the fence, then came a crushing blow from behind and another scream rent the night air.

2

"It's time, John. They need you."

As his eyes flew open, John Graham bolted upright in bed, drawing in a sharp breath. Blinking in the darkness, confusion crashed over him as a hand reached out and groped the mattress next to him, seeking the source of that ever-so-familiar feminine voice he'd longed to hear again. His desperate search ended in vain; the opposite side of the bed was cold and empty. Gone three years now, he would never see his Nancy again. Not on this side, anyway.

It had seemed so real. He tried to tell himself it must have been the tail end of a dream—it must have been—but that didn't seem right. What else could it be? If not a dream, why else would he hear her voice now? A voice he'd wanted to hear for so long. Why now? Why had it drawn him from a fitful slumber?

After a moment, he noticed a familiar pressure swelling in his bladder; it seemed to call to him more often in the night as the years progressed. He sighed, letting his eyes drift over to the clock on his bedside table. Squinting into the glow, the clock's cerulean numerals pierced the darkness, proclaiming the ungodly hour.

Two-thirty.

Sighing as he whipped the covers aside, John watched the

spectral white sheet slowly deflate across the emptiness beside him. A void once filled by the love of his life. His chest tightened as he tried to suppress the recurring pain swelling within him—the ache flowing from his fractured heart after his wife's passing.

His feet screamed as they brushed the hardwood floor, then he paused, finally registering the unusual sounds drifting up from the yard. He turned to the window, staring as if he could see through the closed curtains. What was going on?

It was common enough for the song of cattle to break up the silence of the night, but this was different. Their plaintive lowing sounded more nervous, as if they were unsettled by something: a new variable or an unknown presence. He took a moment to analyze the noise. He didn't detect fear, so he doubted it was a predator. When was the last time a predator got in with the herd, anyway?

If not a predator—

Eyes narrowing, he pushed his lean frame to his feet and shuffled across the room, grunting as aching joints protested.

Could it be thieves?

Long had he feared a day would come when he'd wake up to discover fewer cows than there ought to be. Though it seemed like something out of an old western, cattle rustling was still a multi-million-dollar concern. As with everything, cattle rustling had only gotten easier with innovation. Instead of driving cattle off on horseback, spending days in the saddle wrangling stubborn animals, crooks could drive away in a cattle trailer in a fraction of the time and sell them a few states away for a tidy sum.

He snatched a pair of old glasses on his way to the window, jamming them on with one hand while reaching out with the other. His eyes trailed the edge of the curtain as he swept it aside, scanning the landscape beyond. In the moonlit pastures to the far right, some of his ladies grazed, mere shadows in the silver-veiled fields. Closer, directly across the drive, a row of outbuildings stood cloaked in darkness save for the occasional dim bulb casting sporadic pools of light on the walls.

At last, the curtain unveiled the bullpens, thirteen large

enclosures set aside for his most valuable stock. And there, in the farthest corral, a harsh light bathed the enclosure, cutting through the expected darkness. That momentary glimpse was enough to propel him into action. Someone was in Old Mac's pen—a shape moving in front of his prize bull. His mind whirred as he snatched his cell phone from the bedside table.

His heart raced. Why would someone mess with Old Mac? Who would—

Kids …

While a full-grown man would've still been dwarfed by Old Mac, this shape had seemed smaller—positively tiny by comparison—it had to be a kid.

Could they be that stupid? Hobbling to the foot of his bed, he sighed as he pulled up the sheriff's number. Of course, they could. As the warbling tone poured from the device, he switched it to speaker, then tossed it on the bed. Waiting for the call to connect, he grabbed a crumpled pair of jeans and stepped into them. All the while, he tried to curb his anxiety and think rationally.

It had to be kids. Who else would mess with his cows in the middle of the night? The foolish teens were probably trying to go cow-tipping or something equally ridiculous. Ever since that new development had started going up across the way, he'd dreaded what an influx of suburbanites might bring. He'd feared a night like this. Why, oh why, hadn't old man Taylor's kids sold him the property instead of those developers? Sure, he hadn't been able to match the exorbitant prices they'd offered, but he would have put the land to much better use.

A housing development, he huffed. Rich folks, willing to commute, slipping further away from the hustle and bustle of the city, fleeing for the safety of the suburbs. He understood the urge as far as it went; the countryside was an oasis. But other problems accompanied an influx of people. It hadn't started at first, but already he'd received requests to quieten his livestock and better manage the odor. Imagine, moving next to a working dairy farm, and not realizing you would have to contend with the corresponding noises and smells.

"Sheriff's office. How may I help you?" A bored voice flooded the speaker.

He snatched the phone and wedged it between his ear and shoulder. "This is John Graham"—he jerked up his pants and buttoned them—"over at—"

"Oh, hello Mr. Graham," the young man interrupted. "This is Rodger Sandrich," then after a slight pause, "I'm a friend of Hailey."

John's brow bunched, momentarily taken aback by the interruption and the mention of his favorite grandchild—not that he'd ever admit it. Memories of a fair-haired teen tumbled through his mind. "Buck's boy?" he asked. When had he become a deputy?

"That's right," Sandrich said, sounding pleased to be remembered. "What seems to be the issue, Mr. Graham?"

The renewed wave of lowing complaints drifting through the window recaptured his attention.

"There's someone out here on my property … someone messing with my cows …" John explained on as he stepped into a worn pair of boots.

"Yes sir, I understand," Sandrich said, his voice shifting to a more neutral tone. "I'll have someone over there right away. One moment, please."

In the lull, John strode over and plucked an old bolt-action rifle from the wall. He didn't expect he'd need to do much more than wave it around. That should send any trespassers fleeing.

"Deputy Hire is on his way. He shouldn't be more than five to ten minutes away."

John groaned—ten minutes was a lifetime; anything could happen between now and then. "I'm going to head out. See what they're up to." After a moment's consideration, he scooped a handful of cartridges from a pouch draped over the gun rack and sent them clinking into his shirt pocket. All but one, which he inserted into the chamber.

"Sir, I don't think that's wise. You should wait until—"

A muted scream drifted up from the yard, seeming to reverberate off the walls. His chest clenched. *What happened?*

What's going on? John informed the young deputy of the latest development as he dashed along the hall, then hurdled down the stairs. Hardwood creaked and groaned beneath heavy footfalls, mixing with the booming clack of his boot's heels.

There was a moment of silence after he'd finished, then the deputy's clipped voice came back, "Do you think anyone's hurt?"

"Not sure," John gasped as he tore through the kitchen toward the side door.

"I'm going to go ahead and dispatch an ambulance as well. They should be there soon."

John barely heard the words over the booming pulse echoing in his ears as he disconnected. Heart thundering, the scream reverberated through his mind as he bolted from the house—the screen door slapping back against the wall with a loud *crack*. All he needed was for one of those kids to get hurt on his property—oh, the liability.

Perspiration trickled off his brow and pooled under his armpits as he bounded across the porch and practically leapt down the stairs. His boots clacked against the concrete path as he landed, then he was jogging across the lawn into the muggy night air.

A lot had happened in such a short time. He tried to understand what he saw—the harsh lamp he'd noticed earlier had fallen aside, illuminating shadowed shapes dancing along the gravel drive and silhouetting a gaping hole torn through the corral's wooden slats.

His breath caught. Old Mac was loose. *Where*—

His eyes locked on the massive shape of his prize bull looming across the drive. The big guy tossed his head, bellowing as he pawed at the grass. Something still had him worked up. John sped up, his legs pumping, burning with the effort, matching the blaze blossoming across his chest. Gasping as he ran, his lungs strained to take in enough oxygen. At sixty-five, though well past his prime, he was still in relatively good shape; he had to be to contend with the burden of running a farm.

Then he noticed a small shape sprawled across the lawn

behind the disgruntled bull; his pounding heart skipped a beat, the burning muscles in his chest clamping down. Hoping it was a trick of the light, his eyes strained to make out the shape—no more than a lump in the grass. After a few steps, the image coalesced into the shadow-cloaked body of a young girl. She was so small, laying there on the lawn—so small and eerily still.

Lightning struck, shooting along the length of his left arm as his ragged breathing devolved. Inky splotches darkened her clothes. *Oh! Good lord.* With that realization, came a sudden pressure, as if the bull had sat on his chest. John Graham's pace flagged, a sudden wave of fatigue crashing over him. Why? His prize breeder had never been overtly hostile. What was the girl even doing out here? What was she thinking? She should have known better than to mess with a bull. Didn't they teach kids anything anymore?

Sparks flew from the ring light as half of it blinked out, then flickered, snatching his attention. And there, cowering just inside Old Mac's corral, silhouetted by the eerie strobing light, was another small shape huddled next to the section of shattered fence. It wouldn't do much good if the bull decided to charge again. They must see that. Look at what just happened. Even at the best of times, a fence was only a suggestion to a ton of angry beef.

He fought the wave of fog swelling over him.

"Rrrrumph!" The loud bellow drew John's attention. Mac's hoof raked the ground, kicking up dirt and sod. The bull's eyes were locked on the cowering teen. John slid to a stop, boots gliding on the damp grass. He was going to charge. Old Mac was going to charge, and the little girl wouldn't stand a chance.

"Mac!" John bellowed, hoping to at least distract the bull.

No such luck. All he got in reply was a peeved snort and a toss of the head. Then Mac widened his stance, lowering his head and letting out another bellowed, "Rrrrumph!"

John cursed as the lightning forked along his left arm again.

Swinging the rifle up to aim was harder than it should have been with his unaccountably weakened arm. Fog rolled over him again, stealing his clarity for a moment before he was able to claw his way back. Traces of red and blue flickered on the horizon, just at the edge of his vision—the deputy. They wouldn't arrive in time.

John clenched his eyes shut for a mere moment as he called upon what remained of his strength—he'd recognized the symptoms, knew what they meant. But he couldn't dwell on them; he didn't have that luxury. He had to stop his prize bull; there was no other choice. He couldn't let anything happen to that little girl. Not another one.

Why, oh why, had this happened?

As Old Mac lunged forward, John adjusted his aim, emptied his lungs, and pulled the trigger. The explosion blended with the bull's truncated bellow, echoing out into the night as his vision blurred, and his Nancy called out to him again.

3

Apprehension swelled within Deputy Roscoe Hire as he slewed his patrol car into the drive, kicking up a wash of gravel. Moments before, a gunshot had rolled across the countryside. What would he find? Had old man Graham shot an intruder? God, he hoped not—the paperwork!

His headlights sliced a path through the wash of pulsing red, blue, and purple light bathing the drive. The gaping hole torn from the fence to the left scarcely warranted a glance. Instead, two shapes caught in the harsh beam of his headlights captured his full attention. A black and white mass lay unmoving in the grass—one of Graham's cows—and not far away, a smaller shape, just as still. He cursed. With the size of the shape, it could only be a child.

He stood on the brakes well ahead of the scene, kicking up a cloud of swirling stone dust. After jamming the cruiser's shifter into park, he flung the door open and hefted his bulk from the vehicle. He reached up and clicked his radio. "Dispatch, this is Sierra Delta Twelve. I'm 10-97. Over," he said, letting them know he'd arrived as he strode toward the compact form sprawled in the grass. His eyes didn't stray from the ghastly sight as he approached. What had happened? The girl couldn't have been older than thirteen or fourteen. Upraised sightless eyes reflected the stars and a film of crimson liquid had seeped from her mouth and nose, contrasting sharply with the emerald lawn.

"10-4, Sierra Delta Twelve. What's the situation? Over."

"Send EMS"—Hire dropped to a knee beside the figure, futilely checking for a pulse as he scanned the girl's body for trauma—"I've got one down." No telltale heartbeat pulsed beneath the cooling skin. What happened? Various superficial contusions marred the girl's body, but none seemed too serious. Obviously, something had happened. He dared not move the body. Where was Graham? *Please tell me Graham didn't shoot the girl. Please.*

"Rescue is …"

He missed the rest when a weak gasp drifted up from behind him, snatching his attention. He grunted to his feet, swinging around as—almost of its own accord—his hand drifted to his service weapon. A man lay several yards closer to the house, shrouded in the bull's long shadow. It was Graham. Hire took two bounding steps before he saw the bolt-action rifle lying next to the man. He slowed, gripping the butt of his pistol.

What else had he missed? What had happened to Graham? Hire knelt over the old man. His chest rose in ragged gasps, but his thready pulse barely registered beneath Roscoe's fingertips. He rose, letting his eyes rake the scene as he reached for his radio. While he reported the discovery, Hire unconsciously brought his other hand up and stroked his bushy mustache, his gaze drifting from Graham to the beefy animal's carcass. Then it clicked, the position of Graham's body, the gun, the crimson droplets spattering the drive. Graham had shot his own bull. Why? He glanced back at the dead girl. Surely, it had been too late for her; had he waited too long?

"… Graham's in a bad way," he concluded. "Better tell those buses to step on it," Hire paused. "And you better get the sheriff down here … she'll need to see this." He'd been hesitant to get the woman involved—they could take care of their town better than an outsider. But he couldn't not tell her. She'd be incensed. Her instructions about major situations had been clear, and he didn't need to draw any more of her ire. She wasn't his biggest fan, anyway.

A low moan drifted from the fence line. Roscoe swung around, ripping his service weapon from its holster and bringing the iron sight to bare on a small shape huddled behind a shattered section of fence. It took a moment to recognize the shape—another young girl; she couldn't have been more than eleven or twelve. She let out a small squeak, ducking her head back behind the slat as if hiding her eyes from him would make him disappear as well.

Upon seeing it was a child, Roscoe jerked his aim away, brandishing the side of the weapon, showing it was safe.

"It's okay," he soothed, extending a hand. "You startled me is all." Getting no response, he tried again. "Are you hurt? What happened here?" He already had a pretty good notion, but it wouldn't hurt to get confirmation.

Wide terrified eyes peeked above the slat, peering first at the gun as he slowly holstered it, then drifted to the shapes sprawled on the ground.

"Is that your friend?"

Another stifled sob burst from the girl's throat. She nodded, mumbling, "Bull got her." That was an understatement.

"What about Mr. Graham? What happened to him?"

"Dunno … he fell."

"He shot the bull?"

The girl merely nodded; she was in shock, that much was clear. He couldn't blame her.

Then he jumped as his radio squawked again, "Sheriff is on her way. ETA five minutes."

"Copy." He sighed as the undulating cry of an approaching ambulance rose in the night.

They didn't pay him enough for this.

Hailey Graham was yanked from the depths of slumber by an incessant ringing. Still half asleep, her bleary eyes searched for the source as she rolled over, only for a painfully bright blue light to lance into her eyes. Cringing away from the harsh glow, she screwed her eyes shut and groped for the offending piece of tech. Who would call her in the dead of night? It wasn't family—the ringtone told her that much—so when her hand finally landed on the phone, she flipped it over to cut off the annoying racket. Whoever it was could just call back at a more civilized hour.

Sighing into the blessed silence, she burrowed her face into her cool pillow and wrapped her sheet tighter around her. Not ten seconds later, the cursed thing erupted in a fresh wave of sound.

"Just answer …" Hailey tuned her roommate out as the girl went on, throwing in a couple of extra curses for her benefit.

"Urghh." Who would call her at such an ungodly hour? Hailey groped for the device yet again, jabbing the volume button to kill the ringer. Squinting involuntarily, she shied away from the new wave of brightness piercing her retina, though with a tremendous effort she forced one eye to remain open as she tried to read the display—the name of the person she fully intended to throttle.

Rodger? Her sleep-addled mind took an extra second to process that before her heart sped up. What was he doing calling her at … her gaze strayed up to the numerals in the right-hand corner. Normally, she'd have been thrilled to hear from him; but what the hell was Rodger doing, calling her at three in the freakin' morning? This was ridiculous, no matter how cute he was.

Hailey jabbed the screen to connect, ready to give him an earful for the unsolicited wake-up call. She slapped the phone against her ear. "What do—"

"Hailey, your grandfather is in the hospital." His urgent tone cut her off and those words, uttered just as she was beginning her tirade, stole the ire from her. Her groggy mind attempted to grasp the inconceivable statement, then her blood ran cold.

"Wh-What?" She bolted up in bed, the last vestiges of her exhaustion evaporating.

"Uggh," Georgie moaned dramatically, rolling to her side in the next bed over. However, Hailey's attention never wavered from the words echoing in her mind.

"There's been an incident at your grandfather's farm ..." Hailey lurched out of bed as he went on. She bounded across the room and flipped on the light. Her roommate's curses were muffled as she burrowed under her pillow. Hailey paid the girl no mind. She had to be just about the worst roommate ever, anyway. The summer semester couldn't end soon enough.

The intervening moments were a blur. As much as she tried, Hailey only absorbed snippets of the conversation as her mind whirred. Rodger prattled on while Hailey threw on the first things she saw—a pair of nylon shorts and her old cowboy boots were added to her oversized nightshirt. Then she grabbed her keys. She had hazy memories of them cutting into her palm as she whipped the door open and fled from the room, leaving the overhead light on and the door standing wide open.

Later, she would vaguely remember asking questions and receiving answers as she rushed through the dorm, but God only knew what had been said. When Rodger ended with what he knew of her grampa's status—which wasn't much—she mechanically thanked him and rushed out into the night.

Groaning, Michael Graham reached over and snagged his phone from the bedside table. He cut off the infernal ringing that had yanked him from a dreamless sleep as bleary eyes found the name illuminated on the caller id. He took in a sharp breath as his heart pounded. Hailey—his daughter's name displayed in bold white letters on the dark backdrop. What was his daughter doing calling him at this time of night? It couldn't be good. Had something happened to her? Was there an emergency?

"Who is it, dear?" murmured a groggy voice. His wife shifted beside him, reminding him to breathe.

"Hailey." Still dreading the call for some inexplicable reason, he had yet to answer it. He finally accepted the connection and brought it up to his ear. "Hailey wha—"

"Daddy! It's Grampa," she blurted. "He's in the hospital."

As he sat up, his world narrowed; every other concern was

pushed to the periphery.

"What happened?"

"I don't really know. I got a call from Rodger. My friend Rodger. He's a deputy now. You remember Rodger, don't you? He's Stacey's brother." A horn blared in the background, cutting off her rambling explanation. "He said something happened on the farm. I didn't quite catch the whole story. But grampa collapsed, and they rushed him to the hospital." The squeal of brakes bled through the line, followed by a muted horn blaring in the background. "I'm heading there now."

"First of all, slow down. You won't do anyone any good if you get killed on the way to the hospital." His wife's bedside lamp burst to life, flooding the room with illumination. The bed shifted, and he felt her presence at his shoulder, her soft breath tickling his neck.

"How did you kn—"

"I have ears."

"Okay." He heard Hailey fighting to control her ragged breathing. "Okay, you're right."

"Good!" His mind spun. "Now, I'll try to catch an early flight, but it'll still be several hours before I can be there."

"But you are coming, right?"

"Of course, I'll be there as soon as I can, baby."

"Okay, Daddy." Relief filled her voice, and her breathing had almost returned to normal. "I just pulled up to the hospital." A brief chiming carried over the line, then the thump of a shutting door. "I'll call you as soon as I know anything."

"Okay, sweetie."

As the line went dead, Lexa spoke up. "What's happened? Is Hailey all right? Who's in the hospital?"

Michael reached over, cupping his wife's cheek as he gazed into her glistening chocolate eyes. "Hailey's fine, hon," he assured, "perhaps a little panicked. It's Dad. Something's happened."

"What?"

Michael grimaced. "I'm not sure. I didn't get a full picture." He squeezed her cheek before rolling out of bed. "He's collapsed on the farm." Michael paced as he relayed the scattered picture Hailey had drawn. But there were still so many unanswered questions. Not the least of which was why anyone would be at the farm at this time of night. What had happened?

He studied the clock. "It'll still be hours before I can catch a flight. And I'll need to call Caleb," he said, already bringing up his brother's number. But he hesitated. What a way to have to wake your sibling.

"I'll come with you," Lexa offered.

He started nodding, then considered it and slowly shook his head. "No ... you have your meeting tomor—" he paused, glancing at the clock again, "this evening—"

"It can wait. It's not as important as your dad."

Michael raised his hands in surrender. "I know, but you've been preparing for the last month. You could really use that contract. Besides, we don't know how bad Dad is. Why don't you wait until tomorrow morning, then bring the twins down with you? We'll make a weekend out of it. Dad would love a visit from the boys. It might be just the thing he needs to raise his spirits."

"Are you sure?"

"Yeah." Already moving on, Michael glanced back at his phone and tapped the screen, his mind creating a list of what he needed to do:

Email his boss.

Book the plane ticket.

Pack a bag.

The languid pulse of red and blue light broke up the darkness as Sheriff Johnson stood, staring at the scene. Yellow crime scene tape fluttered in the light breeze, its rustle merging with the mournful lowing of cattle. What a mess. Even now, hours after the incident, she couldn't quite wrap her head around what had unfolded.

A thirteen-year-old girl; dead—the victim of some stupid stunt. Another young girl was so traumatized she hadn't been able to complete her statement—much of what they got was undecipherable due to intermittent episodes of weeping. And they'd rushed old man Graham to the hospital in critical condition. It appeared to be a heart attack, possibly even as he killed his own prize bull. The massive animal lay dead over yonder, blood soaking into the grass. It was so big they'd had to call for a crane to remove the carcass.

She grunted. *What a circus.*

Several of her deputies had been consigned to barring a salivating press, rabid for answers. Luckily, Graham had been rushed away before any reporters had arrived, but they'd still been processing the scene when the first news van appeared. The broken body of Mallory Rockwell had been on full display, caught in gory detail. She'd had to have her deputies drive the press back to a more respectful distance, which only drew complaints and questions about what they were hiding.

She'd ignored their grumbling; freedom of the press was all well and good, but that didn't extend to trampling a crime scene. Was it a crime scene? She'd have to treat it as such until she was certain.

While the fervor had long since died out, the odd, unlucky cub reporter still haunted the outskirts of the scene, demanding transparency, insisting any new tidbit of information be shared immediately.

Johnson huffed. It wasn't like she was deliberately keeping things from them just to spite them—not that she wasn't tempted—her department was still trying to get a handle on things, still searching for answers.

A broken phone had been recovered inside the shattered corral, half buried in moist earth, presumably belonging to Mallory. There had also been an HD action camera, though it had a cracked lens and a shattered screen. She could only guess at some of the night's events until she could get someone to pull the video from either device. She reconsidered all the facts she'd gleaned again for the umpteenth time.

Across the street, the upper story of Bethany's house was visible, looming above the decorative fence. As best as she could tell, the two girls stole from the residence in the middle of the night. They'd probably assumed there was less chance of being discovered trespassing, or otherwise deterred. About that, at least, they'd been right.

Between the time the call came in and when her deputy, Hire, arrived, the old man had rushed out to confront the intruders. She could only imagine what went through Graham's mind when greeted with the broken body of the young girl. What a sight. It was no wonder his heart had seized. It didn't look good for the man. She'd received word from her deputy at the hospital that Graham's granddaughter had swiftly arrived and taken up residence in one of the waiting rooms. The poor thing.

And poor Mallory's family was beside themselves with rage and sorrow. The father had already demanded Graham be brought up on charges, if he survived, threatening to sue anyone and everyone. It didn't seem to matter that everything they'd learned so far pointed to the incident being the girl's fault. There'd even been a wild suggestion that old man Graham's entire herd be slaughtered. She wouldn't allow that; it wouldn't be justice, only revenge.

"Sheriff." Her radio crackled. "Sheriff, are you there?" the fuzzy voice came again.

"Johnson here, what is it?"

"I have news on Graham." The static cleared and the voice became recognizable; it was Perkins, the man she had at the hospital.

"Report." Please let him be okay. Please.

"He's gone." Sighing, she cursed. "He coded thirty minutes back, but they just called it."

She slumped. Another death. The night's events had doubled the year's death toll, bringing it up to four. Two had been natural causes—old age—and arguably, so was John Graham's. But the girl? Johnson sighed.

As the hours crawled by, Hailey sat in the waiting room, curled into one of the ubiquitous vinyl chairs. Hugging her knees to ward off the chilled air flooding through the vents, she stared blankly at the far wall, mind roiling as the occasional tear still trickled down her cheek. Neither the vague buzz of florescent bulbs nor the cloying disinfectant pervading the sterile room detracted from the terrible thoughts warring in her mind— horribly unimaginable dreads.

Arriving scant minutes after she'd received the call, Hailey had found herself whipping into the hospital's parking lot—she must have set a new land speed record from the campus; it was a miracle she hadn't had an accident. Other than the vague knowledge that she'd sped the whole way, she hardly recalled the trip. Everything since Rodger's call had been a blur.

And as fast as she'd gone, she was already too late; she just hadn't known it yet. She'd only been allowed a fleeting visit with her grampa—mere moments. It hadn't been enough; would never be enough. Even if he lived another sixty-five years, it wouldn't have been enough.

She sniffed, hugging her legs tighter to her chest as she thought of the warm smile she'd been greeted with when she'd flown to her grampa's side and hunched over his bed. Grampa had tilted the oxygen mask to the side, reaching out to her, beckoning her to him. His raspy voice had uttered her name, but it had been too much for him and he was forced to lower the mask back into place, instead squeezing her hand while she tried to give him the usual reassurances.

It didn't make sense; he'd been so weak. She'd never seen him so weak, and it broke her heart. He was a vigorous man, always had been. As far back as she could remember, Grampa had always been hard at work around the farm, always occupied with some task or other—frequently accompanied by a 'helpful' little girl, who often proved more of a hindrance.

He had to be okay—he just had to.

She couldn't have been there for much more than a minute before the beeping started. The pulse monitor had screamed as the steady terrain of hills and valleys fluctuated wildly, becoming an unreadable tremor. The alarms whipped doctors and nurses into a frenzy, and they came swarming into the room. Pushed aside, Hailey had huddled in the corner, all but forgotten in the melee. Cursed only to watch as they forced a tube down her grampa's throat, stripping away his warm, deep voice.

Then they'd noticed her. Her gaze never left his sad eyes as she was practically dragged from the room. If she'd known it was the last time she'd see him, she would have fought harder, insisted she be allowed to stay in the room.

She'd spent an eternity forgotten in the hallway as they'd tried to stabilize him. Hours later—or was it minutes—the team trickled from the room with good news. One kindhearted young doctor had joined her on the floor; she couldn't even remember sitting down.

"We've stabilized him for now, but he's not out of the woods yet," she'd said.

Hardly paying attention, Hailey had craned her neck, trying to peer into the room. "Can I see him?"

"Not right now. We've got to run some tests; besides, he needs to rest."

"I can't go home."

"You don't have to, but I think we can find you a more comfortable place to wait."

The sympathetic young woman led her to a waiting room. After a while, one of the other doctors had appeared, discussing tests and procedures, then reviewing next of kin and legal decisions. She'd listened, only half aware, mechanically answering whatever she could. Then it was time to call her father again. That hadn't been easy. She only had vague recollections of that conversation as well.

"… Daddy, they think Grampa's had a heart attack …"

"… they're running tests …"

"… don't know if he'll make it …" That last had been the hardest.

Her dad couldn't get there until noon at the earliest. She'd understood that, of course, but had somehow hoped for a miracle; that he could've just transported directly to her side. As it was, she'd resigned herself to a solitary night of restless tension.

Hailey's eyes flicked to the wall clock yet again; it must have been the thousandth time in the last few hours. So many hours, so long alone. She'd dreaded the thought of being by herself, almost as much as the thought of waking a friend. She could have called someone, she knew. Any number of her friends would have rushed to the hospital just to sit with her; be by her side. But she didn't want that, couldn't stand being a burden.

How many times had the doctors popped in? Every time a mixture of anxiety, hope, and fear roiled within her, an unwinnable battle waging in her gut. Then she'd received news of another episode, after which they'd rushed him to emergency surgery. Coronary rhinoplasty and stinting—*no, that wasn't right, was it?* She couldn't think straight.

A movement drew her eye as a tall, lithe man slipped into the room. Half expecting it to be the doctor with news, good or ill, disappointment flared within her for a moment, when she saw it was only Rodger. Her fuzzy mind tried to make sense of his sudden appearance. Then her heart swelled, chest tightening she tried to fight back tears.

"Rodger? What are you doing here?" Her eyes darted to the wall clock. *What time is it?* Her numb brain took a few moments longer than it should have to work out the cipher. A quarter past six.

"I just got off," he said, scanning the chairs next to her, then the rest of the room. His brow crinkled. "Are you here by yourself?"

She nodded, taking in his angular face: the brilliant emerald eyes, the mussed straw-colored hair that just happened to stay in place all day, and the thin stubble running across his square jaw. "Dad's flying in. But he won't be here 'til later."

Rodger nodded, shuffling over. "If you don't mind some company, I could sit with you awhile."

Aw. That was so sweet. "I don't mind." She shook her head as more tears trickled down her cheek.

Rodger slipped in next to her, wrapping an arm around her. "How are you?"

She merely shrugged as she leaned into him. There wasn't

much more to say.

"Have you heard anything?"

She slowly shook her head. "Not for a while. They took him to emergency surgery a while ago …" He listened intently as she told him what little she remembered. She paused, then finished, "I don't know what I'll do without him."

Rodger squeezed her shoulder, and her heart fluttered. "You can't think like that. I'm sure he'll be—"

The doctor bustled into the room, locking eyes with her, a grim expression etched in the deep lines of his dour face. Before he even said a word, the dam broke, and tears flowed from Hailey's weary eyes. She knew.

4

Hailey hunched behind the steering wheel of her old Dakota, sitting in the hospital parking lot as a vague sense of unreality clouded the edges of her mind. She was numb with shock. How was her grampa, her rock, gone? How did that make any kind of sense? He'd been so healthy, always so healthy. The tall, trim man had appeared as if he'd live forever. It just wasn't possible. Couldn't be possible. Yet, why would the doctors lie? Why would Rodger play along?

They wouldn't—that was the simple truth.

It was as if a gulf had opened within her chest and the only things spilling in were despair and grief. The weight of it pressed down on her. She'd lost her hero. Her anchor. The man she trusted above any other. She already felt herself drifting toward that chasm.

Hailey squeezed her eyes shut and attempted to push the swirling anguish away. Now she had to call her dad yet again, had to let him know. How could she tell him his father had passed? In a daze, Hailey extracted her phone. Her thumb scrolled through her contacts, looking for her father, then tapped the green phone beside his number.

He answered on the first ring. "What's the news, Hailey,"

"Daddy, Grampa is gone," Hailey tried to hold in a sob.

With a deep sigh, she could almost hear his remaining hope melt away.

"I see," he murmured, then paused for a moment.

"Daddy—"

"I'll be there in a few hours. Lexa will bring the boys tomorrow."

"Daddy, I don't know what to do."

"I know honey; I know. Neither do I." He sighed heavily, obviously fighting to maintain control. "Have you been up all night?"

"Yeah."

"You should get some rest."

"I have to milk the cows."

"Every day?"

"Twice a day,"

"Can you take care of the livestock? Do you know what to do?"

"Of course, I've been helping Grampa with the cows for years."

"Right. Sorry. I knew that. I need you to hold down the fort. Can you do that for me?"

"Yes, Daddy."

"I'll see you soon, sweetheart."

After that uncomfortable task was complete, she reached for the ignition, only to find the keys still there, and the truck running. She sighed and grabbed the shifter. She needed to be home.

By the time she'd pulled her old pickup off the blacktop and turned onto the gravel drive, Hailey regretted refusing Rodger's kind offer to drop her at home. The short drive had been a true test. The weight of her loss blended with a wave of utter exhaustion. And she still had work to do.

Gravel popped under her tires as the pickup crawled past the shattered corral fence that had been part of Old Mac's pen for so many years. Traces of crimson spattered the ground across from the broken fence; she didn't know who it belonged to and tried not to think about it.

Poor Old Mac. Hailey had known him all his life. Though she'd always been told to stay away from the bulls when she was younger, she had often snuck over to visit with the big guy. He'd never been more than curious with the young intruder, eyeing her through the slatted fence and allowing her small hand to reach in and stroke his muzzle.

Ten years ago, the then two-year-old bull won the title of Supreme Champion at the state fair, surpassing his sire, who'd won a slew of championships himself. Grampa had been so proud. She could still remember the beaming smile as he proudly waved the ribbon around the house. Gramma, long since gone, had been beaming as well, even though the bull's prize overshadowed her award-winning homemade rhubarb pie.

The win had added another lucrative aspect to her grampa's business as well. Farmers from across the tri-state area had paid a hefty fee to get one of their ladies a 'date' with Old Mac. And the big guy never lacked for dates. Old Mac was popular; he must have personally sired hundreds of calves—the number of offspring catapulted into the thousands when you included artificial insemination, another of her grampa's side hustles.

She tore her gaze away from the ruined fence. It didn't matter now. Mac was dead; Grampa was dead. She had to pick up the pieces.

Hailey continued past the collection of bullpens before coasting to a stop next to Grampa's new, gleaming black Ram 2500, parked in front of a line of barns and outbuildings. The first and largest of the outbuildings was the parlor barn. Though the building had only been added five years earlier and had the latest equipment and specifications, the facade was a portrait of distressed crimson siding with white accents that complimented the farm's simple wooden fences and weathered white farmhouse to give Grampa the rustic esthetic he preferred.

Hailey cut the engine and was immediately greeted by the lilting cadence of protesting cattle. Eager for the day's milking, the ladies huddled along the fence beside the barn. Her appearance only spurred them to greater volume. Ever the clock watchers, cows were notorious and would complain loudly if their human attendants were late for the milking or feeding.

Hailey groaned, resting her head on the steering wheel as the chorus of low calls faded into the background. How would she get on without her grampa? Oh, she could slog through the work, no matter how hard; it was the idea of doing it all alone that gave her pause. Now she understood how he felt after Gramma died.

She only lingered for a minute or two. There was no point in delaying the morning's work—besides, she had a feeling the cows wouldn't stand for it. That was all she needed: disgruntled livestock.

"Okay, ladies, I'm coming. I'm coming."

Then her door creaked open, and she went inside.

While the parlor barn was built to administer to the cows, they only had access to about half of the structure, including a large holding pen, the milking parlor, and a six-foot-wide corridor running along the northern edge of the barn dubbed the return alley. Leaning against a stainless-steel gate, Hailey waited in that wide corridor as the steel door trundled open, clattering and rattling as it coiled overhead. The rolling door served as both entrance and exit for the herd.

"Come on, ladies," she encouraged as cattle poured in, still bemoaning the wait. "I know. I know, girls. I'm sorry I'm late." They seemed unsatisfied with her apology. As the press of protesting cattle flowed past and into the holding pen, their bulk jostled the gates to either side of the passageway, sending a clangor rising off the rattling metal.

Hailey's eyelids seemed to have gained weight as she yawned into the clamor, halfheartedly struggling to keep count as they passed, making sure all the ladies made an appearance. For the most part, she could count on them to turn up—they seemed to enjoy the process, plus the lure of the sweet cake was strong—but occasionally, one would fail to show up. Luckily, there weren't any missing today. She didn't need the added headache of chasing one of the ladies down on top of everything else she was dealing with that morning.

After the final cow lumbered through, Hailey detached the

thick metal gate and swung it across the lane, simultaneously securing the jostling cattle into the holding pen and opening the return alley for their ensuing departure. Sixty-odd cows in all waited in the space. Not an enormous herd, but enough to suit their needs. *Her* needs. There had been plans for expansion until the pandemic put a hold on them. She might need to revisit that, but for now, she had enough to deal with.

With the cattle safely waiting in the holding pen, she turned to a few tasks she had to complete before she could begin the day's milking.

Hailey went around front and detached the milk transfer line, switching it from the wash system to the bulk tank. The milk cooling tank stored thousands of gallons of milk, keeping it fresh and agitated, ready for the tanker to pick up. Only the crown of their massive stainless-steel bulk tank jutted through the wall in the front hallway; the rest extended into the next room, almost filling it. She ducked into the machine room on the other end of the tank and switched on the pumps, then headed around the corner into the changing room, passing her grampa's office— she dreaded going in there.

The changing room was a large space that doubled as a break room for Grampa's many permanent employees—namely, her. On one side, a bank of lockers lined the wall, and on the opposite side was an old couch where she'd spent many an hour.

Standing in front of her locker, Hailey stripped out of her mismatched outfit, then paused, inspecting her reflection in the mirror mounted inside. Five-eight and slim, she had broad shoulders—toned from years of farm work; she also had the uneven tan that went along with hours in the sun in a variety of outfits. She drew the hair off the sides of her heart-shaped face, bringing it up and snugging it into a ponytail. Though she wouldn't be confused for a supermodel, she was pretty enough. *Plain*, but pretty. Despite being red and puffy from hours of intermittent weeping, brilliant sapphire-blue eyes gazed back at her. Her grampa's eyes, her father's eyes. She idly fingered a large, raised mole perched along the side of her nose between her wide-set eyes. When she was younger, it had brought scorn from some of her classmates and she'd wanted it removed, but as she'd matured, she became more accepting and grew to regard it as unique.

The grumbling calls of cattle drifting through the building urged her to hurry. She slipped into a dull gray jumpsuit with the farm's logo embroidered on the back, topping her uniform off with a pair of waterproof rubber boots.

A wave of lowing complaints swept over her when she finally whipped open the door to the parlor. She paused. Was it her exhaustion, or did they seem even more impatient than usual? *I mean, I am late but—*

She shook off the thought; that was it. The schedule; had to be.

Bare concrete and stainless-steel equipment adorned the milking parlor, and beyond that, cattle jostled restlessly in the holding pen across the room. Hailey eyed them as she bounded across a narrow alley, slipped through a pass, then trotted down into a depression that seemed to be hewn into the surrounding concrete. Commonly called the pit, the depression put the cow's belly at eye level, allowing for better access.

On either side of the room, five milking stalls were set up for side—or tandem milking. Not only did this give the operator a side view of the udder, but it also put the cows at ease by allowing them to see what you were doing, thus fostering a better working relationship with the cattle. They hated having anyone in their blind spot.

Hailey prepped the stalls, pulling each vacuum pump cluster off the wash trays, and letting them dangle on a cord in front of the stalls. Water trickled from the silicone-lined milk claws; evidence that the automatic wash cycle had run after the previous milking session.

Automation streamlined the operation, allowing one person to milk the herd if needed. On the far side of the pit, Hailey pressed a button to start the sequence and the rear gate of the nearest stall swung open, then the parlor's entry gate parted to allow the first cow to wander in. Thoroughly accustomed to the process—and lured by the promise of a sweet treat—the cow lumbered to her own stall, taking her place before the gate closed behind her. Then the automated sequence opened the next gate, admitting another cow, then another, until all five stalls on the left were full.

Sensors read the RFID (radio frequency identification) tags, telling the system how much cake to drop—the more milk a cow gives, the more cake she gets. As the cows munched their treats, Hailey started the sequence on the opposite side, then crossed to the front of the pit, snatching a pair of blue nitrile gloves as she went—she had to be sanitary—milk production depended on the health and happiness of their ladies. While the second wave of cows flowed in, she moved to the first cow in the line. Hailey drifted through the motions as she had done hundreds, thousands of times before, letting the animals' contented lowing wash over her and blend with the buzz of pumps to lull her mind. There was a comforting repetitive order to the entire process.

She took a clean cloth and wiped down the teats, then sprayed the first squirts onto the floor. Known as stripping, the action simultaneously signaled the cow to let down her milk and presented a sample for Hailey to check. Luckily, the pure cream color was the correct hue. If there had been clotting or any sign of discoloration, she wouldn't have allowed the possibly contaminated milk to be transferred into the bulk tank. As it was, she slipped the silicone-lined vacuum hoses over the teats on each quarter of the udder, then moved to the next animal in line, then the next, following the same process over and over. After she had the first five going, she crossed the pit and performed the same procedures on each cow in that group.

By the time she'd finished setting up the second group, the first five were going strong. She waited, letting the pumps extract the milk, then one after another, as the milk dried up, the clusters automatically detached, leaving a film of disinfectant solution behind, and the automated system opened the exit gate for each stall in turn. As the freshly milked cows plodded toward the exit, the entry gate parted to admit new cows to take their place.

Her eyes strained to remain open as cow after cow passed

by. It seemed like a never-ending wave of cattle, but that was only her fatigue talking. Exhaustion battled within her by the time the clusters fell from the final cow, and the gate released her. Hailey blinked, yawning as the vacuum pumps kicked off, putting an end to the incessant humming, and the last vestiges of white liquid were carried away. Then Hailey began the now tedious task of prepping the parlor for the evening milking session by placing the clusters into the wash tray's self-cleaning nozzles.

She was so intent on retreating to bed that, for the first time ever, she did a truly poor job of rinsing out and spraying down the stalls.

The morning's work had gone smoothly enough, though the rumble of the vacuum pumps almost lulled her into a doze. Or had it? She could have sworn there were times when the clusters came off almost as soon as she'd slipped them on. But it made no matter.

She staggered along the return alley to make sure all the cows had departed, then reset the gates and lowered the barn door. Hailey fought to stay awake as she slogged through to the rear of the barn; there was one task she'd yet to complete before she could drift off into the sweet oblivion of slumber.

She had to feed the calves.

Hailey prepped the milk cart in the calf kitchen, filling it with fresh pasteurized milk drawn from the bulk tank, then wheeled it out to the calf shed next door; an open-aired structure housing all the calves until they were ready to join the herd. A line of calf pens just inside held the youngest calves, only a few of whom were still bottle-feeding. For those, she filled a fresh bottle and slid it into its holder, letting them get to it. The rest were served their milk in a large bucket hanging outside the stall. She watched for a moment as the calves poked their heads through the bars and greedily inhaled their meal.

The final group of calves was in a large rearing pen at the back. The ten calves milling around the space mooed in welcome. Troughs running along the barred pens still held food from the previous night; the calves always had more than they needed. Hailey went ahead and topped them off.

That task completed, Hailey replaced the milk cart, then lumbered back through the milking barn, stripping out of her jumpsuit as she went. She forwent a shower, opting instead to crash on the old orange and yellow plaid couch in the changing room.

After sprawling on the sofa, Hailey peered at her phone. Apparently, the news of Grampa's death hadn't filtered out to her friends yet. Once it had, she was sure she would be flooded with condolence calls and messages. She didn't feel like dealing with that, so she shut the device down and curled into the cushions, snuggling under an old threadbare sheet. Besides, as her father said, she needed rest.

Half expecting to dwell on her loss for hours, it couldn't have been more than a minute before she'd drifted off.

5

"Hailey, honey!" Her father's voice drifted in through the open door, echoing off the walls. Hailey groaned and rolled over, snuggling deeper into the old couch. The plush, cushioned fabric cradled her in its warm embrace. "Hailey!" There was a note of panic creeping into her father's voice.

She fought through her fatigue to respond. "In here," she croaked.

"Hailey?!"

She cleared her throat and tried again. "In here, Dad." This time it came out louder, clearer. And the corresponding footsteps thumping along the concrete hallway told Hailey her dad had heard her. His silhouette appeared against the light flooding in from the hallway.

"Oh, thank goodness," he said, flicking on the light. She groaned, cringing away from the sudden brightness. "I got here, and you were nowhere to be found. The house is unlocked and open. No sign of you. Your truck is here, and Dad's, so I figured you hadn't gone anywhere. I started to fear the worst. What are you doing out here?"

For a moment, her heart skipped a beat as her father's features came into focus. Looking down at her were her grampa's worried, compassionate eyes—the same wide-set blue eyes she'd inherited; the strong jaw; and matching chestnut hair. As her vision cleared, she was able to spot differences: a softer sculpt to her dad's stubbled jawline, a lack of age lines hewn into his features, and an absence of gray that had been steadily creeping through Grampa's rich brown hair.

"I'm fine, Dad." She groaned, turning over. "I was just tired, so I decided to crash here." Her eyes strained to remain open. "What time is it, anyway?" she murmured into her pillow, feeling the coolness soak into her cheek.

"It's almost one. Are you going back to sleep?"

"Yeaaa …"—her response trailed off into a yawn. "Maybe a couple more hours. The cows don't need to be milked again until six thirty."

"I'd feel better if you came up to the house," he said.

"Ohh, but Dad—"

"No buts," he interjected. "Come on, it'll only take a minute."

"Fine," she sighed, stretching under the sheet. The smooth fabric against her skin reminded her of something else. "I need to get dressed."

"Alright." Her dad turned away and his footsteps retreated.

Hailey drew the thin sheet off her torso and stretched in the prickling chill as she set up. Eyes still straining as she blinked against the fresh glow, she searched the floor for her clothes. She padded over to an oversized t-shirt and a pair of nylon shorts laying scrunched up along the opposite wall and slipped them on.

Her dad was waiting in the hall when she shuffled out, bare feet padding against the chilly concrete. He glanced down at her outfit, brow crinkling, face forming into the ghost of a smile, but he didn't say anything. She didn't blame him; her faded maroon t-shirt clashed horribly with a pair of lime green running shorts. The pair of worn cowboy boots cradled in her arms completed the curious ensemble. She must have been a sight in the hospital. *Is this really what I was wearing last night? Rodger saw me like this.* She shook it off, suppressing a yawn.

"Come on, hon."

Dad led her out of the barn. As a wave of heat greeted her, she squinted into the bright sunlight, somehow much brighter than the rays seeping into the barn through the many windows. Gravel dug into her bare feet as she picked her way across the drive. The whitewashed farmhouse shone in the midday light, floating on an emerald sea. The shadowed eves of the house were a welcome reprieve against the intense sunlight. Hailey barely glanced around the drafty old house as she creaked up the porch stairs. The coolness from the deck's shadowed floorboards soaked into her feet, dispersing the last traces of discomfort from her barefoot walk across the gravel.

After the intense sunlight, she shivered slightly and squinted into the dimness of the gloomy house, her sight slowly returning as she padded through the kitchen and the dining room to the living room. Hailey stopped at the foot of the stairs; turning to her dad, she yawned and said, "Make sure I'm up by five."

"Okay, hon."

She plodded the rest of the way up the creaking stairs, eyes locked on her feet as she ascended each step. Three bedrooms upstairs and one down; it was much too large a house for one old man. She wished she hadn't moved out. She sighed; she'd wanted some freedom, wanted to experience college like the other kids. How foolish! Her grampa would have made a much better roommate. Could she have prevented this? She would never know, and that would always haunt her.

If she could only go back …

Leaning on the kitchen counter, Michael Graham's mind roiled as he gazed through the small picture window above the sink, his eyes roving out over the property: barns, bullpens, and the pastures beyond. There were a lot of questions to mull through. Not the least of which was what they should do with the farm. He was in a quandary—had no idea what he should do. His father wouldn't have wanted them to sell the place, that much he knew. He also knew Hailey would want to take over the farm. This had been more of a home for her than anywhere else they'd lived. But did he want that for his daughter? What else was there? It wasn't like he had any idea how to run the place; he was wholly inadequate to the task—wouldn't even know where to start. So much had changed over the last twenty-odd years.

Though the farm had been in the family for generations, neither he nor his brother had grown up there. It wasn't until Michael was seventeen, almost a senior in high school, that he and a thoroughly disgruntled little brother were dragged out to the country. It was fine for his father, who was just returning home from an extended stint as an engineer. But for him and his little brother, it was incredibly unfair.

It was in his senior year, upset by being displaced and missing his home and friends, that his little surprise came. The young woman, a girl really—they'd both just been kids—hadn't wanted the baby, but being raised in a Christian home, couldn't bear to get rid of it. He thanked God every day. His Hailey had been his whole life for years. The sole reason for living. He couldn't imagine a world without her.

When the girl's parents found out about the pregnancy, they'd disowned her. Even after so many years, he still couldn't get over that callousness. And they called themselves good Christians. Where was their love and mercy? His parents, while they hadn't been especially pleased, took Hailey's mother in, and cared for her until the baby was born. Then she'd left. Just disappeared one day, leaving him with a newborn daughter to care for at only eighteen. He hadn't been remotely ready, but he'd had the support of his parents—and free childcare—in those tough years, as he worked two jobs to put himself through college. His parents had been a constant source of strength through those difficult times.

He still couldn't believe his dad was gone. This whole thing was too much. And the death of that young girl—whispers were already reaching him about the unrest it'd sparked in the community.

Gravel popped like firecrackers outside, drawing his attention to a vehicle pulling up the drive. Michael glanced at the wall clock: a little after two. It was still too early for his brother to show up. Caleb wasn't due to arrive until at least four. Michael craned his neck, peering through the kitchen's small window, looking for the source of the noise.

A two-toned SUV crept into view. Accentuating the sparkling champagne paint, a coat of deep mahogany cloaked the hood and front fenders, before tapering into a bold stripe—trimmed underneath by gold—which ran back to the taillight. Centered across the doors, the legend SHERIFF lay in bold mahogany letters, followed by a golden shield perched on the front of the passenger door, seeming to straddle the gold trim.

What now? Michael sighed. What did they want? He watched a young man climb from the driver's seat. Tall and blonde, he stood, straightening his uniform as he looked around the yard. The young deputy's gaze fell upon him, hovering at the window. The man gave a slight wave and headed for the side door.

The deputy came to a halt at the screen door and nodded to him. "Mr. Graham."

"Yes?" Michael replied hesitantly. *Why is the sheriff's department here?*

"My name is Rodger Sandrich," the man said, pointing unnecessarily at the name etched into the tag perched across from his glimmering badge. Michael's mind spun; he'd heard that name before. And recently.

"I thought I'd come and extend our condolences on behalf of the department. We're very sorry for your loss."

"Thank you." The young man seemed to sense his confusion.

"You may not remember me, but we've met before. My sister Stacey used to be good friends with your daughter."

Memories came flooding back; the towheaded children, appearing more like twins, often accompanied Hailey as they traipsed across the countryside. In later years, the mention of his name would be accompanied by a deep blush flooding his daughter's face. And the night before—

"You were the deputy who called my daughter last night."

"Yes, sir, right after I heard of the incident."

"And sat with her all night in the hospital."

"Not all night, sir, just after I got off shift."

"Still, I appreciate that. She sure didn't need to be alone." Remembering his manners, Michael added, "Come on in." Hinges creaked in protest as the old screen door swung open and Rodger stepped inside. "What can I do for you, Deputy?"

"Well, Mr. Graham—"

"Call me Michael," he interrupted.

"Yes, sir ... thank you, Michael." The young man nodded. "I was actually just stopping by to see how Hailey is doing." Neck craning, Rodger peered around the room as if trying to spot Hailey.

"Oh, I'm sorry ... she's still asleep."

The young deputy nodded gravely. "I thought she might be."

"I'll let her know you stopped by." Michael hesitated a moment, then bulled on, "Can you tell me what happened last night? I'm still unclear on the details."

"Of course, sir ..." Rodger spent a few minutes relaying the events of the previous night.

"That poor girl. How's the family doing?"

"Not well, not well at all." Rodger didn't let on how much of an understatement that was.

Back at the station, Sheriff Kimberly Johnson sat at her desk, rewatching the recovered video for the fifth time. Captured the night before on one of those compact action cameras, the video revealed the events in stunning high definition. With lights washing her in a heavy glow, the stocky teen preened in front of her phone, straightening her cute outfit—the last she'd ever don. Then Mallory backpedaled and centered herself in the frame; a couple of seconds ticked by before the music started, tinny in the night air, almost drowned out by the vocal cattle. The girl moved to the beat, making exaggerated gestures typical of the videos she'd seen online.

Obvious in the background, though shrouded in a faint grainy mist, the bull expressed his agitation at the intrusion. Hadn't she realized the bull was aggravated? Had she even noticed? Either the girl hadn't recognized the signs, or she'd ignored them. Then the bull turned and the girl behind the camera gasped. The animal spread its legs, hunkering as it bunched its shoulders and glared at Mallory. But the silly girl kept dancing.

Once it started towards them, it was too late; the first high-pitched cries rang out behind the camera. Bethany dropped the camera at this point, its lens cracked, and the picture spun to catch the farmhouse in the frame, fortunately missing the visual of the teen being gored. The audio was bad enough. Panicked squeals, heavy breathing, a sickening wet *squelch*, then a loud series of almost simultaneous explosive cracks as the bull tore through the wooden fence—using the girl's body as a battering ram.

Johnson shuddered at the thought.

Mallory's light rig fell out of frame, half shattered, sending sparks flying—that must have been the point when Mallory's cell phone cracked as well. Johnson had sent the device to a specialist, hoping to retrieve any of the girl's own video. She wasn't sure how those apps worked. Did it store the video on the phone's drive? Hopefully so. Though not crucial, the footage might shine some further light on the night's events.

Through the speakers, another scream rent the air, this time from Bethany, the only survivor of the night. The bull's legs flashed by. Mercifully, Mallory wasn't visible there either. Johnson knew it was at this point the bull deposited the girl's limp form on the lawn not far away. Gravel scraped beneath Bethany's feet as the girl scampered away, and the bull circled back, trotting into frame.

The agitated animal paced back and forth, in and out of frame for the next minute or so, before the old man barreled from his home. Most of the detail of Graham's pale face was lost in the low lighting, small artifacts in the video obscuring whatever expressions he wore. What must he have thought when he was greeted by a loose bull and a dead teen on his lawn? The bull ignored the running man, intently focused on something off-screen. Bethany. The irritated animal began raking a hoof across the ground, getting ready to charge again. The man slid to a stop, bringing up the weapon as the bull bellowed its rage. A shot rang out in the night and the massive animal collapsed on the screen, followed moments later by Graham.

Johnson groaned as she stabbed the spacebar, pausing the playback just as the strobing red and blue lights of her deputy's patrol car flickered across the screen, bathing everything within range. She didn't want to see the moment that idiot Hire had almost shot the other girl.

Like many in her department, Roscoe Hire was a holdout from the previous administration and was a lousy deputy. Though not corrupt like his former boss, her predecessor, he had no energy, no drive. He was just biding time until he could retire. She longed to be rid of him, however; she had no grounds to dismiss him. She shook the thought away. There was nothing she could do about that now. Besides, she had other worries.

To dispel the flocks of reporters swarming in from the tri-state area, she'd had to assign more people to help patrol the area around the farm. Still, the press made a nuisance of themselves, trying to ferret out the tiniest bit of dirt on John Graham or his family. Insinuations ranging from negligence to murder flew from people's lips, sweeping across town like wildfire. Accusations of carelessness and criminal neglect raged from strangers and neighbors alike. "Graham should have had such a dangerous animal destroyed long ago." It didn't matter that the bull had never shown any sign of aggression before that night. She'd checked.

This was just what she needed. Many were already questioning her qualifications with her upset victory over the former sheriff coming on the heels of a major scandal. And now this. She'd have to walk a fine line through this situation to come out on top. If she could just release this footage, many of her problems might disappear. But no matter how much she might want to leak it, no matter how much it would simplify her life, she wouldn't do it. She was a professional. Instead, she decided to push the politics aside, resigning herself to the drudgery of investigations and interviews that would come over the next several days and weeks.

And that wasn't all, social media was already flooded with condemnation. Threats came flooding in, and John Graham was their target. What else was happening on his property if such things could happen? Rumors spread of a madman indiscriminately waving an assault weapon at children, endangering them by firing wildly. Still others, called in to question the whole idea of farming. "There is no reason for them to have cattle in the first place." "These beautiful animals should be free to live in peace, unaffected by man's voracious appetite for flesh, or worrying about themselves or their calves being murdered and consumed for sustenance." Calls for his imprisonment by the public—it didn't seem to matter he was already dead—were stacked up with threats of legal action by the young lady's family. Her dad was creating an especially large fuss. The man was threatening to sue the county and Graham's heirs, as well as demanding the entire herd at Cracker Farm be destroyed.

She couldn't imagine losing a child; it had to be horrible. But it just wasn't Graham's fault, nor his heirs. The girl had clearly been in the wrong. Perhaps if Graham had housed the bull behind steel bars, that may have prevented the whole episode. But then again, the girl had been inside the pen when she was gored. According to those she'd asked, nothing could have guaranteed the bull's captivity. If the bull wanted to get out, it would get out. Neither wood nor steel was anything more than a suggestion to a two-thousand-pound animal.

Sheriff Johnson shook her head.

A commotion downstairs yanked Hailey from a peaceful slumber. *What?* Bleary-eyed, she stared around the room, trying to find its source. *Where am I?* It took her a moment to remember why she lay sprawled on her stomach in her old bed, now one of her grampa's guest rooms. The realization crashed down on her anew. A wave of grief swept over her, despair seeping into her entire being. Tears leaking, she ignored the commotion, rolled over to her side, and curled up, letting herself drift off again.

"Is she still in bed?" the voice pulled her from the fog of slumber again.

"Shh! You'll wake her."

"It's not my fault she's still asleep."

"That's not the point," the voice hissed. "It's rude."

Hailey Graham let her eyes drift open. The lithe forms of her twin cousins stood framed by the doorway. She stretched under the sheet, her limbs rubbing against the smooth fabric. "Hey, guys," she mumbled, smiling at the two. While their faces mirrored each other, the fifteen-year-olds couldn't be more different. Chloe embraced her Scandinavian heritage, letting straight white-blonde hair fall and drape around her shoulders. Zoe, on the other hand, seemed to like color; her bobbed hair was currently a mixture of warm black with blue highlights. While the color accentuated her cobalt eyes, Hailey couldn't understand why she'd do such a thing.

"What time is it?" She yawned, letting her tired eyes drift closed. "When did y'all get here?"

"Just now," one twin said.

"It's almost five," the other said. Without looking at them, it was hard to distinguish the voices.

"I better get up." Hailey groaned, stretching. "I have some work to do before milking time."

"I could help you," Chloe said meekly—she didn't have to see them to know who had said that. "Milking the cows ... if you want."

"That would be nice, Chloe, thank you."

"I can't believe you're going to help her," Zoe said. The divergent styles weren't the only thing, emotionally the girls were miles apart. Whereas Chloe was introverted, shy, and sweet; Zoe was boisterous and outgoing, and more than a little self-absorbed. "It's a despicable industry." She was also a vegan. Opposed to any form of animal exploitation. Used to her vehement criticism, Hailey let Zoe's comments slide past. "I can't believe our grandfather was involved in abusing those poor animals."

"Abuse?" Heat prickled within her at the suggestion Grampa would abuse his animals. Hailey's eyes narrowed. "What are you talking about now?"

"What else would you call it?"

"Farming …"

Zoe harrumphed. "You keep them locked up inside year-round, trapped in tiny pens, unable to see sunlight or get fresh air. You hook them up to some machine, constantly stealing milk that should rightfully go to their calves. Who, if female, are forcibly impregnated; forced to give birth over and over. But that's not near as bad as what you do to the male calves. It makes me sick just thinking about it."

Confusion clouded Hailey's weary mind, dampening some of the heat building within her as she shot a look at the twin. "What are you talking about? What is it you think we do to the male calves?" Surely, she wasn't upset that most were castrated; sounds like that would be right up her alley.

Zoe sighed and rolled her eyes. "Everyone knows that male calves have no place on a dairy farm. You just ship them off, sell them for meat. Veal. Don't let the poor creatures have any kind of life. If Grampa was still alive—"

"You have no idea what you're talking about, do you?" Hailey snapped, finally tired of Zoe's babble.

Her young cousin's eyes went wide at the uncharacteristic rebuke. "Well, I—"

But Hailey wasn't having the best day, so she bowled over her. "A. We don't kill male calves. That would be a waste. We raise quite a few; our bulls fetch a good price. Others we castrate and raise—"

"For slaughter. And that's any better? Cutting off their balls and—"

"B," Hailey interrupted again. "Our herd is not cooped up, 'packed in some barn their whole lives, milk constantly being drained.' Our cattle are free roving, grass-fed." Hailey gestured to the window. "If you would just glance outside, you'd see we have hundreds of acres of land out back for them to roam and feed."

"But, milking them; you're torturing them."

"C," Hailey raised her voice. "We don't torture the cows. Milking them causes no pain whatsoever. It actually relieves the pressure building in their udders. They line up for it, eager to be milked." She decided not to mention the bribe of sweet cakes fed to the cattle as they were being milked—best not to muddle the issue. "Which you would know if you had ever visited Grampa." At those words, the tears her young cousin had been fighting finally burst out, and Hailey realized she might have gone too far.

"It's not my fault Dad and Grampa didn't get along," the girl cried.

Hailey leapt to her feet and rushed to Zoe, enveloping her in a hug.

"I know, I know. I'm sorry I said that. It's just what you were saying; Grampa loved his cows. He would have never abused them. He gave them the best life he could."

6

As Hailey padded down the stairs, she let her fingertips trace the worn wallpaper, smiling at the memories of Gramma and Grampa when she was younger and the paper newer. When she was growing up, she'd loved to race up and down the wooden stairs, peering at all the ancient sepia pictures glistening on the wall. Her fingers wiped layers of dust from the glass. After Gramma died, Grampa let the place go a bit, focusing more on his livestock. She still couldn't believe the things Zoe had been saying; Grampa was a good man. Now he was gone, too. Both her grandparents. The ones that mattered, anyway. She supposed her mother's parents were still around somewhere, but neither had wanted anything to do with her or her parents ever since her mom ended up pregnant. Then her mother left—without even having a chance to get to know her.

Hailey sighed; it was too painful to think about. That had been hard when she was younger. She was convinced something was wrong with her—why else couldn't they love her? When Gramma got wind of it, she'd sat her down and set her straight.

A smile flickered across Hailey's face, remembering her gramma's reassuring words as she passed through the main foyer and angled through the dining room toward the kitchen.

"… I don't know. I just want you to consider what Dad—"

"Good morning, sleepyhead," her father announced as she rounded the corner, cutting off whatever her uncle had been saying. Her father, Aunt Sierra, and Uncle Caleb stood around the island in the center of the kitchen. Unlike the stairwell, the kitchen was clean. There was no dust covering the walls or cabinets, instead, it just looked aged. The faded cabinet doors needed to be sanded down and repainted; the stove, while mostly clean, needed a deep scrub to remove the black circles atop it; and the dishwasher needed replacing, having given out years before.

"Hey, baby, how are you?" Dad glanced at the clock hanging above the oven. "It's not quite five yet."

Her stomach grumbled. "Yeah, the twins found me." She stepped to the fridge; the gleaming chrome appliance looked incongruously out of place, added only a couple of months before. Hailey blinked, opening the door as she rubbed the sleep from her eyes. "I'm okay."

"Are you hungry? I can make you something to eat."

"Yeah, I a—," she croaked, then coughed, then tried again, "I am a bit hungry."

"What would you like?" Her dad filled a cup with cool, clean water from their artesian well, and offered it to her. "I could make you a sandwich real quick."

Hailey took the glass and drank deeply. The cold liquid soothed her parched throat. "A sandwich sounds great." She smiled.

"What are you up to?"

"I have some stuff to do out in the barn before the next milking. I didn't exactly finish earlier."

"Hey, listen." Pressure built in her chest at the sudden intensity of her father's tone. Was he going to give her more bad news? Did he want to sell the farm? "After everything that's happened, I don't think you should be milking alone."

The tension in her chest dissolved, but confusion swamped her. "What do you mean?"

"I don't like the thought of you being alone out there with all those massive animals. Look what happened to that little girl."

Ohhh. "The girls won't hurt me."

"I'm sure you're right. They wouldn't hurt you … intentionally, but they're big animals. They could hurt you without really meaning to."

She just gave a halfhearted shrug—it had been known to happen. "I really don't think I have anything to worry about."

"Be that as it may." Dad lifted his hands, showing her his palms, clearly not wanting to argue. "I think it's for the best."

"What do you want me to do?" Hailey grudgingly acquiesced. There was more she might have said, but she didn't feel like arguing either.

"All I'm asking is that you don't go out there alone. Bring one of us with you."

She smirked. "Y'all want to help me milk the cows?"

"I wouldn't say *want* is the right word," her uncle said, "but we will."

Her smirk transformed into a smile at his grudging tone. "Actually, the twins are going to come out with me after while."

"You've got to be kidding," Caleb barked, the surprise in her uncle's voice evident. "Little miss, 'meat is murder' is going to help you?"

"Well, no. Chloe is. I think Zoe's just coming out to make sure we aren't torturing the animals"—Hailey waved airily.

"So, I don't suppose this means the sanctimonious lecturing will end," Aunt Sierra said. "But perhaps she'll lay off on the milk and cheese."

"I wouldn't get my hopes up too much. By the way, Hailey, how many cows do you have to milk?" Uncle Caleb's face shifted, taking on an almost hungry look; surely, he wasn't thinking about eating them.

Hailey suppressed another yawn. "We milk around sixty, twice a day."

Caleb's expression transformed, scrunching in confusion. "Only sixty? It seemed like more."

"Oh, there are more cattle in the herd. Quite a bit more. We have tons of steers, some almost ready for market. There's a new crop of calves from this season, last season's stock are still too young to breed. Grampa also had the bulls."

His face brightened at the news.

Hailey yawned, stretching. "I'm going to go get dressed."

"Okay, hon, I'll have your sandwich waiting for you when you come down."

"Thanks, Dad." She gave him a quick kiss on the cheek, then turned on her heel and strode away.

As soon as they heard Hailey's footsteps thumping up the stairs, Michael's brother started up again. "Like I was saying … think about what Dad would have wanted." Minutes earlier, Caleb Graham had bulled through the screen door, Sierra and the twins in tow, acting like the last few years hadn't occurred. Caleb and Dad had gotten into it again at Mom's funeral. As far as Michael knew, the two hadn't spoken but a handful of times since. And here he was claiming to know what Dad would have wanted. And he couldn't be more wrong.

"What Dad would have wanted?" Michael echoed, before laying into his brother. "Are you really going to stand there and tell me that Dad would have wanted us to get rid of the farm?"

"I know … 'the farm has been in our family for five generations,' right?" Caleb parroted their father's words.

Michael shook his head. "You know, he wanted Hailey to take over. He was well aware neither of us was interested."

"He didn't plan to die so suddenly," Caleb countered.

"I know he was thrilled when Hailey started showing such an interest, but she is still quite young," Sierra added. "He would have wanted her to finish school."

"Surely, you want your daughter to finish college," Caleb urged.

"Well, of course, I do," Michael said, wavering as his eyes swept his brother and sister-in-law. They had already begun to team up against him. And it wasn't like they weren't bringing up valid points—he'd already begun wrestling with the same doubts—but he didn't like that Caleb had started pressuring him so soon. It only added to his stress. He knew Hailey dreamed about taking over the farm, but he wanted her to get a degree, experience life, try new things. Perhaps she'd find something she liked better. It was an awful burden to saddle on a twenty-year-old. So, he demurred; "I just don't think we should bring it up today. She's been through enough for one day, don't you think?"

"We understand," Sierra agreed, nodding slowly.

Michael stepped back, crossing his arms. "Besides, I think Hailey should have a say."

"I'm not suggesting we sell it out from under her," Caleb said, though Michael suspected that was exactly what his brother had been hinting at. "We should consider it, at least. We could probably get an outstanding price from some development company looking to add another subdivision. Just think about it."

Michael gave a slight shrug. Money—it was always about money with Caleb. His brother was never the best with his finances and lived well above his means—up to his eyeballs in debt.

Caleb let his mind drift as the GPS guided him through town. The small college town had grown since his high school years—when he'd been uprooted and stranded—but not enough for his tastes. He mulled over the unproductive discussion with his brother. Didn't Michael see they should get rid of the place? What was he thinking, humoring his daughter's desire to be a dairy farmer? He couldn't really be considering letting his daughter waste her life, could he?

Caleb had a much better use for the farm and the herd. And what better place to start than the local feed store? With the cows, the dairy equipment, and especially the land, they were sitting on a small fortune. Several square miles of land. Three sections. He envisioned the area bordering the lake cleaned up and turned into waterfront housing. They would make a killing, and half of that was his.

But that was long-term; in the short term, he needed some

liquidity to come up for air, which was where the cattle factored in. When Hailey told them how few milkers they had, his heart sank a bit. It might not be enough. But apparently, that was only a fraction of the herd. There were younger cows and steers, ripe to sell for meat.

He'd done some quick research on the way out, discovering that each of the milkers could be worth upwards of twenty-five-hundred bucks. Bulls could be worth up to twice as much. It was a shame Dad had been forced to kill the old bull; he would have been worth a fortune. There had to be others worth a tidy sum.

Before long, he was directed into a small lot; Bud's Feed Store emblazoned in green on the building's white walls, below that the individual words: Grain — Feed — Seed. The building's pockmarked wooden walls were worn with age. A truck sat idling in front of an open loading bay near the rear as a forklift unloaded pallets full of eighty-pound feed sacks. That was another thing: he couldn't guess how much it cost to feed the cattle. Hopefully, they could get rid of the animals before they had to buy any more feed. What a waste.

When he yanked the glass door open, a wave of cool air buffeted him, pushing back the worst of the summer heat. A bell tinkled above as a rush of smells filled his nostrils: grain, wood chips, and plastic—exactly the mixture of aromas he might have pictured in a feed store. A dozen feet ahead, a massive wraparound counter floated like an island on the vintage hardwood floors running throughout the building. On the far side of the checkout counter, a row of pallets ran along the center of the double-wide main aisle stacked with various brands of heavy feed bags. Shelves to either side stretched the length of the building, filled with odds and ends—anything you might need on a farm. Most of the items were as foreign to him as anything.

"Hi, there!" The high-pitched voice came from the left, near the end of one aisle. "How can I help you?" A young woman stepped into view, hands swiping dust from her worn jeans. She couldn't be that much older than his daughters. She was short, with enormous eyes and a brilliant smile on her round face.

"Yeah uh, is Bud here?" Caleb asked, gesturing idly to the name painted in tall letters on the front of the counter.

A warm giggle escaped from her lips. "You must be new in town."

"Why do you say that?" Caleb asked as the heat rose to his face.

"There is no Bud, or at least there hasn't been for a long time. I'm not sure if there ever was. It's just the name of the place." She kept that annoying grin on her face as she strolled toward him. "Mrs. Wills owns the place now, but she isn't here. She's on vacation. Her husband took her to Hawaii for their twentieth. Can you believe that?"

Ignoring the information download, Caleb glanced around the store, then took in the name etched in delicate cursive letters on the tag pinned to her smart green polo.

"Cassie, is it?" He nodded at her tag.

Her eyes shot down to her tag, and she frowned. "No. They misspelled it. My name is Kaycee." She proceeded to spell it for him. "Mrs. Wills said I have to wait another three months for a new one." Kaycee, not Cassie, stamped her foot. "Can you believe that? It's like she thinks I won't last that long."

"Is there someone else here? Perhaps a bit—"

"Older?" Leaning on the counter, the girl's eyebrow rose, and her mouth pressed into a thin line as her eyes bore into him. "I'm sure I can help you with whatever you need."

"I'm sorry." He'd offended her; that hadn't been his intention. He was off to a great start. "You wouldn't happen to know where someone could buy or sell livestock?" He paused, glancing around again. "… perhaps a bulletin board or some classifieds?"

"What are those?" she responded. He blinked at her. After a moment, she broke into a sly smile. "Juss kidding. Come around here." Her voice was melodious in her amusement. Caleb's eyes tailed her as she strolled around to the opposite side of the island counter. Waving for him to follow, Kaycee's smile bloomed a bit brighter. "Come on. The classifieds we have cover the whole tri-state area. For local sales, we have a bulletin board around here." She waved for him to follow her again. This time, he did. Sure enough, on the opposite side of the counter, a bulletin board held advertisements. "There's just about anything you need: livestock, farm equipment, labor. You were looking for livestock?"

"Yes." His eyes traveled to the section she indicated. "Livestock, cattle."

"You looking to buy? There's tons of good cattle in this area."

"No, I'm actually looking to sell a few," Caleb murmured.

"You could always go to the sale barn."

He gave her a perplexed look; her smile brightened, and she explained. "The stockyards off Route 9, north of the college. They're kinda hard to miss."

Of course, why hadn't he thought of that? Tack it up to inexperience.

"Or … the ag nerds … uh, the students from 4-H and FFA are always looking for livestock." Kaycee pointed to an advertisement stapled to the board. A row of paper tabs lined the bottom edge of the sheet, a telephone number written in a neat script. Caleb leaned closer and ripped one off. "We also have several excellent butchers around." Kaycee gestured toward another row of advertisements. "It depends on their age. How old are they? How many are there?"

Without thinking, Caleb explained, "See, my dad just died, leaving us a herd."

Her head cocked back. "You mean Mr. Graham? He was one of our best customers. Poor guy. You're one of his sons? And you're going to sell the herd?"

Caleb rocked back on his heels. He hadn't considered how well-known his father was in town. It would be just his luck for his plans to come out before he was ready. His mind raced, trying to salvage this.

"No, no. Not all of them. Just want to slim down the herd a bit."

Her face lost its surprise.

"Oh, I'd ask Hailey if I were you. She'll know where to go.

She helped Mr. Graham with the cattle."

"I plan to. I'm just doing some research, trying to help out, you know," he hedged. "I have a lot to learn."

As she nodded, his fluttering heart settled. Had she bought his explanation?

Hailey led her cousins out to the barn; Chloe followed eagerly, Zoe somewhat more reluctantly. Hailey was excited. She didn't get to see her cousins nearly as much as she would have liked. In fact, it had been more than a year since she'd seen the twins. She glanced at Zoe's hair. They'd changed a lot in that time.

In the changing room, Hailey held out an old jumpsuit for Zoe.

"I'm not putting this on," Zoe roared. "It's hideous!"

Hailey's eyes roved over her cousin's outfit. Her jeans had enough holes, they looked to be falling apart, and the shirt she'd changed into had a caricature of an annoyed cow with the slogan 'dairy is udderly ridiculous'—the bright green fabric clashing horribly with her blue and black hair. In Hailey's eyes, Zoe didn't have a valid argument, but for the sake of harmony, she let it pass.

"Working with cows can be messy. You don't want to get your"—Hailey's gaze flicked over Zoe again—"outfit dirty."

"I wasn't going to help. Like you suggested, I'm just observing. I still don't think it's right what you do to these poor animals."

Hailey's eyes narrowed, and she sighed. "Uh-huh." She offered the jumpsuit to Chloe.

Chloe took the outfit and let her eyes trace the room. "Uh, where's the bathroom?"

"Oh, right through there," Hailey pointed out a door at the end of the changing room that not only held the toilets, but a couple of showers as well.

"Okay," Chloe said, taking the jumpsuit and slipping through the door.

After she left, Zoe rolled her eyes. "She's so modest. She

won't even change in front of me."

"There's nothing wrong with that."

"Whatever." Zoe shrugged before turning and leaving the room.

After slipping into her own jumpsuit, Hailey met her cousins in the hallway. Chloe had pulled up her hair to match Hailey's, and her roomy jumpsuit draped off the girl, several sizes too large for her thin frame. Though she looked ready.

A brief tour of the facility garnered awe from Chloe and more criticism from Zoe. Though, when she first saw the baby cows, for just a moment, Zoe had gotten that dewy, dreamy-eyed look reserved for every type of baby animal. She had even assisted one calf, using her fingers to guide the calf's mouth toward the bottle. For half a second, Hailey thought she was getting through to the girl. Then she fell back to her usual dour demeanor.

"A calf should drink its own mother's milk," Zoe complained. "In fact, they should be the only ones drinking the milk. Besides, it's cruel to separate a calf from its mother. They scream and cry for each other for days."

The girl didn't seem impressed when Hailey explained that the calf shed's open-air design seemed to reduce the distress caused by separating the calves from their mothers, allowing them to at least see each other. She'd merely sighed when Zoe told her how ridiculous that was. Like many of her age, Zoe knew best—the girl wasn't open to any contradictory viewpoints.

By the time they let the cows in and circled back to the milking parlor, Hailey had had just about enough of her cousin. Though she'd promised herself she wouldn't, she was about to tell Zoe off again. Luckily, it didn't come to that.

As Hailey started wiping off the first cow's udder, Zoe let out a disgusted snort and said, "I can't do this."

Eyes narrowing, Hailey studied her cousin. "Do what, exactly?" She hadn't done anything all day.

"I can't just sit here and watch you molest all these cows."

Cocking her head, Hailey blinked at her cousin. "Molest the

cows?"

"What else would you call it? You're just—just groping them."

"I see," Hailey blinked. Groping the cows? "We usually call it milking, but, you know, whatever."

Zoe snorted, turned, and, without another word, left the parlor.

Hailey turned to Chloe, who was trying to stifle her laughter. "I better get back to groping the cows." She was fast realizing Chloe was the good twin. "Care to help?"

Her cousin snorted, breaking into peals of giggles, but edged closer to help.

A shame—Zoe hadn't lasted long enough to see a single cow milked.

"What we do first is strip them …"—Hailey demonstrated as she explained, squirting a stream of milk onto the black floor mat. She trailed off halfway through her explanation when Chloe snorted. Her cousin's face was red, and muscles danced at the corners of her mouth. "What is it?" Hailey allowed a reluctant smile to creep across her face.

"First groping, now stripping," Chloe breathed, barely able to contain her mirth. "What are you doing to these poor cows? Better not tell Zoe." Chloe broke into renewed peals of laughter, and Hailey couldn't help but join in.

After leaving the feed store, Caleb dialed the number printed in neat script on the strip of paper, and his brief call put him in touch with an adviser for the local FFA chapter (formerly Future Farmers of America). Sally Jessup proved to be an enthusiastic, sweet-natured woman with a melodic voice. Though he'd had his pitch laid out this time, not wanting to make the same mistake he'd almost made with young Kaycee, it hadn't come to that. When he'd brought up the possibility of selling some cattle, she'd invited him right down to the ag barn.

It only took Caleb a few minutes to reach the local high school. There was one thing to be said for small towns; unlike the sprawling metropolis where he lived, it didn't take long to get anywhere. The Agricultural Education Barn sat beside the school, in the southeast corner of the campus, nestled between the practice stadium and the main parking lot.

A short, heavyset woman met him in the parking lot, greeting him warmly. As he shook her plump hand, he introduced himself.

Her face fell. "Graham? As in John Graham?"

"Yes, he is—was my father." Again, his father's legacy proceeded him.

"I'm so sorry for your loss. It was such dreadful news."

"Yes, thank you," Caleb agreed. With the obligatory, empty condolences out of the way, it was time to get down to business. "So, your organization might be interested in some of his cattle?"

"Well, not the FFA itself," she said. "That's not exactly how it works."

"No?" though he tried to suppress his emotion, Caleb was sure his confusion was evident. "Sorry, I'm not sure how this all works."

"I'll be more of an intermediary, between you and the parents," she explained. "John Graham's cattle are outstanding stock. I'm sure there will be plenty of interest. Come inside, I'll show you the facilities. Since we're a smaller community, the ag barn serves both the FFA and 4-H clubs …" Sally Jessup babbled as if following a prepared script. Half listening, Caleb followed.

Entering through a side door, the pungent odor of numerous animals assaulted his senses. The temperature inside the prefabricated metal building was only slightly cooler than the sweltering summer sun outside. Rows of galvanized-steel stalls to the left held any number of animals: pigs, goats, sheep, and along the far wall, a double row of larger pens held cattle.

"This is the *sand pit*." Sally indicated a training area stretching almost the width of the building, ringed by an oxidizing metal pipe fence. "It's where the students learn to show their animals. It can be quite a struggle … let me tell you." Inside, a young teen held a pig whip, tapping a hog lightly, trying to lead it around the ring. However, the young woman's diligent effort garnished poor results—the hog appeared to lead the girl more than the other. A man leaning against the fence nodded to them as they approached, then went back to encouraging his daughter.

Sally stopped, smiling warmly at the girl before gesturing around the building. "As you can see, the animals have a suitable home while the students care for them and prepare them for show." Caleb suppressed a wince; he wouldn't have wanted to live here, but then again, he wasn't the one that had to.

He let his gaze wander for a few moments as he slowly nodded, then steered the conversation back to a more relevant topic. "So, there will be an interest in my father's cattle?"

"Oh yes, Cracker Farm cattle are some of the best in the county. Best in the state, even. I think it's great that you're willing to share some of your father's cattle with the students."

The young lady being led by the hog looked around. "Ms. Jessup, it's not working," she complained.

"You're doing very well, Amy. It just takes time."

"Am I doing it right?" Amy asked.

"Just a second." Sally turned to Caleb. "I'll be right back. Duty calls." She moved closer to the girl, murmuring soothing words and tips.

"You're looking to sell some show cattle?" The girl's father sidled up to him, sticking out his hand. "Sorry to eavesdrop. Robert Ellison."

"No trouble at all," he replied. "Caleb Graham." Grasping the proffered hand, he was greeted by a firm grip.

"Graham, that wouldn't be John Graham over at Cracker Farm?"

"Yes, he was my father."

The man's face took on a sympathetic air. "I'm sorry for your loss." Without pausing, Robert continued, "I live in Cimarron Acres …" Seeing that Caleb hadn't immediately grasped the connection, Robert elaborated. "The housing development across the way from your farm."

"Oh, yes. Those are some wonderful homes."

"Yes," he agreed. "Anyway, every time I'd pass by, I'd marvel at the quality of your father's herd."

"That's nice of you to say." Pride swelled within Caleb, despite having nothing to do with his father's accomplishments.

"My daughter, she's eleven now, has been wanting to get into 4-H for a while. What better way to start than with one of John Graham's show calves?"

"Of course," Caleb agreed, eager for the sale. "What are you looking for?"

"You wouldn't happen to have a calf sired by Old Mac? I mean, I'm sure any number of your cattle would do, but he was a show winner years ago, and has sired many since."

Caleb suppressed a grimace; he should have looked over the records earlier. "I'm not exactly sure, but why don't you stop by tomorrow morning, and we'll see what we can do."

"Will do," Robert grinned. "I might have a buddy that will want to tag along as well."

"The more the merrier," Caleb said, grinning. He had all evening to get acquainted with the stock.

7

Billowing curtains of mist churned around the twin torrents of water as Hailey and Chloe hosed down the parlor's gleaming stainless-steel stalls and equipment, then the bare concrete floor, blasting all the dirt and manure down the drains—giving it a little more attention to make up for her poor show earlier. They were just finishing rinsing the parlor when Uncle Caleb appeared.

Hailey cut off her spray, and Chloe quickly followed suit.

"How's my little girl doing?" Caleb called.

"Hey, Daddy," Chloe said, beaming.

The milking hadn't gone much smoother despite having an assistant, but Hailey didn't feel the need to share that. Though the girl tried, Chloe had been more of a hindrance than a help, at first—constantly seeking reassurance. Initially, Hailey thought it was fear of the animals holding her back, that she was intimidated by their size—and her cousin *had* squealed and darted back the first time a hoof shot out. But she soon realized Chloe was more afraid of hurting the cows. The milking claws also seemed to intimidate her, and Hailey had to explain the devices. Demonstrating it on a finger to show it wouldn't cause any harm. Regardless, Hailey was happy for the company. They'd gossiped like schoolgirls.

She wondered what her uncle must think. Chloe was thoroughly disheveled. With her muck-spattered jumpsuit swallowing her thin frame, and her frizzed hair escaping in strands here and there, the girl looked a sight. Not to mention the greenish-brown stain sweeping across her forehead that looked suspiciously like manure.

"You look …" Caleb's eyes flicked over his daughter once more. "Exhausted. Did you have fun?"

"Oh, yeah." Chloe gave him a brief account of everything they'd done, then turned to Hailey. "Is that it? Are we finished?"

"Just about. I have a couple more things to do. Why don't you go get cleaned up?"

"You sure? I can stay and help."

"Nah, it's okay. You go on."

Pride showed in Caleb's eyes as he watched his daughter scurry off.

After she'd gone, he turned to Hailey. "I thought I should get to know more about the herd. I have a few questions."

Hailey perked up. "What did you want to know?" The way he'd talked earlier; she hadn't figured her uncle would want anything to do with the business.

"Can you give me a brief overview of everything you do here? How you do it." His eyes lost focus for a moment. "For example, how do you keep track of the cattle? You must have a way, right?"

"Of course. Good question. Come on, let's go to the office. I'll walk you through it."

As she led her uncle through the barn, she rattled off some of the basics: the daily yield of milk and how their computers used RFID chips embedded in their ear tags to keep track of the cattle, as well as the composition of the herd and its management. She spoke of growing their own grain silage to keep costs down. And what they had to do to store feed for winter. By the time she led him into Grampa's office, she figured he knew more than he'd ever wanted to know.

"Now, you wanted to know how we keep track of the ladies. This is the herd management computer," Hailey explained.

"There's another in our vet office. And they're networked throughout the building and accessible by these." She pulled out a tablet from a charging station. "All the RFID data feeds into the system. Milk statistics, analytics, and so on."

She was so focused on the explanations, it wasn't until she was sitting in Grampa's chair, pulling up the program on the tablet, that Hailey realized this was the first time she'd entered his office since his death. Sorrow crashed over her, but it wasn't quite as sharp as earlier. Her uncle's interest had reminded her that Grampa would have expected her to manage once he was gone. To care for his charges.

Hailey blinked back tears as she opened a program on the tablet. With her uncle perched over her shoulder, Hailey tabbed through the information. "Here we have a list of the cattle with all their info: their id, age, bloodline, and history. It also keeps track of the milk production for the ladies, as well as the semen production for the fellas." Selecting one animal at random, she scrolled through the data. "For example, this heifer," she shot a glance to Caleb and explained, "that means she's a female under two years old, yet to calve—um, she hasn't given birth." He nodded for her to go on. "Anyway, she's getting close to fifteen months, which is about the time we'd usually breed her. Let's see, she was bred on the farm. We list the mother's ID and the name or ID of the sire—we don't name all of them—as well as *their* parent's history. It's easier to keep track of those born on the farm, but every farmer has some kind of comparable system. Grampa only dealt with pure-blood Holsteins and was a stickler for documentation. We have a copy of all the papers in the filing cabinet." She hooked a thumb over her shoulder.

"So, say the big bull that died. What was his name?" Caleb asked.

"Old Mac?" Hailey smiled wanly.

"He was the prize winner, wasn't he?"

Her smile brightened. "We actually have several champions. But he is the one that won Supreme Champion at state. Grampa's pride and joy." At those words, her smile turned rueful.

Caleb nodded. "Was he still having children?"

"Oh yes, the big guy was still quite popular." She gave her uncle a wry smile. "He never lacked for companionship. Grampa would acquire several heifers every year for him. You know, to keep the bloodline fresh. We still have several of his offspring, and with AI—um, artificial insemination—we're able to breed more. Though I'm not sure we should …"

"I have another question."

"Shoot," Hailey said, thankful to get away from the topic.

"Why do they all have horns?" Caleb's eyes narrowed. "Isn't it dangerous?"

"Not enough to justify the expense and effort of removing them. Besides, Grampa didn't like causing the animals any undo pain or distress."

"Speaking of pain and distress, cutting off their balls didn't qualify?" He shifted uncomfortably.

"Oh, we never cut them off. We use a device that stretches a thick rubber band …" Hailey trailed off as he paled. "Suffice it to say, it's totally painless."

"I'll take your word for that." Caleb shuddered, bringing a smile to her face. "Thank you. I think I have everything I need to know for now. I'm sure I'll be coming to you for more soon."

"No problem," Hailey replied, tapping through the tablet. "Glad to help."

"Can I borrow one of those?"

Hailey glanced at the tablet in her hand, then at her uncle. "Sure." She passed it over.

"What are you up to now?"

"I was actually going to hand milk one of the ladies. I didn't like the look of the milk when I stripped her."

"Stripped?"

She smiled and took a moment to explain; that was a popular question.

"So, there was clotting?" Caleb surmised. As she nodded, he continued, "Is it bad? I mean, is the animal in danger?"

Hailey slowly shook her head. "Not necessarily. But it might be an early sign of mastitis—an inflammation of the cow's mammary glands. If it is, it can be treated with antibiotics. We'll just have to watch her. Either way, we don't want her milk added to the bulk tank."

Caleb nodded. "Tell you what. Why don't I join you?"

"Yeah?" Hailey perked up. Maybe Caleb did want to help out.

"You can teach me how to milk a cow."

She smiled. "Yeah, okay."

Hailey switched the light off as they exited the room, then led her uncle out back.

She directed Caleb to a small row of stalls intended for animals that needed special attention while she went to grab a bucket. The thin stalls held the animal sideways and their gates only had two horizontal metal poles, one at the top and another midway down, allowing easy access to the underside of the animals. As she rounded the corner, her uncle came into sight. He'd pulled a stool around and sat beside one stall in front of a bovine, face in the tablet. The only problem was it was the wrong stall.

"Um, Uncle Caleb," Hailey said, trying to suppress a grin. "I don't think you want to milk that one."

Eyes flitting from the screen, he looked at her quizzically. "What? Why not?"

"That one's a bull."

Hailey couldn't help but laugh as Caleb lurched to his feet, stepped back, and tipped the stool, sending it clattering to the ground.

Caleb turned, a sheepish grin slipping across his face. "I think you're right."

Fighting hard to control her laughter, Hailey nodded to the next stall over. "Come on, I'll show you."

The gurgling growl of the four-stroke engines filled the boy's ears and fumes wafted up as they raced along the blacktop on their four-wheelers. Air rifles strapped over their shoulders; they'd been in the woods down by the lake doing target practice.

Frank pulled to a halt. "Is that the farm?" he asked, seeing several cows grazing in the field.

"Huh?" Collin replied.

"The farm where Mallory was murdered. Is that it?"

Collin blinked at his friend. *Murdered?* "Yeah, we're on the western border of the old Graham farm. But, hey, I don't really think—"

"We should do something."

"What are you talking about?"

"Teach them a lesson," Frank said.

"Teach who? Old man Graham is dead."

"No dummy, teach the cows a lesson."

"Like what?" Collin asked, trying to understand what his buddy was on about.

"Mallory was nice and really cute. I was going to ask her out this summer," Frank explained, unslinging the rifle as he climbed off his ATV and looked for a likely target.

Collin's breath caught. "What are you doing?" he asked.

"I'm going to teach these stupid cows a lesson."

As Frank brought the air rifle to his shoulder, Collin launched off his own four-wheeler, lunging for him. His foot caught on the front fender, sending him toppling to the rough asphalt where he scraped the skin from his palms and banged his knee.

Frank took his eye off the target as he pumped the rifle. "Nice one," he said, smirking, then drew a bead on the cow again.

"No! Frank, don't ..." Collin seethed, clinching his hands, hissing as the shredded flesh burned with the air and movement.

"Calm down, man. It's not like I'm going to kill it," Frank chided. "I doubt I'll even hurt it."

"It's cruel," Collin protested. As he bounded to his feet, a fresh wave of pain lanced through his blood-covered knee, joining the ache pulsing from his palms. "Besides, you don't want to make 'em mad."

Frank didn't even glance back as he replied, "You can't be serious. Are you really afraid of making these big, dumb animals mad?"

"Well, what do you think happened to Mallory?" Collin seethed as he hobbled toward his friend.

"That was a bull. It's different," Frank chided, then squeezed the trigger.

The metal pellet streaked from the barrel, lancing across the yard. It struck one cow in the ribs as Collin finally reached Frank and yanked the weapon down.

"What did you—"

A bellow cut Collin off moments before the cow charged. The enormous ink-smeared animal closed quickly. Too quickly. Both boys cursed as they dashed back to their ATVs. Collin's palms screamed against the rubberized grips as he kicked his to life.

Frank shot ahead, forcing Collin to catch up.

Another angry bellow rose behind him, and Collin turned and witnessed the cow leap cleanly over the barbed-wire fence. The animal's hooves smacked against the asphalt, then it turned in their direction. He whipped his head around, revving his engine as he tried to catch Frank.

He shot another glance back. The ink-stained monstrosity surged after them for about a hundred yards, then it slowed. Unwilling to take any chances, he revved his engine again, but he hadn't been paying attention to the road. His ATV had drifted toward the side of the lane. A jolt startled him as the tires slipped off the pavement to the left. Collin whipped around, jerking his steering bar too far to the side, overcorrecting. The ATV lanced across both lanes and slammed into the ditch beyond, tumbling end over end and launching Collin into the air before he came crashing back to the earth.

He hurdled down and struck the ground hard, bones snapping like twigs. Pain bloomed throughout his body as the air exploded from his lungs. Fighting to catch his breath, Collin's vision blurred as he watched Frank hurtling away, pleading silently for his friend to return.

Frank didn't know how far he'd traveled before he'd noticed Collin wasn't with him any longer. He'd just turned and realized his buddy wasn't there. Fearful, Frank let off the accelerator, and let his ATV drift to a stop in the middle of the road as he peered over a shoulder, looking for any sign of the cow or his friend, then stood up on the footrests and scanned the road.

How had that cow moved so quickly? It shouldn't have been possible, but for a time, the thing was actually gaining on them. Frank shuddered as goosebumps swept over his body. He fought to control his breath as seconds became minutes: one, then two, then five before he finally decided to see what was keeping his friend. Frank turned the four-wheeler in a wide arc and slowly retraced his path.

Several minutes later, the brush along the road thinned and an overturned ATV came into view, laying in the field beyond. Frank hopped off his four-wheeler, throwing one more quick look around to see if the cow was coming, then he bounded across the ditch and sprinted toward Collin's broken body.

As he ran, Frank dug his cell from his pocket and tapped nine-one-one. He dropped to his knees next to Collin, surprised to see the other boy's chest rise and fall as he labored to breathe. As the call connected, his eyes locked on the smoking remains of Collin's ATV. It was a miracle he was still alive.

Frank wondered how he was going to explain this.

One thing was for sure; he wasn't going to mention the cow. He couldn't; not without explaining how all this was his fault.

Hailey sat with her family, lounging around the living room, sated from a delicious cheeseburger casserole; one of many dishes dropped off by sympathetic neighbors when Caleb spoke up. "I think we should discuss the next steps," he said.

"So do I," Hailey agreed. "If you guys could assist me as I transition into the job, it would be really helpful. You know, pick up the slack here and there until I get the hang of it. It's very important to set a consistent schedule." She glanced around the family to gauge their reactions. "It's better for the cattle. And as much as I know about the farm, Grampa still took care of certain things."

"I'll help," Chloe announced.

"What didn't he let you do?" Zoe asked; likely ready to express outrage at any insult to liberated women. Then Hailey noticed a swift shift in her expression as she changed tack. "For that matter, why would you want to? Why would you want to be a part of a patriarchal industry that exploits females, steals their babies, robs them of dignity … uses them up until they're no longer of any use, then murders them for meat?"

"Zoe is just upset she didn't get to grope the cows," Chloe taunted.

"Grope the cows?" Sierra asked. "What are you talking about?"

"I was the one who decided not to," Zoe huffed.

"Probably afraid you'd like it too much," Chloe said. "She hates boys enough."

"I don't hate boys," she countered. "They're just weasels."

"Enough you two," Caleb called, cutting off any further argument, then turned back to Hailey. "Let's get back to the topic at hand. Now, I think it's …" he trailed off, looking to his wife.

"Admirable," Sierra prompted.

"Yes," nodding, Caleb continued, "It's admirable that you want to take over the family business, but you're still in college."

"Who's going to run it? You?" Hailey asked, with more than a hint of mirth. "Let's face it, I'm the only one in this family that's ever had any experience working on a farm."

"We know that," Sierra soothed. "And I'm sure you would do a wonderful job. It's just …" Hailey's eyes flicked between her aunt and uncle, narrowing.

"It's an enormous commitment," her uncle added. "You won't be able to travel, you can't take any vacations. You'll be too tired to hang out with your friends. You'll be required to be here every day. Day in and day out. All to care for and feed the animals."

"Caleb," her father grumbled in warning.

Her uncle continued, ignoring him. "Earlier, we were discussing the merits of downsizing, or perhaps even selling the place altogether—"

"You want to sell the farm?" Hailey's voice rose; her eyes flitting between her aunt and uncle. "Is that why you wanted to know about the animals? Because you want to sell them?" She looked at her dad. Her dad, who always had her back. Her dad, who told her she could do anything she wanted in life. Her dad, who was now looking sheepishly back at her. Hailey's heart fell, and her voice softened. "You too, Dad? You want to sell?"

"I haven't made up my mind yet—"

"But you're leaning toward it?" He opened his mouth to answer, but she didn't let him. "Grampa would have wanted me to stay," she pleaded. "He would have wanted me to look after the animals."

"If you call what you do—"

"Not now, Zoe," Hailey cut her off without looking.

"Fine," Zoe grumbled, then jammed her earbuds in and cranked up her music.

Hailey's eyes bored into her dad's. "I know he would've wanted me to take over."

"I know honey, I know. It's just—you're so young."

"I can do it."

"That's not the issue."

"It's not?" she scoffed.

"Of course not. I have every faith you could run the business. The question is, should you have to? Should you have to take on this massive responsibility? Is it because you want to, or because Dad wanted it? I know how he was, always extolling the virtues of the business, talking about the proud line of farmers who've worked this land—"

"Overlooking the fact that he abandoned the farm for decades," Caleb cut in, grumbling. "Only coming back when his own father grew ill."

"Caleb, now is not the time for that," her dad chided.

"He was following his dream," Hailey said, jumping to Grampa's defense.

"I just think it's hypocritical that he simply expected one of us to take his place," Caleb argued. "He practically disowned me when I turned him down."

"I believe it was the way you turned him down he took issue with." Her father waved a dismissive hand through the air. "But the issue now is—"

"When our Hailey here started showing interest, I'd never seen him happier," Caleb said. "After that, he welcomed me back as if he hadn't pushed me away in the first place."

Hailey had suspected the reason her grampa and uncle didn't get along, but had never known for sure. To her, it had always seemed Uncle Caleb was the cold one, but if Grampa had—

Hailey shook her head; it didn't matter. Grampa was gone. And Caleb wanted to sell the farm. Grampa's farm. Her farm.

"I want to," she blurted.

"You want to?" Dad asked.

"I want to run the farm. I have since I was little. Sure, Grampa encouraged it, maybe even expected it. But I want to at least try."

8

After being up the previous night and sleeping most of the day—as you can imagine—Hailey's schedule was way off. She had stayed up a couple of hours later than usual, hoping it would help get her schedule back on track. But with the outcome of the farm up in the air, she still spent several hours idly studying her moonlit ceiling. Worrying about the farm's future; her future.

When she did eventually drift off, she fell into a restless slumber and woke up more tired than she had been when she'd laid down. But that didn't matter; she had a job to do, and she intended to prove to everyone she could do it—including herself.

She rolled out of bed and lumbered to the bathroom. Steam billowed from the opening door, revealing a fog-coated shower streaked by rivulets of condensation that left long furrows tracing the length of the glass door.

Who else would be up so early?

Preening in front of the carelessly wiped mirror, brush inches from her silky blonde hair, was a familiar shape wrapped in a fluffy white towel: her cousin Chloe.

The girl whipped around.

"Oh, sorry," Hailey mumbled and started to close the door.

"I forgot to mention the lock is broken."

The girl's startled expression morphed into a small smile.

"No, it's alright. I'm just finishing up; come on in."

"Um, okay?" Hailey's brow knit. "Are you sure? It's just …
last night Zoe said—"

"Oh, what did Zoe say?" Chloe scoffed.

"Just that you're super modest."

Chloe's smile crept into a smirk, and her eyes brightened.
"That's not it at all."

"No? I mean, it's okay." Now Hailey was totally confused,
and the residual haze of fatigue didn't help. "You changed in the
bathroom last night, and she said you won't even change around
her."

"Oh, it's not modesty, it's this." Parting her towel, Chloe
unveiled her side. Along her upper ribs was a crisp, black tattoo.
A line of runes etched into an especially thick strip of alabaster
skin: ᛒᛁᚢᛗᛁ. With what looked like a pair of little green leaves
growing from the top of the last character.

Hailey darted forward to study her cousin's ink. "What does
it mean?"

"It's basically my name in runes … or as close as I could
figure; I had to research it myself. *Chloe* means 'blooming' in
Ancient Greek, right?" Hailey just nodded. "And the word *blómi*
means 'to bloom' in Old Norse."

"And you have the little green sprout. That's so cool," she
cooed. "But where did you get it?" Hailey stepped back and
gazed into her cousin's eyes. "On that note, when and how did
you get it?"

"One of my friends has a sister who's a tattoo artist," Chloe
said, beaming. "We talked her into giving them to us a couple of
years ago—well, it was more like we begged and pleaded until
she got tired of us asking, but same thing."

"A couple years? You've had this since you were thirteen?
And neither your parents nor sister know?"

"I've gotten good at hiding it, you know"—Chloe secured
her towel around her and turned to her cousin—"I choose
swimsuits and bras that'll cover it and tend to change alone, just

in case. However, like yesterday, I don't always bother with a bra—with these 'squito bites, I don't exactly need one." She grimaced, waving a hand over her chest, then shrugged. "You know."

Hailey caught herself unconsciously nodding.

"But I still have to be careful. You know how Mom and Dad are. They really don't like tattoos—they'd prolly disown me. And Zoe, well, she would either pressure me into helping her get one or else tell on me first thing. With her, you never know." Chloe's face tightened. "You're not going to tell, are you?" she asked; worry suddenly filling her voice.

"Oh no, of course not. I'm just surprised, is all."

Chloe let out a sharp sigh, and a smile crept back across her face. "You know, I've been so scared they're going to find out. Sometimes I'm not even sure it was worth it. But other times, it's so thrilling to know I'm keeping this secret from everyone. It hurt like crazy too. Apparently, along the ribs is one of the most painful spots. I wish I'd known before ..."

"I can imagine, this hurt plenty"—Hailey revealed a caricature of a plump baby cow etched into the skin on one side of her belly—"and it wasn't on bone."

"Oh, that's so cute," Chloe cooed.

"We can both keep a secret from Zoe."

"I don't know what made her like this." Chloe's face morphed into confusion. "I miss my twin. We used to be inseparable, you know? The only ones to know each other's secrets. Then one day, when we were about twelve, she was just different. Not only did she 'let slip' some of my secrets, but she started keeping things from me, confiding in new people. After that, we just grew apart." She frowned. "I've missed that. I've missed having someone to trust."

"You can trust me," Hailey insisted.

Hesitance and hope sparked in Chloe's eyes, as if she were battling to believe her. Finally, one side appeared to win out, and she blurted, "I'm gay." A mask of dread seemed to fall over her with the whispered confession as her shoulders hunched.

Hailey blinked. Why was that such a big deal? She was

shocked, but only because the confession came from left field. She'd almost let an obligatory 'Are you sure?' escape her lips, but thought better of it.

Hailey stepped forward and enveloped her cousin in a powerful embrace. "I'm glad you told me. That must have taken guts."

Chloe melted into her embrace. "Nobody knows."

"Thank you for trusting me enough to tell me."

"Mom and Dad would kill me. You know how religious they are. Well, Mom is, anyway. I think Dad just goes along with her." Chloe was babbling now.

"Oh, honey, your parents love you. You must know that." The girl just shrugged.

After a minute, Chloe stepped back, looking as if the weight of the world had been lifted from her shoulders. She'd found someone to trust, and Hailey would never do anything to betray that.

"I better finish getting ready," she said as she floated from the room. She stopped and stuck her head back around the corner. "I can help you with the cows again, right?"

"Of course."

"Good," she chimed. "How long will it be? Are you going to take a shower?"

"I'll be down in a few," Hailey said. "I usually wait to clean up until after the milking is done."

Chloe gave her cousin a wry moue. "Why didn't I think of that?" She shrugged and disappeared.

When she entered the kitchen some ten minutes later, Hailey was greeted by her father, uncle, and cousin.

Tipping the coffeepot, her dad poured her a cup, asking, "How do you like it?"

"I'll take care of it."

As her father passed her a mug of the scalding bitter liquid, his eyes flitted to her cousin. "And I'm assuming Chloe is going to help you milk again?"

"Yeah, then I have classes today," Hailey said as she prepared her coffee, adding plenty of fresh milk.

"That's good. I'm going to go to the city and pick up your mom and brothers at the airport."

Stepmom, Hailey didn't object. "When are they coming in?"

"A little after noon." He grimaced, not looking thrilled with the round trip of more than two hours. "I have a few hours before I need to leave. It should give me more than enough time to get there. Besides, I want to swing by a few places while I'm out."

In Hailey's peripheral vision, she glimpsed her cousin perk up, but the girl didn't say anything.

Dad turned to his brother. "What about you, Caleb? What are you going to do today?"

"I thought I'd stick around the house this morning. Keep an eye on things."

"Are you guys still planning on visiting the funeral home this afternoon?" Hailey asked.

"Yeah, as soon as Mom gets here. Can you watch your brothers?"

Her brow scrunched. "What time will it be?"

"By the time we get back, it should be about two—two thirty …" A gleaming light of recognition shone in his eyes. "You'll still be in class, won't you?"

"Yeah, and I already missed yesterday. I can't miss today."

"I'll watch the boys," Chloe said.

Dad turned to her. "Are you sure? They can be a handful."

Caleb swept a hand through the air. "Chloe can handle them … now if it was Zoe. She might have them help her release the cattle into the wild or organize a cattle revolt."

"She wouldn't do that; would she?" Hailey let her concern show. "I mean, freeing the cattle?"

"Nah, I'm just kidding." Caleb smirked, "On the other hand; *Vive la bovin révolution!*"

Worries allayed, Hailey rolled her eyes at her uncle as Chloe groaned.

With the morning's schedule more or less ironed out, Hailey took Chloe along to start the day.

Caleb couldn't believe his luck. After the milking, Hailey had cleaned up and left for class, and at his suggestion, his brother ended up taking Chloe with him into the city. Ridding him of three obstacles. After that, all he had to do was have his wife distract his remaining daughter. So, he'd asked Sierra to take Zoe into town.

He placed a call to the gentleman he met the previous day, and before long, an enormous GMC pickup pulled into the drive. Rays of sunlight glimmered off scarlet paint and gravel popped under the truck's weight as the vehicle crawled up to the milking barn. As they pulled to a stop, Caleb slipped out into the warm morning sun, tablet in hand.

Four people piled out of the pickup, then introductions were made. Robert Ellison was accompanied by his daughter Lily, an elfin girl of about ten or eleven. Lincoln Peretti, a tall, slender man, had accompanied his son, Jeremy, who looked to be about the twin's age, maybe older. Pleasantries were traded and the obligatory condolences were expressed before he got down to business.

The tiff the previous night hadn't deterred him. Half of this place was his now, and it was about to pay off. He'd done some further research into the animal's worth and figured out that the older the calves were, the more he could get. You wouldn't get much for a newborn, only about fifty bucks a pop. Their value seemed to be contingent on how much you spent taking care of them—feeding them and fattening them up increased the price.

As Caleb ushered them through the barn, he asked, "So, what are we looking for?"

"I'd like to see your steers. Somewhere between six and seven months," Jeremy said. "Preferably, one sired by your champion, Old Mac."

Caleb nodded at the young man. "Of course. We have several." He'd spent the last evening looking through the tablet, studying what they had. Then he turned to young Lily. "And what about you, little lady?"

"I want a calf, a girl."

"Not too young," her father reminded her. "Freshly

weaned."

Not as much of a profit, but not bad. "I think we have what you need."

As soon as they stepped into the calf shed, they were greeted by a chorus of high-pitched mooing. Lily squealed and ran up to a pen holding one of the youngest calves. "He's so little."

"He's bigger than you are," her father said.

"Can I feed him?" Lily asked, ignoring the jibe.

"I'm sorry, sweetie, they've already been fed."

"Ahhhh." Her adorable face shifted into an exaggerated frown—complete with a jutting lower lip.

"Come on, Lily," her father urged. "Let's pick out your calf." And just like that, Lily's frown rebounded into a brilliant smile, revealing missing teeth.

As Lily's father led her around to peruse the calves, Caleb led Jeremy and Lincoln out of the shed and back to the pens where they kept the steers. Almost immediately, Jeremy's eyes locked on one steer.

"What can you tell me about that one?"

Thanks to the handy dandy tablet, Caleb had answers to all their questions. "Let's see," he typed in the ID embossed on the tag. "Okay. It appears he's six and a half months old. Yes, sired by Old Mac."

Curious about the newcomers, and as if realizing they were talking about him, the steer edged over.

"It all looks correct. The legs are straight and wide … muscle looks good. Strong back and smooth shoulders. Deep-bodied and thick. He's level, and well-balanced." The boy turned to his dad. "What do you think?"

His father nodded, but shrugged. "It's up to you. It's your project. By rights, he should have already had one picked out," Lincoln chided, turning to Caleb. "He's been procrastinating a bit."

The boy barely paid him any mind. "I was waiting for the best." Jeremy craned his neck to get a different angle. "And I'm lucky I did." The kid turned to him. "I'd intended to ask your father for a peek at his stock a couple weeks ago, but it's summer, ya know? The time just slips by."

The kid asked to have the animal weighed, and Caleb happily obliged. With the help of the soon-to-be new owner, the young bovine was steered out of the pen, along the alley, and onto the scale. Apparently, the weight was satisfactory, because after a bit more poking and prodding, then a brief discussion of payment, they came to an agreement, shaking hands.

Caleb left the little guy in a catch pen to get acquainted with his new owner while he and Lincoln returned to the Ellisons. Father and daughter were both peering into the pen housing some of the older calves.

Lily noticed him and darted over, bowling into him and squealing, "I want her! Right there!" She pointed. "Number three-two-four. I'm going to name her Lodi. Little Miss Lodi …" Caleb tuned the rest of her babble out as he haggled with her father.

While not a gold mine, the three-month-old calf still drew more than a newborn. Caleb grinned; he'd sold two cows, both at the upper end of the price spectrum. Even better, both men had seemed delighted with their purchases. Hopefully, he could expect more sales. It was, after all, his first day.

The men helped Caleb hook up the cattle trailer to his dad's new Ram 2500 and get the cattle loaded. The trip to the ag barn took a few minutes. Unfamiliar with the monstrous rig he hauled, Caleb took it easy. He was in no hurry.

Sally Jessup and another woman met their little group at the ag barn. Maryanne Salazar was one of the local teachers, as well as a volunteer for 4-H. Caleb stood back and watched as the women helped Jeremy unload the cattle. Bribing the young cattle with a sweet treat, the trio led the steer, then the calf, into their stalls.

A rambunctious Lily Ellison bounced around in the pen, going from petting to hugging and stroking her 'Lil Miss Lodi' while gabbing away at her teacher, asking spitfire questions, barely waiting for answers.

As he watched, Caleb was approached by two more parents, each wanting a look at his stock. He happily obliged.

9

The ride back to his father's—his farm—in the roomy rental car had gone smoothly, though, with his niece and the twins in the car, Michael Graham hadn't had a chance for a frank discussion of the next steps with his wife. Little ears always seemed to overhear more than you'd like them to. His eyes found the trio in the back seat; Chloe's creamy alabaster skin and cascade of blonde locks stood in stark contrast to his boy's smooth golden beige complexion and straight dark hair, a legacy of their mother's mixed Filipino heritage. His niece sat between Aiden and Alex, entertaining them with tales of cows. She seemed to be taking quickly to the animals—she'd even asked him to help convince her parents to let her stay the summer to help Hailey.

His chest constricted at the thought of decisions still to be made. The funeral arrangements should be fairly standard. It was the farm's disposition he dreaded contemplating; though he'd been unable to get it out of his mind, he had yet to come to any conclusions.

Once he pulled into the drive, his twin boys strained in their seatbelts, taking everything in with large, round eyes. Living halfway across the country, the boys hadn't been able to visit their grandfather as much as he'd have liked. Though when they had made it down, his father had dutifully doted on the boys.

"Moo cow!" they chorused. "Moo cow, moo cow."

By the time he'd parked and opened the child safety doors, the twins were bouncing in their seats, having escaped their harnesses.

"Can we see da cows?" one said.

"Can we? Can we, pweese?" the other begged.

"I'll take them," Chloe offered. "While you and Aunt Lexa get settled in."

Michael could see the hesitation flicker across Lexa's features. Another reason they'd refrained from visiting too often was the size of the animals. The massive beasts could trample their little boys in a heartbeat, without even realizing it.

"Just to the fence line, for now, Chloe," he offered, gazing at his wife. "We can take them to see the calves later." Lexa nodded at his suggestion. Though still hesitant, the trepidation had faded.

"Okay, Uncle Michael." Chloe held out her arms. "Come on boys, hands."

"Just for a few minutes," Lexa called as they ran off.

"Okay," Chloe called back.

"She won't let them get hurt, will she?"

"Of course not, honey. Chloe's the good one."

"And you're sure that's Chloe?"

"Trust me," he said, smiling. "You can't get the two mixed up." Unlike his own boys, who were still so alike, they both constantly had to check. "You'll see."

Michael hauled their luggage inside and up the stairs, dropped the twin's luggage in the hallway, and directed Lexa into the small guest bedroom they would share; eager to discuss what weighed so heavily on his mind.

Hailey could only take so much. Classes had been a nightmare. Consumed with her grampa's death and the disposition of the farm, Hailey still hadn't checked her phone by the time she'd got to school—much less troll social media—and was surprised by the vehement scorn she'd received once she'd shown up. Before she even knew what was going on, cold looks and barbed words were hurled her way.

She'd quickly learned of the massive backlash sweeping across the net after poor Mallory Rockwell's death. Luckily, a ring of friends flocked around her, offering supportive and consoling words, insulating her from the worst of the scrutiny. Hailey tried to put her head down and bull through the day, intent on letting this mess wash over her.

And it had worked for a little while, but surprisingly, her breaking point had come, not from the naysayers, but from a sudden wave of well-wishers and belated condolences. She'd been so perplexed at the shift, it wasn't until the third random person came up to offer his condolences and support that she found out about the video sweeping the media. Somehow, someone had leaked a video shot that night. The footage showed Mallory Rockwell, clearly and knowingly, trespassing on Grampa's land. Old Mac's agitation was plain for anyone to see. Yet the girl ignored clear warning signs while using the riled bull as a backdrop to perform some stupid stunt for the sake of views.

And just like that, the media's narrative pivoted, changing with the evidence like a leaf on the wind. They praised John Graham for his swift intervention, commending him as if they hadn't just been his largest critics—killing his own prized bull had likely saved more lives. And social media followed suit.

While the footage vindicated her grampa, it was too much for Hailey. Tears poured from her eyes. The whole situation was too much. Her mind whirred, whiplash at the abrupt change of tack. Villain to hero in a couple of hours.

She left early, eager to see her brothers, dad, and even her stepmother.

When she pulled up, her brothers were pressed against the fence with Chloe while a herd of curious cattle huddled around, inspecting the newcomers, and leaning in to receive loving pats from the boys. Hailey smiled—such gentle animals.

The sound of Hailey's truck drew their attention. Chloe

grabbed the squirming boys to stop them from darting toward her as she coasted to a stop. As soon as she opened the door, Chloe released them, and the twins hurtled toward her. "Haywee, Haywee, Haywee!"

Aiden and Alex were scooped into loving arms, and she carried the squirming twins into the house as the two screeched over each other, fighting for Hailey's attention.

"Listen, I want to hear all about it, but I have to go to the bathroom. I'll be right back."

"Hurry!"

"Hurry!"

Grinning at the warm welcome, Hailey bounded up the stairs. Halfway along the hall, her father's voice brought her to a screeching halt.

"… want to sell. But I don't know, Lexa, maybe Caleb's right. This might be what's best for everyone."

Eyes widening, Hailey's chest tightened even as her thudding heart threatened to burst out of her ribs. Dad wanted to sell too? If so, she had no hope of keeping the farm. Her ladies. Was it Lexa? Was she trying to get him to sell too? What gave her the right? Hailey's blood boiled.

However, Lexa's next words threw her for a loop. "I think we should give Hailey a shot."

What? Hailey gasped. She covered her mouth, sure it had to have been loud enough to hear downstairs, but they didn't seem to notice.

"What about college?" Dad asked.

"What about it?"

"I don't think she can do both. It's a lot of work. There'd be a lot of changes. It might take a while to adjust."

"So, she takes a semester off, then restarts with a lighter schedule until she gets acclimated," Lexa countered. "Or … I mean, really, what harm would it do if she took a couple of years off to follow her dreams?" Who was this woman, and what had she done with Hailey's stepmother? "She can always go back if she decides to. I'll continue to help with her tuition. What would be the harm in letting her try?"

Hailey was surprised by Lexa's words, guilty for inadvertently eavesdropping, but surprised all the same. She hadn't thought her stepmother particularly liked her or approved of her. There had always been strife between the two—but now that she thought about it, perhaps that had been her fault.

She'd been thirteen when this new woman had shown up in her dad's life, in both their lives, demanding—stealing—more and more of her dad's time. Then they'd married, without even asking how she felt—though she supposed by that point her feelings had been clear enough. Not long after that, they'd been forced to uproot and follow Lexa to the city, pulling her away from her grandparents and friends. While that hadn't been as bad as she'd feared—she'd still been able to visit often enough with it being a little more than an hour away—Hailey hadn't ever forgiven her stepmom for that, no matter how wonderful the career was or how happy it made the woman.

Then the twins came. Driving more of a wedge between the two strong-willed women. The twins drew ever more attention from her dad and stepmom. And she was called upon to be a babysitter whenever they required. She'd always loved her twin brothers; it hadn't been their fault who their mother was.

Then, to make matters worse, a couple of years ago, Lexa's career had threatened to drag them all across the country. It had only been through Grampa's intervention and assurances that she'd been allowed to live with him and return to the small town for her last year of school.

But now, her stepmom was standing up for her; encouraging her father to let her take time off from school. And the tuition—Hailey hadn't ever considered the money—both her dad and stepmom had comfortable jobs, sharing the bills and responsibilities, but she'd always just assumed that her tuition came from her dad's income.

"… don't need the money," Lexa said.

Caught up in her musings, Hailey had missed a portion of the conversation.

"Caleb and Sierra are intent on selling. And as he keeps reminding me, half of this place is his."

"Oh, screw Caleb. It's your brother's fault he can't manage his finances, not yours. It's not your fault he lives above his means, and it's certainly not Hailey's. Why should our daughter miss this chance?"

Our daughter? Hailey's heart leapt. Is that really how Lexa felt? Had she been at fault all this time? The sudden realization of how horribly she'd treated the woman swamped her. Her mother. That stopped now.

"He'll still get his share of the profits. And, if worse comes to worst, we may have to sell some cattle or land to placate him or even buy him out. I'm sure we can work up some kind of payment plan."

"I don't know if he'll be content with that. He seems to think the land is worth a fortune. He intends to sell to some real estate developer."

"Well, that's his problem, isn't it? Besides, your father was smart. With the trust he set up, both you and your brother have to agree to sell."

Heart soaring, mind fuzzy with equal parts hope and disbelief, Hailey Graham continued to the bathroom, then flew down the stairs to rejoin her brothers. Though still ashamed over eavesdropping on her parents' conversation, Hailey couldn't help being grateful that she had. A load had been lifted from her. They were seriously considering letting her run the farm; it was practically a done deal—good thing she didn't have to break it to her uncle. She smirked. But even more important, and more comforting, was the realization of how Lexa felt about her.

Chloe sat on the living room floor, playing with the twins. Along with a herd of plastic cattle, Grampa had collected a wide array of vintage die-cast 1:16 scale farm vehicles. Gleaming metallic, forest green paint contrasted against yellow trim, shimmering in the brightly lit room. His collection contained more than a dozen unique models of tractors and many types of farming equipment for them to haul. From the harvester and silage wagon to a hay bailer. There were plows, wagons, and augers, a disk harrow, and even a grain elevator. Many of them she'd played with as a child, but many more had been added since—some of them he'd restored himself. He'd been planning to unveil a new Prestige Edition Four-Track Tractor. Her chest constricted. He'd never get to see the joy on the boys' faces when he presented it.

The pressure in her chest intensified. Grampa was gone, and the boys would be lucky if they even remembered him. Blinking back tears, Hailey scanned the rest of the room. Zoe lounged in shadow in her accustomed place on a recliner in the corner, earbuds in, and her phone's ever-present blue glow washing over her face. On the couch, Sierra absentmindedly watched the boys play while Caleb studied a combine from Grampa's collection.

Her heart skipped a beat; if he knew how much they were worth—

She'd once run across one at an antique store, and its exorbitant price encouraged her to look them up; the value of some of them had taken her breath away. She'd confronted her grampa, asking him how he could have let her, or the boys, play with them. His jovial response had been, "… they're toys, toys are meant to be played with."

She couldn't bear the thought of Caleb hocking them. They weren't his. She wouldn't let him.

Luckily, Mom and Dad thumped down the stairs—it was bizarrely refreshing to think of Lexa as Mom. The commotion drew Caleb's attention, and he set the toy down, then rose to his feet.

"You guys ready?" Caleb asked, looking at his watch.

"Yeah." Dad's eyes fell on her. "Oh Hailey, you're here. I thought you had a class."

Hailey took a deep breath. "I kinda … blew it off." She suppressed a wince, dreading his reaction after the support they'd just voiced, albeit behind closed doors.

Dad blinked, then nodded, waving it off. "It's okay, I understand. Can you help watch the boys?"

"Nope."

"No?" His brows crinkled.

"Chloe's going to be in charge until you get back," she

deadpanned, then broke out in a gleaming smile, "I'm going to play with my brothers."

Slow smiles spread across Dad and Lexa's faces. "Well, don't be too hard on your babysitter."

The two couples left, and Hailey got down to some long-awaited playtime.

10

On his way home, Michael reflected on their visit to the funeral home. The director had been maddeningly obsequious, willing to bend over backward for their comfort, as most were. Dad already had a plot reserved next to their mother's which helped. They'd picked out a nice but plain coffin. He found it annoying that Caleb automatically gravitated toward the least expensive options, yet he knew their father wouldn't have minded.

Michael hoped they hadn't scheduled the viewing too quickly. He knew his brother just wanted to get it over with. And to a certain extent, so did he. But it was more the desire to lay his father to rest than be done with the matter. After the uproar involved with the young girl's death, it felt best. They'd scheduled the visitation for the next evening and the funeral for noon the day after. In the small community, it should be easy to spread the word.

His father had been so well respected that, even before the truth leaked with the videos, there had been rumblings that people from around the tri-state area, especially his fellow farmers and ranchers, would ignore the media outcry and flock to the small town to pay their respects. With the truth leaked, and the news cycle now trumpeting his dad's innocence, he expected even more would show up.

Michael came home to find his three children, a twenty-year-old and twin four-year-olds cuddled up in the downstairs bedroom, taking a nap. While one niece was still in the living room, straightening up, rearranging his father's vintage farm toys, the other was nowhere to be seen, probably off engrossed in her phone as usual. It was nice to have the family under one roof, even if tragedy had precipitated it.

The next few hours proceeded without incident—Hailey was attentive to her brothers and much more cordial to her mother than usual; could it be the loss of her grandfather that prompted the change? Around six that evening, Hailey and Chloe disappeared into the barn once more. When Chloe popped in again sometime later, she had an invitation so exciting the boys could barely contain themselves.

"Is Hailey out there alone?" Michael asked as Chloe barged into the living room, a muck-stained jumpsuit draping around her lithe frame. He'd specifically told her he didn't want her out there alone.

"Huh?" Chloe paused and glanced out toward the barn. "Oh, yeah. She's just finishing up and wants to know if the boys want to come out and help her feed the calves."

"Can we, can we?" the boys chorused, jumping up and down. "Pweese, pweese."

"Of course, you can," Lexa said.

"Yay!" they squealed.

"Why don't we all go?" Michael asked, scanning the room.

Zoe peeled her gaze from her phone. "No, thanks." No surprise there—she'd wanted nothing to do with the animals.

"Are you sure?" Lexa urged. "It could be fun."

"I'm sure." The blue glow of Zoe's phone illuminated her features, accentuating a look of contempt she didn't bother trying to disguise.

"Why don't Caleb and I go grab some food while you guys are out?" Sierra offered; her face unusually pale.

"Yeah?" Caleb asked. "We still have plenty of leftovers from the neighbors."

Sierra winced. "I want something hot and fresh."

"Sure, hon," Caleb said, giving her a relaxed shrug, "if that's what you want."

"Pizza, pizza," the boys said.

"Hush now, boys," Lexa chided, hugging the rambunctious twins to her, then turned to Sierra. "What were you thinking?"

"Actually, pizza sounds wonderful."

"Yay!" the twins chorused.

Zoe peered around from her phone. "Don't forget—"

"Yeah, yeah," Caleb agreed. "Vegan for Zoe."

Satisfied, Zoe returned to her screen as the rest of the arrangements were made. Michael hoped neither of his boys would be so withdrawn and sullen in their teens. Though Hailey had gone through quite a tumultuous phase herself.

While Caleb and Sierra went to pick up takeout, Chloe led Michael, Lexa, and the boys out into the milking barn. Hailey was just finishing spraying down the walkways as they entered. Grinning, she gave the boys the grand tour on their way through the structure. She ended the tour by ushering them into a spartan room. "… and this is the calf kitchen."

"Where are dey?" Alex asked.

"This is where we prepare their meals," Hailey explained.

"Do da mommy cows cook, too?" Aiden called.

His daughter let out a warm chuckle. "No, silly. The mommas make all the food the calves need in their bellies." She poked him in the belly.

"Meelk," one called.

"I wike chocowate meelk," the other said. "Do the baby cows wike chocowate meelk?"

Hailey let out another delighted chuckle. "No, they like their milk plain."

As she prepared the milk, she summarized the process. The boys were far too excited to get more than the basics, but he and Lexa soaked it all in. Before long, Hailey had the milk cart, or milk taxi as she called it, prepped and led them out back to see the calves. The open-air structure allowed a healthy cross breeze—augmented by an array of droning fans—to dampen the worst of summer's gentle breath.

Greeted by the sight of so many baby moo cows, the twin's faces lit up. The curious, awkward young cows crowded forward, allowing the boys to pet them. Hailey had a grand time helping the boys bottle feed the calves. The twins were especially thrilled and wonderfully disgusted by the way Hailey had them help feed the youngest cows. After Hailey showed them it was safe, they delighted in sticking their milk-coated fingers into the babies' mouths and leading them to the bottle.

When Hailey introduced a pair of calves to the calf pen in back, everyone watched in amusement as the calves pranced around the open space, getting used to their new hay-strewn floor and nuzzling their new pen mates. Hailey left to grab some of their food, something she called calf starter.

Alex was so enamored with them, he loudly counted each.

"... eight ... nine ... ten," he cried. "Ten baby moo cows."

Walking up as he finished, Hailey came to an abrupt halt, her face going blank as confusion swept over her. She extended a finger, ticking it as she counted the cattle, then her eyes went wide.

"What is it, Hailey?" Lexa asked, worry creeping into her tone.

"That's not right."

"What's not?" Michael asked.

"There are two missing," Hailey explained.

"What? Are you sure?" He couldn't help himself. Nor did he blame Hailey for the exasperated look she gave him.

"Yes, Dad. I can count. There were ten in there this morning, and I just added two. There's supposed to be twelve now."

"Could they have gotten out?" Lexa asked.

"Well, yes. Cows are surprisingly good at escaping."

"Really? I didn't realize."

Hailey nodded. "They're consummate escape artists. If there's a way out, they'll find it," she said as she walked across the building, scanning the other rows on the off chance she'd missed two calves wandering around, then leaned over the south gate to check the alley running between the outbuildings and the bullpens. "But there would be signs," she murmured.

"An open gate or something?"

"Or something." The gate rang as Hailey smacked it, then turned back to them. "But they couldn't have gotten far," she said as she passed, striding to the opposite fence to scan the fields.

"Do you think someone S-T-O-L-E them?" Lexa asked, glancing at the boys, who had, as yet, remained oblivious to the situation and their sister's worry.

Hailey glanced at her stepmother, then shrugged slightly. "I mean … it's possible." Hailey looked perplexed as she shook her head. "But … it's a lot of effort for a couple of calves. I mean, they couldn't be worth much more than a few hundred dollars."

Michael's brain clicked at the information. *He wouldn't have.*

"… Any one of the ladies is worth almost ten times as much. And the bulls even more."

"And none were missing?" Lexa asked.

Michael felt heat prickling in his chest.

"None of the milkers, for sure. And I didn't notice any missing bulls." Hailey turned to Chloe. "Did you see anyone around today?"

The girl shook her head. "I went with Uncle Mike to pick up Lexa and the twins."

"Can you run and ask Zoe? I need to check the rest of the herd."

Chloe raced away, followed by Lexa and the boys, as Michael accompanied his daughter out to check on the herd. In the pit of his stomach, he had a terrible feeling he knew who'd taken the missing animals. But would Caleb have done that? Could he be so cruel?

Chloe caught up with them near the steer pens, where two more animals were missing. Apparently, Zoe had gone into town with her mother and hadn't seen anything suspicious either.

Caleb let his fingers tap out a loose beat on the steering wheel as he and Sierra waited on their order. His mind was awash in ideas as he pondered how to profit most from the farm. The land would probably be worth the most. He couldn't wait to get rid of those pesky animals. His brother would have to do the right thing. He would eventually listen to reason. Michael couldn't possibly want Hailey to toil away as a farmer.

So intent on his musings, Caleb hadn't realized how quiet Sierra had been until she spoke. "I found a copy of your father's trust," she blurted.

"Oh?" Caleb asked, still only half listening. Perhaps the college might want to buy some of the land for student housing; that could bring a tidy sum. Or—

"It isn't what we expected."

"Hmm?"

"The trust," she said, "your father changed it."

"Oh? How so?" Dad had probably added Michael's twins to the thing. The last time he'd brought it up had been before the birth of the boys. And his daughters might get something. He'd be sure to put whatever they received to good use.

"Caleb, look at me," Sierra said.

He did. "Dad added the twins, did he?"

"Well, yes, but that's not what I was talking about."

For the first time, Caleb noticed the pinched expression contorting his wife's otherwise lovely face.

His brows knit. "What is it?"

"He left Hailey more than we expected."

"That's not surprising. He always had a soft spot for her. And she was great at ingratiating herself with the old man. What are we talking about here? A couple of grand?"

Her pained look deepened.

He squinted, worry building. "What? How much? He was well off. Wasn't he?"

"He left her a third of the farm. And a sizable nest egg to help in lean times."

Caleb blinked, his breath seizing in his chest. "A third?"

"That's not all. In the past few years, he'd invested heavily in expanding the farm, purchasing more land, and upgrading the equipment."

"Well, the land must be worth a song. Even if I have to persuade Michael, we can just—"

"That's just it! All three of you have to agree to sell the farm."

The fist clenched over his heart. "What?" Caleb's anger boiled.

"Plus, she's in charge of the dairy operation. The disposition and welfare of the cattle solely depend on her."

"What was that old man playing at?! He left a girl, barely twenty years old, a third of *my* farm? *My* inheritance. Not only that, but he gave her the run of the operation and the decision of whether or not to sell." *More power than either me or my brother.* "How could he do such a thing?" Caleb raged.

"I don't know."

"Where is this document?" Caleb was fairly shouting now. "How do we know it's real? Could Hailey have doctored it?"

Sierra winced. "I don't know about that, but …"

"Tell me," Caleb took a deep breath, allowing his tone to return to a semblance of normal. "Tell me you didn't show it to anyone."

"Of course not! I hid it in the back of the closet."

"Good—"

"—But if it is genuine, I don't know how we can keep it from them."

"It'll at least buy us some time. Hopefully, enough to come up with a plan."

Caleb slammed his palm into the steering wheel and cursed.

11

After the pesky pressure that had built up in her udders during a tranquil day of grazing was released, the young mother moseyed over to the calf shed for a visit. Through the cold steel bars, she could see the scattering of calves frolicking in their pens. She watched them at their play for a moment before she noticed that something wasn't right. Her plaintive cries failed to produce her missing calf. Where was she? She was always here. Had always been here.

She caught only a faint whiff of her calf as she bounded back and forth along the fence, crying out in distress again; only this time, the mournful cries of another young mother joined hers. People were about, but they didn't seem to notice their distress.

After a time, receiving no reply, the young mother focused on the lingering traces of her missing offspring, using her extraordinarily keen sense of smell to guide her as she set off along the fence line, searching for a trail.

After a long week grinding away at his nine to five, Sam was looking forward to retreating to the lake to spend a long weekend with the wife and a pair of rambunctious kids. Thank God for summer break; he didn't know if he could have waited any longer for his kids to get out of school. Though, as it was, their constant bickering was threatening to drive him over the edge already.

"Mom, Sammy touched me—" came his eight-year-old son's falsetto voice.

"Did not!" his daughter replied indignantly.

"Did too!"

"Stay on your own side," his wife chided distractedly. Her face was buried in her cell, scrolling through her social media.

"I am!" his daughter complained. "He's the one messing with me."

"Nuh-uh."

One of Sam's eyelids twitched as pain lanced across his temple. As if the argument wasn't enough, the setting sun was already playing havoc with his vision. It had drifted to just the wrong angle, rendering the visor useless at the moment, as the sun's piercing rays flooded through the small gap over the rear-view mirror, only amplifying his worsening headache.

As they raced west toward Lake Drive, the line of decorative privacy fencing fluttered by, obscuring most of the luxurious development to the south. Sam grumbled. The entitled jerks didn't even want the likes of him to glimpse their palatial homes. It wasn't fair. Sure, he'd love to have been able to afford a spread in Cimarron Acres, to provide that for his family, but with his meager salary at the plant and his wife's laughably incommensurate pay as a teacher, they'd never be able to afford it.

Before long, the vinyl ramparts ended, replaced by an untidy, overgrown field of corn. Sam peeled his gaze from the shabby crops flashing by, shifting to the side as he tried to block the worst of the glare flooding into the windshield.

The disagreement in the back grew in volume during his reverie, each of his wonderful kids sniping at each other, trying to bring down their parent's fury on the other. How his wife expected the two to share a tent this weekend was anyone's guess, but she hadn't heeded his warnings.

The argument came to a head when a loud *smack* echoed

through the truck's cab. As one, he and his wife whirled around to see his son cradling an arm and bawling, and his daughter staring wide-eyed and open-mouthed.

"Sammy hit me," he blubbered.

"DID NOT!" she screamed back.

Their son removed the protective hand, unveiling a perfectly formed red handprint on his upper arm.

"I didn't." Little Sammy turned, wide-eyed, eyeing her parents pleadingly. "I swear, I didn't. He hit himsel—" She stabbed a finger ahead—"Daddy, watch out!"

Sam whipped around in time to see a pair of ink-stained cows trotting onto the road ahead. He threw a protective arm across his wife as he stood on the brakes. Tires squealed, and he left at least an inch of rubber coating the road as the truck skidded to a stop no more than five feet from the apathetic bovines. The cattle merely kept their pace, loping across the road. Breath coming in ragged gasps, heart pounding, he turned to his wife. He was sure the panicked expression on her pale face was a mirror of his own.

His heart restarted, and he whipped around, snarling, fury lancing from his eyes. He was about to lay into both of his children, until the teary-eyed youngsters cowered from his wrath, both trying to suppress sobs. He closed his eyes and took shuddering breaths, working one fist as he fought to control his anger, then took them both in.

His daughter cowered in the seat behind him, trying to make herself smaller, attempting to disappear into the corner. His son did the same on the passenger side, still cradling his left arm. Then something clicked; Sam had noticed it a split second before the cattle had appeared, but he hadn't quite had the time to fully process the information. The red imprints marring his son's upper arm were all wrong. For the fingerprints to be on the outside of his upper left arm like that, the slap would've had to come from the right. There was no way his daughter could have done that. Heat boiled within him again, but he quashed it.

"You can't cause a commotion like that while we're driving," he said as calmly as possible, still seething. Now wouldn't be the right time to lay into the boy. He'd have to have a man-to-man talk with his son this weekend about lying.

Right now, it was just a miracle they were still alive.

He turned to his wife. "You better call the police. Tell them about our wayward cattle."

Still trying to catch his breath, he started off again.

12

"Hey diddle, diddle, the cat and the fiddle,
The cow jumped over the moon;"
Hailey poked each of the twins in the belly at the end of each line, sending up gales of giggles.

"The little dog laughed, to see such sport,
And the dish ran away with the spoon."
Poke, poke.

"That was Gampaw's favorite nursery rhyme. Gampaw and Gammaw's. I remember them reciting it to me when I was your age as they tucked me into bed."

"I miss Gampaw," Aiden whined.

"I know, honey. So do I."

"Is Gampaw in heaven, with da angeuls?"

"Yes, Grampa's in heaven, with the angels."

"Wilw he have cows?"

"I think so," Hailey smiled, then kissed each of her brothers. "Good night, Aiden. Good night, Alex." She tucked them tightly under the thin sheet of her full-sized bed. It dwarfed the boys, leaving plenty of room for the pair.

"G'night, Haywee," the twins chorused sleepily.

"Wilw you weave a wight on?" Alex pleaded.

"Of course, I will, sweetie," Hailey assured, striding over to a special night light she'd dug out just for them. As Hailey flicked the switch, a pocked silver orb glowed to life with a small black and white cow floating above. Under the harsh yellow glow of the overhead light, the new source of illumination made little difference until Hailey flipped the light switch, plunging the room into semi-darkness.

"And weave da door open?" Aiden begged as she was pulling it closed.

Hailey chuckled. "Of course. Now try to get some sleep. We have a busy day tomorrow."

"Can we feed da baby cows again tomorrow?"

"We'll see." Hailey wasn't sure when the boys woke up, but she might be able to push the feeding back a bit.

Pulling the door to within a few inches of the jam, Hailey listened to her brothers as their excited whispers faded. God, she needed to spend more time with them. Then it hit her; as hard as it had been to visit before, it would be harder now—near impossible. Perhaps she could hire a hand or two to help occasionally. She and Grampa had done most of the work themselves, only bringing in help when it was absolutely necessary. And while that cut down on the expenses, it also broadened their responsibilities exponentially. She'd have to study the books; see what she could work out.

Considering the books as she descended the stairs, Hailey hadn't noticed the gradually rising voices until she was near the bottom. The conversation suddenly filled her ears, rocking her back.

"I can't believe you would do such a thing without asking," Dad said.

"Why would I need to ask you?" That sounded like Caleb.

"I meant discussing it with me."

"Are you sure you didn't slip and say exactly what you meant?"

Hailey rounded the corner to see her father and uncle squared up in a whispered argument.

Caleb continued, "Like I need my big brother's permission to do anything."

"That's not what I meant, and you know it," Dad said. "I'm saying it wasn't *solely* your decision to make."

It appeared her father had gotten to the bottom of the missing cattle. Hailey huffed. Uncle Caleb had sold them.

"Half of this farm is mine now!" he cried. A curious look passed across Aunt Sierra's face.

"And the other half is mine!" Dad interjected. "And don't forget about Hailey."

"Oh? What about your precious daughter?" The bitterness dripping from Caleb's voice surprised Hailey. Where had that come from?

"She's your niece, and she deserves a say in what happens here," Dad grumbled, making it clear he didn't appreciate Caleb's tone.

"What does it matter? We're going to sell, anyway."

"We never decided that." Her dad glanced at his wife. "In fact, Lexa and I are thinking we should let Hailey try her hand at running the farm."

"You can't be serious!" Caleb's ire flashed at her. She hadn't realized anyone had noticed her enter the room. "She's still in college. Besides, she has no business being a farmer. Maybe if she was a boy. But even then, are you really willing to let your daughter ruin her life to follow some stupid dream?"

"No dream is stupid!" Zoe's unexpected outburst drew all the attention in the room. "Even though I don't like what she's doing here—it's wrong to exploit these animals." Zoe's eyes flitted to meet hers, and she nodded, then looked back. "Hailey has every right to follow her dreams, especially if she's *just a girl*"—Zoe added air quotes to the final three words.

Hailey was taken aback by this uncharacteristic show of support from such an unlikely source.

"Now, you know that's not—" Caleb tried, but was cut off by the increasingly irate twin.

"God Dad, sexist much?"

"Don't talk to your father like that," Sierra warned, steel creeping into her tone.

Zoe scanned the room, taking in her whole family as they

stood there gaping at her. "Fine," she blurted, then spun and strode from the room.

"Where do you think—" Sierra started.

But Caleb cut her off. "Let her go." He waved a hand languidly through the air.

"Uncle Caleb," Hailey probed, taking a step forward.

"What?" he snapped.

She jerked back as if slapped, taken aback by his vehemence, but pushed on. "Well, it's not so bad you sold a few of the steers, but the young heifers are worth a lot more to us in the long run as breeders and milkers. We're very selective about which ones we sell and to whom."

"If I wanted to hear your opinion, I'd ask."

"Caleb!" Dad growled.

"This is something we need to discuss amongst ourselves," Caleb said.

"Can't we get Grampa in the ground before you all start fighting?!" Chloe cried, then bolted from the room and out into the yard.

"Chloe's right, I think we should put a pin in this until after the funeral," Dad grumbled. "And I don't want to hear of any more missing cattle."

"Or what?" Caleb asked.

Her father just glared at him for a moment, then turned away. "I'm tired. I think I'll go to bed."

"Do whatever you want." Caleb stalked over and flopped on the couch, as he said, "Just leave me to do the same."

The TV blared to life as her father stomped up the stairs. Lexa sidled up to Hailey, took her elbow, and guided her into the next room. "You gave the twins your bed. Where are you sleeping tonight?" she murmured.

Hailey's eyes flitted to the couch, her uncle sprawled along its length, the television's volume bar increasing.

"I'll get—" Lexa started.

"No!" she said. "No. Chloe's right. We don't need another fight tonight."

"But where else—"

"I'll just crash in the barn." Lexa gave her an incredulous look. "Grampa put his comfortable old sofa in the break room."

"Are you sure?" Lexa dithered. "Caleb hasn't seen me step into the ring yet."

"Yeah, I'm sure." She smiled at her *mother*, for that's really what she was.

On an impulse, Hailey stepped up to the woman and wrapped her in a tight embrace. Lexa's body stiffened for a moment before she reciprocated the hug. She couldn't help but smile brighter, picturing the surprised look on the other woman's face. It was one of the few times she'd initiated a hug.

"Thank you for believing in me," Hailey murmured.

After a moment, the two pulled apart, and Hailey couldn't help but notice the tears leaking from the other woman's eyes.

Hailey smiled and went out to find her cousin.

"Sierra Delta Twelve, do you read?"

Deputy Roscoe Hire was yanked out of a daydream; or had he been dozing? It didn't matter. There wasn't much else to do out here. The speed trap along Route 9 was too well known amongst the locals, and few out-of-towners even used the old highway with the interstate only a few miles further east. There couldn't have been more than a few vehicles pass him in the hour he'd been stationed there.

Roscoe Hire languidly unclipped the mic from the dash.

"Copy dispatch, Hire here."

"Hire, we've got a 10-54 out on Cracker Road, east of Cimarron Acres."

Roscoe groaned, letting his head fall back into the headrest and closing his eyes. Livestock on the road. And, of course, he just happened to be the closest unit. He sighed; *consigned to animal control again.* He was a deputy, for God's sake.

"Understood. What have we got?"

"Someone almost hit a couple of bulls."

"Bulls?" Hire repeated with renewed interest. "Plural?"

"That's what was reported."

"Copy that," Hire said, sighing as he slammed the mic back onto its hook.

As with any rural town, it wasn't uncommon for them to deal with escaped livestock now and then. He'd seen all number of things; everything from chickens to cows crossing the roads. He'd even encountered the occasional bull, but he couldn't remember having two loose at the same time.

Of course, his thoughts strayed to Graham's Cracker Farm, and the grisly events at the place a couple of nights before. He shuddered at the thought; that scene was one he wished he could forget. Could it be the Grahams' animals? Had they misplaced more livestock? For their sake, he hoped they hadn't. That was all they needed.

He couldn't help but hope it was a prank.

Hire reached for the gear stick, but before he jammed the gears into drive, his eyes wandered over to the cardboard box laying on the seat. He needed a fix. He opened the flimsy container and drew out a gooey treat. The donut was from a local baker, a kindly middle-aged woman who was happy enough to supply him with free—if day old—pastries. If she hadn't been his mother's age, he might have welcomed her not-so-subtle flirting.

He passed the glorious hunk of sugar and carbs to his other hand and licked his fingers clean before flicking on his lights, then yanking the gear lever down into drive. After checking the way was clear, he pulled out onto the two-lane highway, munching on his sweet treat.

Less than a minute later, he turned at the intersection of Cracker Road—unsurprisingly named for the Grahams' Cracker Farm—and old Route 9, which coincidentally marked the southeast tip of the Grahams' property. The massive spread ran up Route 9 and stretched over to Lake Drive, and the lake on the west, extending some two-and-a-half to three square miles—one of the biggest farms in the area.

Hire slowed a quarter mile later as he approached the first hint of cattle fencing at the intersection where University Drive's nice four-lane paved road ended, morphing into County Road

15—not much more than a dirt lane running north through the Graham property, marking the border of their dairy pastures.

Hire let his mind drift again as the vehicle crawled along, scanning the fence line for any breaks or gaps. It was only a few minutes later that Hire rolled past the old Graham Farm. The old man's granddaughter was outside near the bullpens, talking to a young blonde. She didn't look agitated, didn't look like they were missing an animal—she even waved as he rolled by. He grunted; surely, if they'd been missing a bull, she would have noticed and been a lot more animated than she was. He'd still seen no trace of any escaped cattle nor a gap in the fence line as of yet, so his suspicions of a prank grew. Could it be the Rockwell girl's father?

He glanced across the way to the neglected cornfield. Or perhaps the cattle had disappeared in there? He shoved that thought aside and continued his leisurely pace along Cracker Road. By the time he'd reached Lake Drive, he still hadn't encountered any loose livestock, so Hire pulled a three-point turn and headed back the way he'd come. By now, he was almost positive it had been a hoax.

The sun was disappearing on the horizon when Hire passed the old Graham place again. He'd still seen no sign of any wayward cattle. He longed to just increase the pressure on his gas pedal and aim back to his secluded speed trap, but he thought better of it—if he missed something, there would be hell to pay. Instead, he pulled into the overpriced new real estate development when he came across the entrance. The name, Cimarron Acres, and the charging bull logo had been adopted from a ranch that used to dominate the area.

Hire kept an eye out for any sign of an animal as he meandered through the large subdivision, winding along the convoluted streets. It wasn't so bad. He let his eyes and mind wander for the next half hour; in that time, no sign of an errant cow had appeared: hide nor hair, nor cow-pie. Then he gave up his search, concluding the call must have been a prank.

He had no way of predicting the tragedies that would occur that night.

13

The last rays of sunlight caressed Maryanne Salazar's skin as she floated in her pool, feet dangling, soaking in the cool water. A light breeze broke up the muggy evening, tickling her lightly toasted flesh, presenting a welcome change from the heat she'd endured most of the day. With her privacy fence and a few strategically placed trees, she didn't have to worry about nosy neighbors spying on her as she whiled away the hot summer days working on her tan.

Languidly, she reached over for her lukewarm lemonade, eyes still shut. This marvelous new floating lounger actually had built-in cup holders, by far the most important feature—much more than the ridiculous shape and color of the thing, at least. She'd laughed aloud when her husband had presented it, seeing the absurd picture printed on the box. A cow. And not just any cow, a black-spattered dairy cow, a Holstein, just like the ones on the farm over yonder. When she'd asked her husband to pick one up, she'd only expected a simple inflatable pool lounger, but she supposed that's what she got for not being specific—and to be fair, she had told him to surprise her. But really, a cow? Still, it was better than the pig or goat he'd shown her; anyway, it was growing on her.

A faint smile crawled across her face; while he'd gone for a ridiculous design, her husband had been concerned about her comfort and had ordered her a deluxe model. It just highlighted Joe's quirky sense of humor, reaffirming her decision to marry him. Besides, it was an obvious commentary on her insistence to volunteer with 4-H throughout the summer. Though she was relieved to have a break from the daily rigors of teaching, she couldn't put it all behind her, so she helped out where she could while she waited to start anew in the fall.

A soft lowing floated through the evening air. Her eyes drifted open, and she gazed to the north; though blocked from view, she could almost picture the dairy farm over the horizon. She surrendered to the weight tugging on her eyelids and settled back into her lounger as she thought about how she'd intended to ask old man Graham if she could bring her class on a field trip out to the farm; it would have been a wonderful educational experience. After the terrible news which rocked the town the day before, she was almost glad she hadn't gotten around to it; she couldn't help but wonder what could have happened to her own students if they'd made it to the farm for the field trip.

Across the yard, the young mother used her large horned head to nudge an unlocked gate. Well-lubricated hinges made nary a squeak of protest as the gate opened. The cow passed from the cornfield into a carefully manicured yard where she was greeted by an expansive emerald buffet. She lowered her massive head to the lawn and ripped up a mouthful of the delicious growth, savoring the wonderful taste.

Mixed with the cloying aroma of petroleum-based plastics and chlorinated water was a hint of the distinctive scent that had drawn her, coming from the woman floating on a monstrosity of colored plastic in the middle of a small pond. This human had come into contact with her missing calf. The woman reeked, not only of her calf and other young cattle but of a myriad of other earthy smells and unfamiliar animal odors. She had something to do with the missing young.

Even with her vision encompassing most of the yard, almost

330 degrees, the cow didn't see any sign of the missing calves. She slipped closer to the woman; she had to find her baby.

The cow trudged down a slanted path, cleverly built along the edge of the pool—oblivious to the purpose of such a ramp—and slipped into the unnatural water. As she submerged herself, something in the pond burned her eyes and left an awful taste in her mouth. She set that aside; she had to continue.

A gentle rocking nudged Maryanne from her doze. Her eyes drifted open; save for a few lazy ripples pushed about by the wind, the water around her was as placid as ever. Had it been a dream? Her body jerking her awake? She blinked and shifted into her inflatable lounger. It might be best if she didn't let herself drift off again; it wouldn't be a good idea to spend the night out in the summer air—she'd be eaten alive by mosquitoes. Even so, her sleep-weighted eyelids drifted closed again., oblivious to the shadow drifting her way under the water's surface.

A familiar, earthy fragrance greeted Maryanne when she was rocked awake moments later. While not unpleasant, the smell was undoubtedly foreign in her pool. As her senses returned, she recognized the aroma of wet livestock. She let her eyes flutter open again. Squinting into the twilight, she couldn't help but wonder if somehow the wind was carrying the odor. She'd never smelled it before, not in her yard.

Pushed by the wind, her lounger had floated into the center of the shallow end. Ever-increasing ripples broke up the previously placid water around her. What was causing that? Had someone joined her in the pool? A tingle of hope swelled within her. Was her husband home early?

Using one hand, Maryanne languidly paddled her float around in the center of the shallow end. She froze, eyes widening when she saw the massive shape approaching. Heart thumping wildly, her mind tried to make sense of it. She forced her eyes to close, screwing them shut for a moment, hoping the shape would disappear when she reopened them. No such luck.

How was it possible?

Water churned under the enormous animal as a cow—an actual cow—paddled toward her. In her pool! With its head and horns gliding along the surface, it looked like a parody of a shark's fin slicing through the water. Stunned, Maryanne lurched back and rolled out of the inflatable lounger. As she plunged into the cool water, it sent a jolt through her, washing away any lingering drowsiness. She came up spluttering, on her feet in a heartbeat, but the cow was still approaching. She backed away, trying to understand.

Her disbelief swelled into anger.

Oh god, if that animal were left in here—if it did its business—she would have to clean the pool, drain it and start afresh. There was no way she would swim in manure-laced water for the rest of the summer. And someone else would be footing the bill, that was for sure.

But what was it doing here, anyway?

And, more concerning by the second, why was it paddling directly for her?

As that pair of wickedly sharp horns glided unerringly toward her, Maryanne's anger dissolved, morphing into trepidation, and then finally fear. It was almost upon her. She had to get away from the cow and those viciously sharp horns. Fighting the resistance of the water, Maryanne spun and slogged toward the pool's edge. Still, the tireless cow paddled, closing quickly.

She made it to the steps built into the shallow end, grabbed the metal bar, and tugged at it to draw herself up. Water cascaded off her body, flowing over the concrete deck as she emerged from the pool. Maryanne spun left toward the house and took a bounding step forward, only for her foot to slip. The pavement came rushing up to meet her and her head struck the lip of the pool.

She was out cold when she plunged back into the cool water.

Tucked away under the eve of one home, a security camera activated, and a solitary blue light lanced out in the darkness.

Long since accustomed to the nightly parade of wildlife, the homeowner ignored the trilling notification; sure it was one of the many opossums, raccoons, or foxes they'd noticed roaming their property. Though if they had checked the feed, they would have been startled by the odd visitor caught on their security system. Large bovine eyes blazed like eerie beacons in the night as it took a few plodding steps through the front yard before another motion sensor tripped—flooding the yard with a wave of harsh light, sending the startled cow trotting out of frame.

Nor was it the only such event. The next day, several homeowners would be surprised to discover what had been prowling outside their homes.

Sally Jessup sat, curled into her comfortable reading chair, the room around her dark, save for the scant illumination coming off her e-reader. Her eyes traced each line, hungrily drawing in each new word of her new shifter romance novel—her guilty pleasure.

"Oh Rodrigo," Esmeralda moaned, as the massive Spanish bull morphed into the form of her secret crush—her ranch hand. No wonder he was so good with her cattle. Esmeralda rushed to the man, falling into his embrace as their lips met for a passionate kiss.'

Sally sighed, drinking up the were-cow story. If only she could find true love like that. But she feared it was not to be. Nearly thirty, she had never had much luck with the fellas. Sure, there had been a few here and there, but they hadn't sparked this kind of passion within her. Her Rodrigo had to be out there, though; isn't that what she'd learned from every romance she'd seen or read?

An unexpected sound tugged her concentration from the story unfolding on the page. Squinting in confusion, she scanned the dim room. Had she just heard the lowing of a cow? Or had it been the novel evoking the memory? It was, after all, an author's duty to call on their reader's experiences. After a moment, without further interruption, she shook it off and her eyes flicked back to the page, searching for where she left off.

'Esmeralda ran her hand through Rodrigo's thick black hair, imagining—'

The muted lowing drifted in through the windows again. Sally grunted, letting her tablet fall to her lap as she turned to the window. It had been a cow. And it sounded close. Almost as if it were right outside, coming from her backyard.

Had there been another escape?

As she was contemplating the possibility, another low call drifted through the window. She sighed. Unfurling from the armchair, Sally rose from her comfortable seat for the final time. She dropped the tablet on the seat cushion and sidled over to the back window. As the blinds parted, she was greeted by a recognizable coal-smeared cow grazing on a patch of clover in her backyard. The motion of the blinds drew the animal's attention, and it lifted its large head. It eyed her, languidly working its massive jaws.

Questions sparked through her mind like lightning. Who did it belong to? What was it doing in her yard—for that matter—how had it gotten there? Had she left the gate open? After that, other thoughts drifted through her mind. What should she do?

She suspected it might have wandered away from the Graham place—it was just over yonder. Had the new owners been lax? It wouldn't improve their image if word of another stray animal filtered through the community. She didn't want to cause any trouble, especially after the death of poor old John Graham. The man's son had been nice enough to provide some cattle for her students and seemed to be willing to sell more. Besides, she wasn't even sure the animal had come from the Grahams' place. She squinted at the bright yellow tags hanging from each ear; perhaps the farm's contact information was printed on them.

She shivered; the thing's large black eyes hadn't drifted away from her as it continued chewing and, for some inexplicable reason, its gaze was unnerving—those deep Stygian eyes locked on her.

Perhaps she should have called the police, but all they'd do was check the tags and contact the owners anyway. And with the incident the other day, the cops might be on edge and end up injuring, or even killing, the poor creature. There was no reason to hurt such a beautiful animal; it hadn't caused any harm. No, she'd check the tags and contact the farm directly.

She slipped into a pair of house shoes, pulled her housecoat tighter around her bulging tummy, and shuffled to the back door. The chime of her alarm system rang out as the back door scuffed against the jam. She flicked on the porch light and peered through the tempered storm door. Save for its head, which had followed her, the cow hadn't moved. Its mouth still worked as its tail flicked back and forth, swatting at imaginary insects.

When the screen door opened, it cried out in protest and the ebony-spotted cow shuffled back a few steps, lowing in complaint. Sally stepped out into the humid night, her eyes tracing the bulky creature as she approached. A pair of wickedly sharp horns protruded from atop its head. She'd be sure to avoid them. Blots of jet black decorated its hide as if someone had spilled an entire bottle of black ink on a fresh page. Her eyes fell to the underside.

She eyed the udders drooping beneath the animal. "You too, huh? I guess you're not my prince charming."

It had shown no hint of aggression as she approached, simply following her with those large black eyes. Jaws continued to work, grinding up the vegetation as a tail swung back and forth. Its seemingly skittish nature set her at ease. For the most part, bovines were docile animals, and Holsteins were known for being an even-tempered breed.

Still, she was careful not to get too close to either the horns or the rear legs as she sidled up to the cow. From her vantage point, she couldn't make out any of the writing on the tag, save for the large 1052 etched in black. As she moved closer, the timid cow shifted, stepping forward and turning away slightly. Sally sighed and took another step; she had to get close enough to make out the minuscule writing embossed on the tag.

The cow moved another step forward and away, drawing Sally even closer. Then, before she realized what had happened, the cow's powerful rear legs were in the air, swinging around to meet her. Pain erupted from her chest as the hooves slammed into her. Something within her ribcage cracked as she was thrown back.

Struggling to breathe, agony flared through her chest for a moment, then the discomfort dissolved as soft, warm earth cradled her and her consciousness drifted, the darkness encroaching into her vision.

As if nothing had happened; as she lay dying, the bovine lowered its head and took another mouthful of delicious clover.

Cradling his teddy protectively to his chest, little Hank Ellison dug a knuckle into his eye as he crept into his parent's room. After crossing to the foot of the bed, a little hand reached up to give each of his parents a good shake.

"Mommy, Daddy," the boy whined, jiggling a foot as he addressed them, "there's a cow in the living room."

"Huh?" Robert woke with a snort. Eyes blinking in the low light, his gaze searched the room until he found his son's silhouetted form. His wife groaned next to him, stirring in the soft blue glow of moonlight playing through the sheer curtains.

"There's a cow in the living room," Hank repeated.

"That's nice, Henry, dear," his wife said, as she gave Robert a distinct *it's your turn* look and rolled onto her side, curling up under the thin sheet.

Robert groaned, desperately trying to hold on to his fading drowsiness as he let his head fall back onto his pillow. "Okay, bud, go back to bed."

"But it woke me up."

"What woke you up?" Robert asked, sighing, his attention finally drawn. Was someone in the house?

"The cow woke me," Hank urged, shaking his foot again. "The one in the living room."

"You were having a dream." His wife's steady breathing told him she had already slipped off again. Lucky her.

"Was not," Hank said.

"It's okay, buddy, it's just a dream."

"Nuh uh, I heard it," he whined. "It broke the TV."

Ellison's body stiffened, his eyes becoming hard as all his fleeting weariness evaporated. "The TV better not be broken … or else a certain young man will be in a world of trouble."

"But I didn't do it," Hank objected indignantly. "It was the cow."

Ellison groaned again as he whipped the covers aside and rolled out of bed. Better to rip the band-aid off. His middle daughter, Lily, had just gotten a calf to raise for 4-H and the first thing his youngest had done was whine about not getting one too. It wasn't fair that both Lily and Amy had gotten an animal, and he hadn't. And to some extent, Robert agreed with the boy, but at six he was just too young to care for an animal.

"Come on, let's get you back to bed." He grabbed Hank's hand and led the boy across the room, hoping the boy was mistaken and his new 4K television was still in one piece. It wouldn't be the first TV broken by his kids, nor probably the last; but what was this business about a cow?

Hank's hand securely clasped in his, Robert led the boy into the gloomy hallway. Had it been a mistake to allow Hank to pick a room so far away? Whereas the girls had each claimed rooms upstairs, Hank hadn't wanted to be quite that far from his parents, but he was also intent on proving he was a big boy and had shunned the bedroom next to theirs, choosing the room at the end of the hall. It had worked out so far, and while he still seemed to appear in their bed most nights, he hadn't woken them so deliberately in some time. They'd need to discuss the matter—tomorrow. Perhaps they could move Hank into the room next door, then shift the guest bedroom to the end of the hallway; that would allow Hank to be closer.

As they passed the arched doorway leading into the living room, movement drew his attention. Were the girls up too? Robert let his gaze drift over, then came to an abrupt halt. Eyes widening, he drew in a sharp breath, not believing what he saw. He let his son's hand slip through his fingers and stepped through the arch.

There *was* a cow in the living room. The massive ebony-swabbed animal had to weigh at least three-quarters of a ton. What in the world? Where had it come from? How had it gotten in? Robert's eyes traced the far wall. Sure enough, the sliding glass doors stood wide open.

Had one of his children left them open? They must have. How else could a cow have gotten in? Or was it some kind of prank? Could it have been the Peretti's—Jeremy or his dad? Lincoln had a bit of a twisted sense of humor, but Robert doubted even *he* would do something like this. Either way, the cow couldn't have opened the door itself. Could it?

"Moo?"

No, Robert decided as the animal's dull, gloomy eyes locked on him and the beast edged curiously toward him, nostrils flaring. It gave out another low *moo*. At the moment, he was too lost in surprise and rage to reflect on how amusing their curiosity normally was. There was a bull tramping around in his living room. There was no telling what damage the thing had caused.

Stepping further into the room, Robert took it in. His gaze flicked to the TV. Sure enough, its screen held a spider webbing crack radiating from the bottom corner. Anger boiled within him. Someone owed him a new TV. And he intended to collect.

"Hank, get the light."

Incensed, Robert stepped forward to meet the beast head-on, peering intently for a name on the animal's ear tags. The animal tilted its head, shying away, forcing him to lean in to read the tags. So lost in rage, Robert didn't think about those viciously sharp horns. Or the animal's massive bulk.

It would be his undoing.

He shot a look back at his son. "Hank, hit the light." Instead of following his directions, Hank shrunk back into the shadows.

The animal shied again, tilting its head away. Robert stepped right up to the thing and snatched one of its ears. Quick as lightning, it brought its massive head up toward him in a sweeping arc. The powerful neck muscles drove one of its thick horns up, piercing his chest at an angle, ripping the air from his lungs even as it gored him. Pain flared, almost too intense to process. As he was plucked off his feet and flung into the air, he vaguely heard a squeal and the thumping of tiny feet. Ellison found himself sprawled across the living room's thick carpet in a growing pool of dark, sticky liquid, fighting for breath from his torn lungs until the agony finally swallowed him.

A loud thump startled Abbey Ellison awake. She took in a sharp breath, rolling to her other side and reaching out for the comforting presence of her husband. But her roaming hand was greeted with absence. Robert wasn't back yet. Studying the clock, Abbey let her fingers trace his side of the bed. It was still warm. What was taking Robert so long? Hank should have been in bed now—and Robert returned. How long ago had Hank woken them? She hadn't thought to check the time.

A squeal drifted through the open door, followed shortly by tiny thumping footsteps fleeing down the hallway. Her son's cry set off alarm bells, prompting Abbey to bound from the bed and plow into the hallway. What had spooked her son? A dull thumping came from the living room. Was his father playing with him? She scowled. It was much too late for that.

Abbey marched through the arched entry, only to be confronted by a horrendous sight. Robert lay sprawled in the middle of the floor, dark liquid oozing from his chest. What happened? Had someone broken in? So intent on her husband, Abbey missed the fifteen-hundred-pound animal hurtling from the sitting room, charging toward her until it was too late. Her mind only registered the pounding steps a moment before impact. She opened her mouth to scream, but with the collision, all the air exploded from her lungs. Abbey flew back into the door frame and slammed her head against the wood. The beast followed, turning as it rose to its rear legs and brought its considerable weight down on her over and over.

As his mother was being trampled, then hours after, little Hank Ellison lay curled in a tight ball under a blanket in the closet in the safe embrace of a pile of stuffed animals, cringing every time he heard the slightest sound. Of the girls upstairs, only Lily heard the animal. The little girl flopped onto her other side and eagerly returned to the dreams of her new calf, little Miss Lodi.

14

Sheriff Johnson let her gaze drift around the idyllic neighborhood as she cut across the carefully manicured lawn. Each of the subdivision's enormous homes was at least two stories of stone-laden walls accented in a mixture of earth tones and surrounded by elegant lawns, a nightmare on the water bill at this time of summer.

Moisture clung to the sheriff's shoes, leaving clear footprints on the driveway as she trudged toward the swarm of first responders congregating next to a gleaming Mercedes—a symbol of wealth she would never achieve—in an immaculate two-car garage. Even in such a small town, there were those that had, and even more, flaunted their wealth.

One of her deputies detached himself from the group as she approached and handed her a pair of disposable cloth booties, which she slipped on before continuing through the garage and ducking into the house.

Inside, she was greeted with the scent of fresh lavender, tainted by a hint of tangy copper. Her gaze swept the entryway to the left. Harsh rays of morning sun flooded through the glass lites framing the front door, projecting bright shimmering shapes on the slate-tiled floors. On the far side of the entry, a door opened into what appeared to be a home office. Straight ahead, an ornately carved staircase wrapped along the far wall, framing an elegant sitting room. And to the right, an arched entry led into the family room, where two of the family now lay dead.

Her cloth booties protected the brindled frieze carpeting as she crossed the sitting room. Before slipping under the arched entry to the family room, Johnson glanced to the right to take in the dining room. A lightly stained table sat on a patch of slate matching the entry. Regrettably, the family would never dine together again.

She shook the thought away and focused on the tableau in the middle of the living room. Baines, one of her detectives, crouched over a body, peering intently at the bloody ruin of the man's chest. Blood had spread around the man, staining the carpet in a pool of dusky crimson. To the left lay another figure, crumpled against an arched doorway, blood pooling around her waist. Divots on the carpet suggested that some of the furniture was askew, and a lamp had toppled to the floor. The massive television mounted to the wall had spider-webbing cracks radiating from one corner. And along the back wall, a sliding plate glass door stood wide open, letting in a humid breeze that rustled the thin curtains as it filtered through the house.

What the hell was happening in her town? First that Rockwell girl gets gored, followed directly by John Graham's heart attack, then, only hours later, Collin Gill has a severe four-wheeler accident—the boy hadn't woken up yet, and his friend seemed to be hiding something. And now this: a double murder. What else could it be?

"Baines," Johnson said.

The well-built man's head jerked up; blinking at her for a moment before his surprise washed away.

"Oh, there you are, Sheriff," Baines said as he pushed to his feet, then straightened his suit jacket, bringing it together to hide his slight paunch.

She nodded. "What have we got?"

Baines stepped over the body and across to her. "We received a frantic nine-one-one call early this morning from the eldest daughter …"—he flipped through his notes—"Amy Ellison. It seems the girls woke up early to take care of their show animals … FFA or 4-H … only to find this horrendous sight in the living room. And a missing little brother."

"A missing child?" Johnson's heart skipped. Why hadn't she been told?

"Don't worry," Baines assured, then gestured across the room, "along with this mess, first responders found the six-year-old curled up in the closet, white-faced and terrified. He may have seen something."

"Has he said anything? Given any indication as to what happened?"

Baines shook his head. "We haven't gotten much out of him yet. He's still in shock."

"The girls didn't hear any commotion down here last night?" Johnson asked, eyes still roaming the room.

"Nothing," Baines said, then he sighed. "They were asleep. Though one thought her dad might have been watching a movie."

"Why is that?"

"She thought she heard a cow. Though she admits it might have been a dream."

Johnson peered around. "Where are the children?"

"We've moved them next door. I have Sandrich over there with them."

"Good." Rodger Sandrich always had an affinity for children. Johnson nodded to the body sprawled across the living room floor. "Any clues? … Anything you can tell me?"

Baines' already thin lips tightened. "I'm not sure yet … this is an odd one." He gestured to the body lying in the middle of the floor. "While Mr. Ellison has a single penetrating wound through his chest"—the detective waved to the other body propped against the arched entryway—"Mrs. Ellison seems to have several to the torso as well as a handful of broken bones—in her hips, legs, and ribs."

"Was she the target?"

"Hard to say." He unconsciously chewed on the inside of his

lip.

There was something he wasn't saying, and his hesitation drew her curiosity. "What is it?"

Baines grimaced, then sighed. "This whole scene is baffling."

"How so?"

"There's … something I'm not seeing. It just … doesn't make sense."

"Have you found a murder weapon? Any indication of what could have done this?"

"Not yet. The amount of tearing around the wounds points to a considerable amount of leverage. My guess would be some kind of spear."

"A spear?" Incredulity flooded Johnson's tone. She'd never had anyone use a spear before.

"Perhaps a javelin. We'll know more once the medical examiner takes a look."

"Do we have an ETA on the M.E.?"

Baines glanced at his watch. "It'll be another thirty to forty-five minutes. Doc Brown was out of town, so we had to call one in from the city."

"Let me know when they arrive." Johnson glanced around the room.

"Sheriff Johnson." Her radio squawked to life. "This is Sandrich. I have an update. Over."

Johnson's hand flew up to her shoulder and depressed the button. "Go ahead, Deputy."

When the speaker crackled to life again, a little girl's tinny voice flooded through. "—puty Sandwich. Deputy Sandwi—"

The call cut out for a moment, then Sandrich came back. "Sorry about that, Sheriff."

In the background, the muted chanting continued: '… deputy Sandwich—deputy Sandwich …'

"That's fine, Deputy. What have you got?"

"The little boy … Hank … finally started talking."

"Did he see what happened?" Johnson asked.

"I'm not sure. All I've been able to get out of him was 'the bad cow did it,' 'the bad cow hurt mommy and daddy.'"

"The bad cow?"

"That's what he keeps saying."

"Thank you, Deputy. Let me know if you get anything else."

"Will do, Sheriff, Sandrich out."

Sheriff Johnson shot a quick look at Baines, then strode over to Mr. Ellison and knelt to get a better look at the wound.

"Bad cow?" she murmured. Her eyes raked the deep gash in the man's ribcage. Now that she thought about it, the wound looked eerily similar to the gore wound left behind on Mallory Rockwell—albeit a bit smaller. Johnson pushed up off her knee and crossed over to Mrs. Ellison. The wounds there too looked almost as if she was gored by a horn.

"Well, it does kind of look like …" Baines rubbed his head, running his fingers through thinning hair as he took a deep breath and let his gaze flick between the two bodies.

Johnson pointed toward the sliding glass door. "Who was the first on scene? Was that open when you arrived?"

"It was," he murmured distractedly, "I made sure to ask …" Of course, he did; he was a skilled detective—always professional. She could almost see the gears working behind his cool gray eyes. She imagined the thoughts rushing through his mind were the same as hers. Could a cow have wandered in? Or, perhaps, the boy had just heard about the attack on the Rockwell girl? That might be the most likely explanation. Still. Could a cow be responsible?

"Were there any tracks … or other signs of cattle around?"

"Not that I noticed." Baines shook his head. "But frankly I wasn't looking … I hadn't considered …" He trailed off, glancing around the room. "There's nothing concrete that points to a cow inside the house, and I didn't see any obvious signs out back. But, like I said, I wasn't looking for hoof prints or anything …"

She read his apologetic tone, and the dismay in his eyes, before his face and eyes hardened.

"I'll take a closer look; perhaps last night's drizzle obscured the tracks." Baines hesitated, his face softening again as he lowered his voice. "Are we really considering the possibility that a cow snuck in here and killed Mr. and Mrs. Ellison?"

"It does seem a little farfetched," she said, releasing a deep sigh. "But at this point, we can't rule anything out. It appears …" Johnson shook her head. "Just let me know what you find. I'm going next door to talk to the children."

What the hell was happening?

Johnson ducked out through the back door, wanting to poke around a bit, to see if anything caught her eye. Her gaze drifted across the backyard as she followed a walkway around the side of the house. There were no telltale signs around the patio or the pool, and the yard was a lush carpet of thick, dew-speckled grass. It wouldn't be easy to find hoof prints in there. What did a hoof print on grass even look like? Still, she supposed she'd have to assign someone to look into it.

Rounding the corner of the house, a pair of her deputies came into view, crouched over a patch of moist dirt. She came to an abrupt halt, their conversation snatching her attention.

"… during prohibition, bootleggers sometimes wore cow shoes," Gilroy said.

"Cow shoes?" came Chambers' incredulous reply.

"Yeah! They were these shoes with carved hoof imprints on the sole … anyways"—Gilroy gave an airy wave as if it might remove the smirk spreading across his buddy's face—"they would wear them as they crossed through pastures so they wouldn't leave footprints for someone to find," he explained. "More than a few stills were discovered from careless criminals leaving behind footprints."

Pushing off his knees, Chambers stood. "So, what are you saying? A bootlegger broke into the Ellisons' house and slaughtered the couple. You hear 'bad cow' over the radio and conclude a 1920s gangster killed them."

"I'm not saying it was a bootlegger per se," Gilroy sighed, shoving to his feet, eyes locked on his companion. "The boy's words just brought it to mind. It could have been someone trying to cover their tracks. Someone trying to throw us off the scent by making it look like an animal attack. I've seen stranger things."

The pair turned and strode toward the front of the house.

"Where have you seen stranger things?"

"Is it any less plausible than an actual cow breaking into these peoples' home and murdering them?"

"A bit, yeah."

"Should I tell the sheriff?" Gilroy asked.

"Are you kidding?" Chambers chided. "By all means, tell her about the print, but leave out any mention of bootleggers or cow shoes."

"I told you; I don't think it was boot…" As his voice drifted away, Johnson pulled her stunned gaze from the pair and strode over to where they'd been crouching. Sure enough, sunk into a patch of moist earth, was the perfect imprint of a hoof.

What the—

15

Hailey stood just outside Old Mac's ruined pen, a bundle of supplies next to her, surveying the remnants of the shattered fence. It was a chore she should have completed earlier, but she'd kept putting it off. For the life of her, she hadn't been able to bring herself to venture too near the wrecked fence. Nor did she like to think about what happened—it was the reason Grampa was dead.

She still couldn't quite believe it. Mac had competed in shows for years, winning prize after prize, and he'd always been so even-tempered—it was a fairly important aspect of the competitions. She'd always known he might become surlier as he got older—that was always a concern with bulls—but he hadn't. Sure, he'd grown a bit grumpy over the years, but they'd been mindful, always keeping a weary distance and giving the big guy enough space.

If it hadn't been for that stupid girl, Mac might not have acted up, and maybe Grampa—

She shook it off and turned back to her chore. It was done now; the bull had killed the girl and Grampa had killed the bull.

Their railed cattle fence bordered the western edge of the drive. While chosen to be ascetically pleasing, the decorative wooden fence had, until recently, fulfilled its purpose. Four evenly spaced one-by-six-inch slats were staggered between thick posts extending five feet out of the ground, about half a dozen feet apart. Because every other slat was offset, Hailey had to remove four support beams to get to the rails.

As the electric drill whirred and screws sprouted from the wood, Hailey considered the merits of replacing the wooden fences with galvanized steel. She wasn't too enamored with the idea—it would be a costly endeavor. And with the fate of the farm uncertain, it might be inconsequential.

After the support beams were removed, Hailey detached the broken remnants of the larger rails. She tested the fence posts, shouldering into them; luckily, they were still solidly anchored into the ground with thick concrete. She took one of her fourteen-foot-long beams, and, after measuring carefully, cut it down to a little over twelve feet.

It wasn't the first time she'd repaired the fence line alone, so she knew how to proceed. She planted a holding screw into the furthest post, allowing her to easily prop one edge of the rail up as she attached the opposite end to its post, then went back and secured the beam to all three posts.

Hailey had zoned out, working hard on the second rail, when she spotted a sheriff's SUV creeping up the drive. Her heart leapt for a moment, hoping it was Rodger, but she quickly noticed the driver was female. She hadn't realized she'd been so eager to see him. Where had that come from? Sure, he was cute, and sweet, and …

Hailey was surprised when the sheriff herself climbed from the vehicle. In her late thirties or early forties, the brunette wore an immaculate uniform—the same tan and brown design as those of her deputies. She had a trim physique and couldn't have been too much more than five feet tall.

Johnson nodded politely as she strolled over. "Ms. Graham, how are you doing today?"

Hailey stood, stretching as she wiped her brow. "Just fine, Sheriff. And yourself?"

"Well, well." She nodded. "How are things?" The sheriff's gaze traced the newly replaced boards and the pile of supplies stacked to the side, then drifted over the rest of the corrals and on back to the pastures. Was that a look of consternation gleaming in the sheriff's eye? Did she think a metal fence would be better? It wasn't a terrible idea. But it'd be so expensive; she quailed at the thought of the cost.

When she spoke, Johnson didn't mention the fence, instead asked about the herd, but she seemed distracted, barely paying attention to Hailey's answers. Her gaze traveled back across the corrals, scanning the fence line and the bulls beyond.

"You wouldn't happen to have any missing bulls, would you?"

Missing bulls? Hailey's heart skipped. Had Uncle Caleb sold a bull as well? She craned her neck as she scanned the surrounding corrals, tallying the animals. Luckily, she came to the correct number. She sighed and returned her gaze to the somber woman in front of her. "No, Sheriff."

"It's just ..." Johnson hesitated, her face contorting into a slight wince as her eyes lost their focus. Was she hiding something? When her attention returned, all hesitancy had fled, and she bulled on, "Last night, we received a call reporting some bulls wandering along the road." Sheriff Johnson tilted her head unnecessarily to indicate the street.

"Are you sure they were bulls?"

"The animals had horns."

Confused, Hailey frowned, and offered, "I mean ... our cows have horns too, but we're not missing any of them either."

"I see." Johnson's eyes traveled back to the herd. "When did you last count?" She glanced past the outbuildings to the cattle scattered across the pasture.

"This morning."

"This morning?" The sheriff slowly nodded, seeming simultaneously relieved yet somehow more concerned. "So, no missing cattle? You're sure?"

Hailey took a moment, not knowing how to answer—if it was even relevant. Finally, she just blurted, "I didn't want to say anything, but ... apparently my uncle has been selling some without our knowledge. At last count, he'd sold four."

Johnson's eyes returned to Hailey, boring into her. "Do they have horns?"

"Um, I mean … the steers were about six months old, so their horns are still developing. I doubt they'd be confused with a full-grown bull. And the calves were only a few months old, still far too young."

"And you counted this morning?" The sheriff murmured, stepping back as her gaze traveled over the fields behind Hailey. She'd lost focus again as if the question was just perfunctory.

"Yes, Sheriff." Hailey didn't understand. All this fuss for a couple of loose cows. And from the sheriff herself. Something else must be going on.

"Be on the lookout, will you?" The sheriff's eyes flicked back to Hailey. "Call me if you see anything."

"Of course, Sheriff."

The scrape of gravel drew their attention to a new arrival. She and the sheriff both turned to see Hailey's dad striding across the drive.

"Is there a problem, Hay?"

"No problem, Dad. The sheriff was just asking me some questions."

The sheriff extended a hand. "Hello, Mr. Graham, I'm Sheriff Johnson," she offered as they shook.

"Michael."

"Michael," Johnson said, nodding.

"This doesn't have anything to do with the other night, does it?" Dad asked.

The sheriff's eye twitched, and she hesitated longer than Hailey would have expected. "No sir, that incident was thoroughly resolved. The video makes that clear …" Sheriff Johnson's lips thinned, drawing slightly to one side of her face. "If I ever find out who leaked that footage …" she shook her head and took a deep breath. "By the way, I wanted to extend my condolences. I should have stopped by sooner, but I've had a busy couple of days."

Dad waved the explanation away. "It's quite alright, Sheriff. Your man Sandrich stopped by yesterday and extended condolences on behalf of the department."

"Did he?" Johnson's lips curved down as she gave a slight nod.

"Rodger came by. And you didn't tell me?" Hailey complained, heart fluttering.

"I better get going," the sheriff said, taking a step back. "Let me know if you see anything."

"Of course," Hailey agreed, then the sheriff ambled to her vehicle, gaze roving over the farm as she went.

Her dad's eyes burned, his curiosity evident, but he refrained from asking until the sheriff had pulled away; only then did Hailey summarize the conversation.

"The sheriff is responding to a call about loose cattle?" He seemed incredulous. She couldn't blame him.

"That's what I thought, but …" Hailey shrugged. By rights, it ought to have been a job for one of her deputies, but this was a small town …

"How's it going out here?" Her dad studied the two rails staggered along the posts.

"I'm halfway there."

"Want some help?"

"Sure," Hailey beamed.

With her dad's help, the final two slats fell quickly into place. After that, Hailey went ahead and replaced the four support beams with new ones. As her dad studied the fence, Hailey wiped away the residue of dripping sweat rolling down her face.

"Have you eaten?"

"Not yet," Hailey admitted.

"You need to eat," Dad chided. "Why don't you clean up while I try to scrounge up some leftover pizza?"

That sounded wonderful. Hailey agreed, and went to grab a quick shower.

They crept toward the sound of splashing, paying little heed to the sporadic cracks and snaps of brush splintering around them as they pushed through the vegetation blanketing the forest floor. Tangles of underbrush and thorny brambles did little to impede their progress, no more than the sections of barbed wire had when they'd bulled through the fence. They were on a mission. They had detected the unmistakable scent of their missing calves not long ago, clinging to someone nearby. It drew them ever forward.

Drifting between consciousness and a light doze, Jeremy Peretti fought his overwhelming desire to drift off as he lounged in the scorching sun in their lakeside refuge. They'd stumbled across the natural clearing hidden in a small cove a few summers before. Only a short hike from the public beaches, large stone outcrops rose around the western rim of the inlet, blocking the cove from the rest of the lake, making it the perfect spot for the county's teens to hang out. That the land was private property didn't seem to matter. Nobody had ever said anything. He wasn't sure anyone knew. Every once in a while, some hapless fisherman would troll into the cove, but would inevitably abandon the place once they spotted the raucous teens. Today, he and his friends had the place to themselves.

While Donny and Allie splashed around in the shallows, Jeremy and his girlfriend, Cydney, were soaking up the sun. It was her idea. If truth be told, he didn't understand the appeal of baking one's skin for fashion, but she liked him tan and that was all it took. She lay stretched out on her belly on a fluffy beach towel, her bikini top untied as she worked on evening out her tan, trying to remove those pesky tan lines—her words. Truthfully, he thought the areas where sun-kissed flesh blended with her natural skin tone created a rich gradient that looked just as good, if not better. However, he knew better than to suggest it. He'd once made an offhand comment about her not needing to roast herself in the sun. You'd have thought he'd insulted her grandmother. "Do you want me to be all pasty and icky?"

He shook it off and surrendered to fatigue again.

When he next came to, the incessant splashing of their friends had stopped, replaced by the murmur of voices as they ambled past, edging deeper into the clearing. He pried his heavy eyelids open, fighting off the drowse, and looked around to see what his friends were up to.

The massive shapes emerging from the shadows were a surprise, to say the least. Two purebred Holstein milkers pushed out of the brush. Jeremy sat up as one of the animals nosed toward his friends, letting her curiosity guide her, and the other edged up toward Cydney—who hadn't noticed the interlopers—and himself. Jeremy scrambled to his hands and knees and scuttled closer to his girlfriend, worried the large animal might accidentally trample them. But it didn't. It stopped short, and its huge head loomed over them as it snuffled experimentally around.

"Mooo?" the cow entreated.

Cydney squeaked as she struggled to her knees, holding her loose top in place with a hand. The other animal abandoned its search of Donny and Allie and, as if noticing the lake for the first time, trotted down to the shore to take a drink.

"Where'd they come from?" Allie exclaimed in awe as another pair of animals crashed into view.

"We're on the edge of the Grahams' property. They must have wandered out through a break in the fence line …"

"Are they dangerous?" Cydney asked, turning aside to retie the string behind her back. Jeremy caught a flash of her chest and his breath caught as it always did at the sight, but he pushed his desire aside, fighting to focus on the large animal sniffing the air around him.

"I shouldn't think so," Jeremy replied as he slowly rose, then helped Cydney to her feet. "Just stay in her line of sight," he said, waving at Allie, who'd been edging toward the rear of one cow. "They don't like it if you slip into their blind spot."

Allie nodded, retracing her steps, and slowly reached out to pat the animal.

The cow in front of Jeremy mooed imploringly again, snuffling the surrounding air, almost as if she were looking for something. Cydney backed away, apprehension on her pale face, as another animal edged up to Jeremy, nosing at his bare chest and giving him a lick. The rough, thick tongue sent a wave of goose prickles cascading across his body.

"Oh, there's no need to be scared," he soothed, smiling as he took the muzzle of one animal in his hands and gave her a good rub. "She's like a big 'ol puppy."

"Puppies bite," Cydney quailed.

"Cyd, it's okay," he assured, "cows can't bite. They don't have an upper row of front teeth." He lifted the animal's head and pulled her bottom lip down. "They have this dental pad they use to grind up their food."

"Stop," she whined.

Jeremy sighed, turning. He understood Cydney had grown up in the city; she hadn't been exposed to farm animals all her life as he'd been. "It's okay, Cyd. She has no reason to hurt me," he explained—not realizing how wrong he was. Along with the scent of his new steer, he carried the scent of both missing calves. He'd helped unload them—he'd always enjoyed helping the younger kids out when he could.

"Mooo?" the cow implored again.

Jeremy felt the tickle of the cow's tongue on his skin a moment before a sharp pain lanced through his lower back and the tip of a horn sprouted from his abdomen. The horn disappeared as the screaming started.

Jeremy dropped to his knees, trying to staunch the flow of blood seeping through his fingers for a moment before he glanced around, fighting to understand what had just happened. He was shocked to find Donny lying atop Allie, trying to shield her body with his as one of the enormous beasts stalked over them, yet they both lay unmoving as purplish welts and red splotches swelled over their abused bodies.

Another scream returned his focus to Cydney, who'd turned and was now sprinting for the lake. One cow followed close on Cyd's heels as she splashed into the shallows, greenish-brown water geysering up with every footfall. For a second, he thought she might escape, but it quickly caught up with her. The large animal head-butted her, sending her sprawling in the shallow water. Her head struck a submerged rock bed with a resounding *crack.*

She lay there, face half submerged in the shallow water as deep red liquid oozed out before dissolving into the murky lake water. His gaze remained locked on the single vacant eye until his muscles gave out and he tipped forward.

Why?

When Hailey ventured downstairs after her shower, she was surprised to see Grampa's lawyer hovering in the foyer, sharing pleasantries with Lexa.

"Mr. Stein!" Hailey beamed at the small, rotund man. "What are you doing here?"

"Hello, Hailey dear," he said, adjusting his thick glasses. As he spoke, Caleb and her dad strolled into the room. "I've come to discuss your grandfather's trust."

Her uncle came to a halt, his face paling as his eyes flitted to her for a split second. "I'm not sure now is a good time to discuss this," Caleb said.

"There are a few changes you folks should know about," Stein bulled on in his usual jovial manner, oblivious to her uncle's discomfort. What was that about?

"Well, I—" Caleb started.

"What changes?" Lexa asked.

"Perhaps we could sit down and discuss it?" Stein said, gesturing at the dining room table.

"Oh! Where are our manners?" Lexa cried. "You must think us rude."

"Of course not," Stein objected. "This is a difficult time for us all."

"Please come in, sit down." She waved to the table. "Caleb, why don't you find Sierra?"

"I'm not—" Caleb stuttered.

But Lexa had already turned back to Mr. Stein and asked if he'd like a drink. Hailey squinted at her uncle as he stalked off. She wasn't imagining it; he was acting odd.

"I'll have some water." The lawyer said, wiping a thin sheen of perspiration from his brow. "It's not getting any cooler out there."

Hailey rushed into the kitchen to grab the water. By the time she returned with a cold bottle, Caleb had reappeared with Sierra, and everybody was settling in around the old wooden table. As she slipped into the chair next to her dad, her twin brothers shot into the room, followed closely by an out-of-breath Chloe. Aiden was scrambling onto Hailey's lap when the last family member straggled in. Zoe hovered by the door, an air of indifference on her sharp, pale features.

"Perhaps we should discuss this in private?" Sierra said, turning to Hailey. "Why don't you take your brothers and cousins into the family room?"

Hailey was about to object when her dad, mom, and the lawyer all spoke up. Each insisting she stay. Mom and Dad, she'd kind of expected, but the lawyer's support came as a pleasant surprise.

"Why can't I stay?" Zoe complained as if the meeting were suddenly the most interesting thing in the world. She wouldn't be denied.

"I want to hear," Chloe said.

"Fine," Sierra conceded, but her look soured.

Hailey's brows scrunched as she studied her aunt a moment before Stein's words recaptured her attention.

"Your father made some changes to his trust in the last few months." The lawyer addressed the brothers. "Have you found a copy of the new paperwork?"

Confusion swept over Hailey. Grampa hadn't mentioned any changes.

"Changes?" her dad asked, shrugging softly.

"New paperwork?" Caleb glanced at his wife.

"I assume you both were aware of the stipulations previously set out in your father's trust. John told me you'd been informed." Despite the nods, Stein eyed Caleb and her dad as he elaborated. "Your father had originally planned to divide his assets between the two of you."

"Originally?" Caleb repeated, shooting a look at Hailey, then immediately returning his gaze to the lawyer, suppressing a grimace as he put on a confused air.

Hailey's eyes narrowed, and she glanced at her father, who looked just as perplexed as her. Why hadn't Grampa said anything? What did this mean? Was her dream dying before her eyes?

"As neither of his sons had shown the slightest interest in continuing the family's legacy, John had been growing increasingly ..." Stein paused, adjusting his glasses as he search for the word, "concerned ... about the disposition of the farm and its livestock." Hailey was surprised when the lawyer addressed her next. "Your grandfather had planned to wait until your twenty-first birthday to announce this, but alas, he didn't make it that long."

Hailey was too nervous to speak.

"Announce what?" Lexa rescued her.

"For several years now, John had been watching your progress as he delegated more and more responsibilities to you. We'd been discussing the possibility, then the likelihood of you stepping into your grandfather's shoes. John was delighted in your interest in the farm and impressed by your hard work and determination ..." Stein paused, grin growing wider as he went on, "He wanted you to continue running the farm." Hailey's pride swelled as she nodded; that was no surprise. Now if she could just convince her dad and Caleb to let her— "And decided to leave you a stake in the farm."

Hailey blinked; that *was* a surprise. But she still wasn't prepared for what came next.

And Stein dropped the bombshell: "He left you a third of the business, thirty-four percent to be exact, a controlling interest. That, along with control of the daily operations."

Hailey's jaw sank as her eyes searched her parents' faces. Would they be upset? Would they resent it? Shock slid over both Lexa and Dad's faces, then morphed into seemingly genuine smiles. She scanned the rest of the room; the twins were bouncing up and down, happy because Mom and Dad were happy. Chloe sat beaming at her, while Sierra's face was still frozen into a shocked expression—perhaps a little too exaggerated—and Caleb's face only showed … Was that annoyance? Yet, it was Zoe's expression that threw her; she had an oddly smug smirk playing across her lips until she noticed Hailey looking at her, then her face morphed into a look of feigned indifference.

Stein picked up, detailing the alterations to the trust as Hailey sat blinking back tears. Her heart raced. A third of the farm? She owned a third of the farm. Not only that, but she would oversee the day-to-day operations. Her dream was secure. They couldn't sell it out from under her.

Despite such glorious news, the next several hours crept by; nobody was looking forward to that evening. Hailey busied herself with odd jobs around the farm—Chloe an almost constant shadow. Other family members popped in to assist throughout the day; Mom and Dad turned up several times, and surprisingly, even Zoe made an appearance when Hailey announced she was going off to check the crops.

Zoe was enthralled with their fields of silage crops, asking all sorts of questions about every aspect of their production, from the types of irrigation and pesticides they used to how to better spend their resources. Hailey was even forced to endure a mini-lecture about the importance of reducing their water footprint. But all in all, it was a pleasant visit with her obstinate cousin. A pretty good day altogether.

And before long, it was time to start getting ready for the viewing. A man from one of the neighboring farms had generously offered to have his son take up the slack while her family was at the viewing. Greg had helped them out from time to time and was set to arrive soon to take care of the cattle. Neighbors were such a great help. His dad had even refused her offer of paying the boy; wouldn't have it, he'd said. While Hailey thought it was kind, she still planned to slip the kid a little thank you.

16

Down at the property line, a grieving father staggered onto the Grahams' land, then crossed the drive. He'd had more than a little to drink: evidenced by his clumsy gait, his uncoordinated movements, and, perhaps most telling, the bottle of Tennessee whiskey he brandished—amber liquid sloshing around the bottom quarter of the container. If anyone were close enough to the man, his breath would've been potent enough to be a fire hazard, as he shouted condemnations and curses, berating the entire town. But most ominous of all was the shotgun slung over his shoulder.

To say Ben Rockwell hadn't taken his daughter's death well would have been an understatement. After days of spouting off, threatening lawsuits, and campaigning to get Graham's cattle destroyed as a public menace, his family lawyer finally impressed upon him the futility of the case, advising him not to pursue the matter and personally declining to take any action. A non-starter, he'd called it. Ben's harrumph turned into a sob. His baby girl was dead and this lawyer he'd known for years, his 'friend,' wouldn't help Ben make the people responsible pay. High school teammates, fraternity brothers, and members of each other's wedding parties—some friend he'd turned out to be.

And then that video leaked, filling the Internet with his

baby's last moments—her death ironically bringing her the fame she'd sought in life. The nerve of them. It was obviously doctored, somehow.

He intended to make the Grahams pay. All of them.

Rockwell continued stumbling up the drive, following the fence line to the place his baby girl died. He'd personally destroy the guilty animal. Or was it already dead? His clouded mind couldn't quite recall. He shook his head. No matter, one bull was as good as the next. And they all needed to be destroyed.

As he approached the pens, he'd expected one to still be shattered, marking the spot where that beast had gored his Mallory. Yet the fence line was intact. He leaned in, squinting. A closer inspection revealed fresh timbers stretching across a section of the fence line. They'd concealed the crime scene as if they actually thought they could get away with keeping such dangerous animals next to a neighborhood of innocents— women and children. He intended to disabuse them of that notion. And when he did, he'd be lauded as a hero by the whole town.

"I'll show them," he slurred.

Rockwell took another swig of fire, then slammed the bottle atop a post with a clunk and unslung his shotgun. It was an older Remington twelve gauge, bought years earlier when he'd fancied himself a hunter—which he was not. He pumped the slide and a crimson shell flew from the breach; apparently, he'd already had the thing primed. He let out a vile curse as he dove for the errant cartridge.

He snagged the shell, but also came up with a handful of debris. He let the stone dust trickle from his fingers as he brought the cartridge up to his lips and blew the grit off, then jammed the cartridge home, back into the loading port, filling the magazine once more. That done, he re-slung the gun and proceeded to the fence, attempting to mount it. He made it onto the first rail just fine, but when he tried to step up to the next rail, he lost his balance and his foot slipped off the board—not unlike his daughter—sending him crashing to the ground. As the weapon's butt struck the hard-packed gravel drive, thunder exploded into the humid evening air. The shotgun clattered to the ground as Ben slapped a hand over his deafened left ear.

Unbeknownst to him, the roar of the weapon carried far and wide; the sheriff's office was alerted, and units were dispatched.

Massaging his ringing ear, Rockwell yawned as his hearing slowly cleared, bringing with it the complaining bellow of cattle. He snatched the shotgun, cursing again as he lurched to his feet, staring daggers at the weapon. How dare it go off on its own? He rethought his approach and, after snatching his whiskey bottle from atop the post, decided to use the gate to get into the bullpens.

He kept a steadying hand on the fence as he staggered toward the wide metal gate. When his weight slammed into the mass of crimson metal, it clanged off the fittings and drew a renewed protest from the nearby cattle. Jerking the latch aside, Rockwell flung the gate wide and stumbled into the alley between the corrals and the milk barn. He threw the next gate open, then turned and squinted down an alley that ran between the bullpens while taking another swig, draining the bottle. He looked at the empty bottle with disgust and tossed it aside; the glass clanking on the hard-packed earth as it bounced away.

His inebriated mind surveyed the layout; two rows of wooden corrals, one on either side of the corridor, held Graham's prized bulls. The bulls that had killed his baby. Rockwell flung this gate open as well and stumbled up to the first pen on the left. He had trouble focusing on the beasts inside; he couldn't tell if the pair of bulls he saw was an accurate count or if it resulted from the alcohol. No matter.

His vertigo increased as the bulls drifted apart, doubling for a second before he could refocus, then dissolving into a pair of animals again. Two then, he mused, well not for long. The massive coal-smeared beasts inside bellowed in agitation at the intruder, pawing the ground and eyeing him with suspicion as Rockwell brought the gun up and anchored it securely against his shoulder. The echoing boom mixed with a roar of pain, then one bull collapsed in a heap onto the floor of his pen. The other animal in the enclosure shied away, doubling again before resolving into a single entity.

He racked the pump again.

Clack, clack. Boom!

Greg had finished milking the herd and was just beginning to spray down the parlor when the first muted explosion bled through a lull in the noise assailing his ears. He cut off the spray and popped one of the earbuds out, eyes narrowing. What was that? It almost sounded like a—but no, that couldn't be. Who would be firing a weapon around here? Was it thunder? Was it supposed to storm today? He didn't recall. He waited for a minute for the sound to repeat before slowly snugging the earbud back in. As the racket he considered music—something his father could never understand—built up again, another thunderous boom reverberated through the building's walls. Eyes widening in disbelief, Greg yanked his earbuds out and rushed through the barn. What was going on?

After the second bull dropped, Rockwell lurched into the center of the alley, aiming across the aisle at another beefy ink-smeared bull. Larger, this corral held more animals, at least half a dozen. He didn't understand why there were so many; weren't they supposed to keep bulls separate? It didn't matter. *Fish in a barrel*, he mused, *bulls in a pond*. He let out a wry chuckle at his own wit—if you'd call it that.

This time, his aim wasn't as good. Most of the buckshot embedded itself into the gate's wooden boards, only winging one irate animal, sending it trotting to the far side of the enclosure as the rest of the bulls scattered. He racked the shotgun again and stumbled toward the enclosure, emptying two more blasts into the milling cattle. As the gun roared, the irate bulls bellowed in pain but refused to go down. Blood trickled from holes peppering the animals, staining their dappled hides with tendrils of deep red.

As two more shots echoed through the evening, Greg slipped from the barn's north entrance, disappearing into the mass of cattle milling around the fence. Hunched low, he shoved through the throng of curious beef, inching up to the gate. When he caught sight of the crazy man taking potshots at the poor cattle, he was only momentarily tempted to intervene—but quickly thought better of it. He'd left his phone inside, and without it or any other way to communicate with the outside world, Greg resigned himself to cowering among the agitated cattle, content to wait until the man left. Someone would have heard and notified the police—they had to be on their way already.

He certainly wouldn't risk himself for these dumb beasts— he shouldered one of the animals as it pressed toward him. He hadn't even wanted to be here. Why did his father have to volunteer him for this responsibility? Hell, he didn't even want to be a farmer. He was just waiting until he turned eighteen, biding his time until he could vanish to college and never have to deal with these endless, mind-numbing chores again.

There were too many bulls jostling around the expansive pen, trotting this way and that. The man's head screamed as one bull split apart; he could have sworn it was a single animal. Rockwell blinked back a wave of dizziness, turned, and staggered back across the alley to find an easier target. Next to the first pen, now holding two gloriously dead bulls, another corral held a pair of thoroughly agitated bovines, huffing and grunting as they hoofed the ground, trying to intimidate him—as if two sides of beef could scare him off.

Rockwell, thoughts still muddled, ignored their threats as he staggered up to the fence. This corral was smaller. Not as much space for the animals to spread out. He yanked the trigger, but nothing happened. He eyed the weapon, blinking at it for a moment before he grasped the issue; it had run dry. Cursing again as he staggered back, Rockwell fumbled with the weapon until he was eventually able to jam another handful of shells into the thing. Then Rockwell took careful aim at the bull again.

Just as he squeezed the trigger, one of the animals from the large enclosure he'd abandoned across the way slammed into its gate, shattering the locking mechanism Rockwell had been unlucky enough to weaken. The explosion of splintering wood and metal drew his wild gaze and threw off his shot. The metal pellets tore a chunk from this corral's gate as well. Though he didn't see that as his gaze whipped around, lighting on the rampaging bull strutting through the shattered gate and blocking him from the exit.

Again, Greg suppressed the urge to do something as the first of the bulls burst from its pen, even though he could see the bulls had a clear route for escape, he still wasn't willing to take the risk. And why should he? He wasn't even being paid. His father had downright refused to let him take anything from the Grahams. It wasn't fair.

Fencing flashed by to either side as Roscoe Hire streaked down Cracker Road: decorative white vinyl to the left and utilitarian barbed wire lining Graham's fields to the right. Several residents of Cimarron Acres had reported shots fired somewhere to the north—that could only mean Cracker Farm. With the wandering bulls called in the previous night, and now this; Roscoe couldn't help but wonder if someone was messing with them. Trying to use the sheriff's department to make the Grahams' lives harder. One individual, in particular, jumped to mind.

Rockwell's heart leapt as he turned from the strutting bull. He had to get away. His first thought was to dash toward the other end of the alley. But as he took in the corridor's length, his eyes widened; it was too far—he'd never make it. Rockwell panicked and launched himself for the first pen; the one where the first two unfortunate animals lay dead. In his haste to scramble over the fence, he lost hold of the gun and it fell, clattering to the ground and sending another gout of thunder echoing through the air, followed shortly by the *thunk* of metal pellets striking wood and the bellows of injured animals.

No less drunk, Rockwell still had better luck scaling the fence this time. However, once he'd scrambled to the top, he lost his balance and toppled into the pen. As the ground rushed toward him, he wondered if this had been such a good idea after all.

Once the crazed gunman dropped out of sight and then didn't reappear, Greg finally felt safe enough to act. Besides, if he just sat back and allowed a score of the Grahams' prized bulls to run amok, he'd never hear the end of it.

Cautiously, yet quickly, Greg straightened and, pushing against the press of dumb beasts, made for the cattle yard gate. Before he committed, Greg double-checked to make sure the man still hadn't reappeared, then reached over to unlatch the gate. All he had to do was dart across the drive and relatch a single gate. That ought to be enough to stop the bulls from getting out; let the Grahams sort out their own cattle.

Yet, as soon as the metal clanged and the gate creaked open, the spectating cows around him pressed forward, their mass and momentum shoving him aside and pinning him against the sturdy fence posts. As the massive creatures flooded by, Greg felt the crush of the animals—bones snapped and agony flared.

Once the pressure lessened, Greg crumpled to the ground. Pain racked his body; he couldn't be sure how badly he was injured. He had to be okay. Even as his consciousness dimmed, a siren blared closer, and a sheriff's car, lights flashing, hurtled toward the farm, flitting in and out of gaps in the hedge wall lining the two-lane road. That was a relief; at least he wouldn't have to wait long for help.

Greg didn't expect what happened next.

Apparently, the man wasn't paying close enough attention, because he'd just barely slowed as the first cow ran out into the road. The cruiser plowed into the animal, sending it flying into the air as the vehicle's hood crumpled and the windshield shattered. The darkness finally consumed Greg, and he lost consciousness without realizing that both the cow and the deputy were dead on impact.

17

Bethany cowered under her sheet, clutching the fabric tightly around her as another peal of thunder rolled across the yard. Shivers shot up her spine, sending her heart into spasms even as her chest clenched, but she couldn't bring herself to so much as glance outside her bedroom window. Because mixed in with the sporadic explosions were the agitated vocalizations of the cattle—the constant mooing across the way was driving her mad.

Where before it had been a quirky consequence of moving out to the country—*Oh look, cows! And I can even hear them*—now it was a dagger to the heart every time the lilting calls drifted through her window.

She hadn't left the house since the incident—refused to go anywhere. Whenever she drifted off into a restless sleep, she would be awakened by nightmares. Screaming, wide-eyed and searching, to find sweat-drenched sheets coiled tightly around her as if she were in the embrace of an anaconda. Panic attacks. That's what the doctor had told her parents—he'd even made a house call. *How quaint*. She knew her parents were worried about her. For the last few days, they'd let her deal with the death—nightmarish, gory murder—of her best friend. Mom had been maddeningly sweet and sympathetic, trying to comfort her, while her dad had likewise been supportive. Neither wanting to come out and blame her for Mallory's death, as they should. But she knew better; while she may not have been solely responsible, she was to blame.

Her best friend was dead, and it was her fault. She'd known better. Been warned. Known how dangerous bulls could be, yet she'd quailed at Mallory's irritated glare; quailed at the thought of ruining Mallory's big idea. She'd known better. She'd—

Bethany sobbed. *Why did I ever let Mallory convince me to let her go?* She knew now, this was why Mallory had insisted she stay over that night. She'd been planning the video the whole time; it hadn't been just a spur-of-the-moment idea like she'd claimed.

Bethany was yanked out of her self-loathing by the squeal of tires, then a deafening *crunch*, followed by a sickening sound of meat smacking against a hard surface. She leapt off the bed and flew to the window. What happened?

Once she ripped the blinds to the side, the sight outside paralyzed her. A sheriff's car sprawled across the road, its occupant unmoving as it blocked both lanes, marring her normally pleasant—though lately unwelcome—view of the rolling fields across the way.

But that wasn't what really frightened her, nor was it the broken body of the cow splayed across the road. The thing that really frightened her, paralyzed her with fear—sent tingles of dread racing down her spine, stripped her ability to fill her lungs—was the tide of cattle flooding across the street. They were after her, heading right for her yard. They'd come to finish the job that nice old farmer had stopped. They were going to kill her this time, and there was no avoiding it.

The final straw fell into place as her father darted into view, cell phone in hand, running full tilt across the backyard toward the privacy fence on the far side. In his haste to assist, he had no clue what awaited him just beyond the line of eight-foot-tall vinyl panels.

He was almost upon the gate when Bethany cried out and the world swam. Her father swung around to face her as Bethany passed out, crumpling to the soft carpeted floor—not knowing the destruction she would sleep through that night. Because sleep she did—the best sleep she'd had in days—as the world around her fell into chaos.

Hand scant inches from the gate, Bethany's dad froze and glanced around. He saw his daughter's curtains sweep back into place over her second-story window. His brows pinched. It was hard to hear anything aside from the roiling tumult, but he could have sworn he'd heard his daughter's muffled cry rise over the uproar. Unfortunately, he couldn't focus on his little girl now— couldn't dwell on the poor thing, still secluded in her bedroom—not when someone could be hurt.

What was happening? What was that horrendous crash? Had the shooter been struck by the car? Or was it someone else? An innocent. Caution had kept him back ... But after that crash ... He shuddered. Even now, part of him was worried. What if the gunman came after him?

Just as his hand brushed the gate, a section of the decorative fence a few feet away exploded, a giant ink-smeared bull materializing from the shower of vinyl shards cascading across his lawn. No, not a bull—he caught a quick flash of udders. He pushed that absurd observation aside—it didn't matter. Because moments later, another tremendous impact shook the fence to his other side, revealing a second massive bovine in a fusillade of splintered plastic.

He backpedaled as his beautiful privacy fence disintegrated before his eyes; crash after crash reverberating along its length, exposing more animals. Then the gate in front of him imploded, sending a wave of vinyl shards crashing over him, and he lifted an arm to shield himself. Through the debris, a beefy animal bore down on him. Black soulless eyes seemed to peer right through him as it lowered its enormous head to charge. Right before the thing hit him, he leapt, throwing his body for the gap between those massive, wickedly sharp horns. The cow mooed with contempt as Bethany's dad hit his mark, then the air gushed from his lungs as the powerful beast launched him into the air.

On his upward arc, he allowed himself a moment to be astounded by the animal's strength—but only a moment—because he quickly realized he was in trouble. Though the cow had thrown him toward the pool, he could tell he wouldn't quite make it. As concrete rushed up to meet him, he reached out and tried to break his fall—if only slightly. He landed awkwardly; the wrist of one arm and forearm of the other plowing into the concrete deck, shattering several bones in each limb. Yet, his desperate ploy worked, and he managed to shift his trajectory, just barely. Even though he avoided cracking his head open on the concrete slab, his noggin still struck with enough force to send stars bursting across his vision.

The stabbing pain radiating through his fractured arms overshadowed the knock on his head as he completed his tumble, plunging face first into the cool water. Pain lanced through his shattered limbs as he fought to right himself. Somehow, despite the raw agony, he managed to flip himself around and kicked off the bottom of the pool.

Nearly blind with pain, his head broke the surface in time to see the stampeding cattle alter course to avoid the pool. Legs kicking desperately to keep his head above the water, he watched in horror as the wave of cows broke east, directly toward the floor-to-ceiling windows overlooking the pool. Then one cow took the turn too wide, and a wall of water crashed over him, obscuring his view of the chaos.

Bethany's mother had looked on from the sunroom, gaping in frozen horror as her husband flew across the yard and hit the lip of the pool before plunging in. During the moments that followed, she watched the growing ripples with bated breath, hoping beyond hope that her husband would reemerge. Seconds stretched like hours, and just when she was sure it was over, sure he couldn't have possibly survived—she'd seen that impact—his bloody head broke the surface, eliciting a tremulous sigh of relief.

Then the torrent of cattle spilled her way, and a new spasm

of dread crawled up her spine. Her heart skipped as she turned and fled. Moments later, a resounding crash erupted behind her as the floor-to-ceiling windows disintegrated, shattering into countless fragments. Chairs, end tables, and a sofa flew across the room around her as if they were dollhouse furniture tossed about by a child throwing a tantrum. Cabinets and bookshelves cracked and splintered, and her pretties were launched across the room, sending a cascade of tinkling ceramic crashing like hail. One chair spiraled through the air, grazing her, before flying past and shattering against the wall.

At the staircase, she gripped the newel post, barely swinging herself out of the way before the first black-smeared beast passed. Her momentum carried her around, and she stumbled up the first few steps, then hip-checked the banister with a *crack*. She lost her grip on the post and ended up backpedaling a few more steps before she lost her footing. Pain lanced from her tailbone as it slammed into the lip of one of the stairs and her back plowed into the balustrade on the other side, cracking several of the wooden spindles.

Sprawled on the staircase, she watched—stunned—as the roiling tide of beef surged past. The large ebony-spattered beasts funneled into the hall, scouring the walls on either side, peeling away swaths of drywall, and battering support beams beneath their immense weight. Moments later, the wave of beef crashed into the entry. The heavy front door proved to be no match for the rampaging beasts, and it exploded outward, cartwheeling across the lawn as the sidelites and transom dissolved into a cascade of splintered wood and glass fragments that sprayed across the entryway and sidewalk.

Then an animal launched itself over the open staircase; banisters no more than a couple of feet in front of her exploded, leaving the railing to either side a ruin of splintered spindles. As kindling cascaded across the foyer, Bethany's mom crab-walked up the stairs to the first landing.

She watched in awe as another animal crashed through the dining room, toppling her grandmother's China cabinet before skidding through the kitchen and slamming into the cabinets.

After the animal fought to regain its feet, it trotted off, leaving fragments of wood and ceramic in its wake. She couldn't help but let the tears flow as she surveyed the ruin that had once been her beautiful home.

The first thing Jean noticed as consciousness slowly returned was an intermittent dripping—*tap tap-tap tap*. She tried to push aside the ache blooming in her temples as she focused on the sound. *Tap tap tap-tap-tap.* It was almost as if someone were trying to send a message in old Morse Code. Bleary eyes fluttered open as she craned her neck up to find the source of the tapping. Crimson droplets trickled up to the headliner, where tiny roses bloomed on the fabric. Dripping *up* to the headliner? A wave of vertigo swept over her, and her perspective flipped as she realized she was hanging upside down by her seatbelt. That explained the tightness across her chest and the pressure in her head.

Now the rough grain of asphalt materialized around her, flecked with shards of glass from her shattered front windshield. No wonder it was so dark. The flickering lights along the dashboard signaled an issue—as if she hadn't already realized something had gone terribly wrong. Had she crashed? She must have. What had she hit? *What had—*

Oh, yeah.

The bizarre scene came flooding back.

She'd been heading home from a long day at work. Traveling perhaps five to ten miles over the speed limit, she'd been about to whip around the corner onto Aberdeen when the weirdest thing happened. The front door of the house on the corner exploded outwards in a mist of shattered glass and wood shards and went cartwheeling across the lawn, kicking up clouds of dirt. That might have been shocking enough if it hadn't been followed by a surge of beef moments later. Cattle poured from a gaping hole in the ruined house, hot on the heels of the metal door as it took its last couple of flips, then tumbled to a stop in a shower of soil. Surprised, Jean's foot had slipped from the gas.

Forgetting she was driving—forgetting anything but surprise as cattle surged from the once beautiful home—Jean let the vehicle coast into the turn, wide eyes locked on the approaching herd. By the time she realized they weren't stopping—weren't even slowing—it was too late. Almost simultaneously, two of the massive beasts slammed into the passenger side of her new subcompact.

She shuddered, remembering the impact—the sickening crunch as the side panels buckled and warped under intense weight—then the shards of glass hurtling toward her as the world tipped.

Her eyes searched the ceiling for any sign of her cell phone as a hand found the catch of her seatbelt. Jean released it, tumbling to the roof, then scrambled over to her phone. There was a massive crack running down its face, but mercifully, it still worked. She peered from the windows, searching for any sign of the mad—they must have been mad—cows as she dialed emergency services.

She had to warn people.

18

When the first reports of gunshots flooded the wire, Sheriff Johnson had deferred, trusting her deputies to handle it. She was already preoccupied with a disturbing situation nearby. She stood at the pool's edge, peering intently into the pink-tinged water where Mr. Salazar had found his wife's body hovering near the bottom. The poor man dove in after his wife and dragged her to the surface—contaminating the scene—in a futile attempt to save her life. Once he'd noticed the clammy, blue-tinged skin, the weeping man had phoned nine-one-one immediately.

Though she couldn't blame him for that impulse, she would have preferred he hadn't disturbed the body. Still, she sighed, it must have been quite a surprise. It was for her. This incident raised the death toll to five in the last three days—four from this particular subdivision—so she had felt it was her duty as sheriff to look into it personally. What was happening to her small town?

At first glance, it appeared to be nothing more than an unfortunate accident, a simple drowning. The open gash at Mrs. Salazar's temple, along with the swath of coagulated, rust-brown blood on the lip of the pool, suggested the cause. But coming on the heels of the gruesome discovery at the Ellisons' home,

Johnson couldn't afford to make that assumption.

The body—having been submerged for hours in cool water—was reluctant to give up its secrets just yet. But the preliminary finding put the time of death sometime the night before, prior to the devastating attack at the Ellisons'.

Before they loaded Mrs. Salazar into the coroner's van, Johnson had taken a good look at the gash marring that otherwise beautiful face and made sure to examine her thin frame for any other signs of injury. Unlike the deaths discovered earlier that morning, this incident had none of the hallmarks of an animal attack. Yet, she couldn't push away the thought that somehow the incidents had been related.

And the foul present discovered nearby did nothing to curb that suspicion. Even now, her techs were bagging a large cow pie they'd found along the border of the neighboring field, just outside the open gate.

Could it just be a coincidence that Salazar had 'slipped' and hit her head on the same night that the Ellisons met their fate— with a pile of dung not fifty feet away?

She ruminated over little Hank's words. "The bad cow did it."

Still, it made no sense. She'd done some research after the grisly scene that morning. Cattle didn't attack like this—they wouldn't wander so far from their herd, would they? Most cattle attacks happened on the farm: in a barn, or out in the pastures. She'd never heard of anything like this; she doubted anyone had.

Could someone be using an overly aggressive cow as a murder weapon? Or perhaps they were simply staging the murders to resemble animal attacks to throw them off? Neither option seemed likely; where was the motive? The only thing these three had in common was … was …

Her eyes narrowed, then widened.

But … no.

4-H.

Why hadn't the realization come sooner? The little girl, Lily, had mentioned a new baby calf. And Mrs. Salazar volunteered at the ag barn, helping the students take care of their animals.

What if a cow had been provoked? What if it'd had its baby snatched away? Did that make sense? The young Miss Graham had mentioned something about her uncle selling some of their calves. But why now? Surely, separating calves from their mothers was a common practice on dairy farms. If that was the case …

Could an animal show such abnormal behavior out of the blue? She shook her head … all it would take was one outlier, one mad cow.

She'd have to speak to Hailey Graham again.

"Sheriff!" A breathless deputy materialized at her shoulder. There was a hint of something glinting in his eyes. Was that fear? What had happened? Now, she concentrated on the flurry of movement that had been playing at the edges of her peripheral vision and glanced around. Across the way, a fireman sprinted up to his lieutenant, the same distressed expression plastered on his face. "Something's happened," the deputy gasped, fighting to be heard over the roil of thunder rolling their way. As she waited for the man to continue, she glanced at the mottled gray sky.

Was it going to storm?

Then the bombshell hit. "We've got a whole herd of cattle stampeding this way."

Her eyes whipped back to the man, and she squinted at him. Cattle again? She opened her mouth to respond, but nothing came out as she merely blinked at the man. What was there to say? Heart racing, she spun and sprinted on the heels of a pair of firemen.

The thundering hooves clashed with the roar of her pulse as she rounded the front of the house, only to catch the tail end of the herd rumbling by.

"Sheriff—" her radio squawked, then the speaker cut out for a moment, "—nson, we're getting panicked calls coming from Cimarron Acres. Reports of cattle rampaging through the neighborhood."

Johnson's hand darted to her radio.

"This is Gilroy, Sheriff, I see them!" the young deputy blurted into his mic as he sped, wide-eyed, toward the rolling tide of beef. The idyllic neighborhood was thrown into chaos as the swell of cattle surged toward him: crashing, jostling, and slamming into each other as well as parked cars lining the street, while residents flooded from their homes to witness the spectacle. "They're headed down Aberdeen. God, there are so many!"

"Where are you?" The sheriff's voice broke through his awe.

"I'm coming up on Galloway," he said, then breathlessly asked an important question. "What do I do?"

His heart thudded in his chest as the tide rose. And quickly. His foot slipped off the gas, but the car coasted ever forward. They'd doubled in size since he'd first spotted them. At this rate, he had only seconds to come up with a plan. And staying the course was not an option. The wave of beef would surely crash over his cruiser.

"Listen, son ..." There was a slight pause over the line, then the sheriff's voice erupted through the speaker, "I need you to turn them." *Turn them?* How the hell was he supposed to do that? "... drive them down Galloway ..." Her words faded as his mind raced.

All he could manage was a whimpered, "How?"

"Whatever it takes, Gilroy!" That was easy for her to say. "Do you hear me? Drive them down Galloway ..." The sheriff's voice continued to blare through the speakers, but he let his focus drift when he realized she wasn't talking to him anymore. He let her make plans as he mulled over his task. He caught words: cul-de-sac, bottle, drive—but he didn't have time to process them as the roar of hooves rumbled closer.

Of the ideas flitting through his mind, only one seemed to have the slightest chance of success. Gilroy gunned the engine as he neared the intersection of Aberdeen and Galloway, then jerked the wheel aside and stood on the brake. His cruiser slewed around, skidding to a stop across the middle of the lane.

The rampaging herd thundered closer, leaving a trail of destruction in its wake.

He jammed the gear lever up into reverse and his cruiser leapt back and slammed into a parked car with a *crunch*. He hoped he wouldn't have to pay for that. But that worry evaporated as the cattle rolled forward. Gilroy's eyes widened as the cattle swelled. Fifty yards, then forty, thirty—they weren't slowing, not even a little bit. His cruiser wouldn't hold up to such an assault. It couldn't, could it? He didn't wait to see. At ten yards, Gilroy scrambled across to the passenger seat and jammed a finger on the window control, then the cattle reached the five-yard mark—fifteen feet—that was too close; what had he been thinking?

He ripped his weapon from its holster and thrust it into the air, pointing it through the opening window, and squeezed off two quick shots just before the windows on the driver's side imploded, splintering into millions of tiny projectiles as the car rocked with the impact of rampaging beef. He cowered against the onslaught of countless glass shards—eyes closed, waiting for the animals to steamroll over him. Yet, after a moment, he was still there, cringing from each fresh jolt as cattle knocked into the rocking car, but still there. He risked opening his eyes and saw a couple of stunned animals shaking off their stupor as the rest of the horde flowed past—east, dashing down Galloway.

Gilroy sighed a curse. It had worked. With a shaky hand, he reached for the microphone—he had to let them know it worked.

He might need a change of underwear—but it had worked.

Sheriff Johnson was in the vanguard of the batch of vehicles speeding after the herd, trying to avoid the minefield of cow pies left to cook on the hot asphalt. It hadn't been more than a minute after the cattle had rumbled past, that she was in her cruiser in pursuit. Even so, the handful of blocks seemed to crawl by as she raced to catch up. All the while relaying orders to her department. *What a mess—*

An entire herd of cattle had escaped. What's more, it had occurred mere moments after she'd pulled at a thread that might connect everything. Was that significant? Was it all connected? Or was it just a coincidence? Following on the heels of the latest body, she couldn't help but suspect it was more than random events thrown together by chance.

Johnson pushed her desire for answers aside; she had to get the immediate crisis under control before she could fully examine the larger picture. She had to figure out a way to stop the cattle—some way to round them up.

Moments later, another deputy called in. "Sheriff, this is Chambers."

She jumped on her radio. "Go ahead."

As she whipped around the corner onto Galloway, completely ignoring the stop sign, Johnson glanced at her deputy's cruiser stretched across the street. The driver's side was a mess of crumpled bodywork and splayed tires. Steam drifted from beneath the hood, and the crumpled rear end was wedged against another vehicle unluckily parked on the side of the road. Gilroy stood, leaning against the passenger side, head in hands; he'd sounded distinctly shaken up, but the kid had done it. He deserved a commendation.

"I'm parked across Galloway, just on the other side of Illawarra," Chambers came back.

"Copy that," she said. "Let me know when you see them."

So far, so good. Illawarra was about halfway along this stretch of Galloway Drive. With any luck, another obstruction in the street would turn the cattle into one of several cul-de-sacs along Galloway—there were three or four if she wasn't mistaken. After that, they could block off their escape and round them up at their leisure. The inspiration hit as soon as Gilroy mentioned his position. It was a desperate plan, but it might just work. Could they be so lucky? Fortune seemed to be favoring them so far—aside from the breakout itself—first with Gilroy's initial success, then with Chambers being in just the right place as he was responding to the shots fired call.

What was up with that, anyway? And why wasn't Roscoe Hire responding? She let off the gas, briefly glancing both ways before rolling past another stop sign, then accelerating again.

Did the gunshots have something to do with their current predicament?

She grunted, pushing the thought aside as she closed on the tail end of the herd, now moving along at a healthy trot. Nervous cattle glanced back at her, tossing their heads and rolling their eyes as they called out and pressed forward.

"Okay, they're coming over the rise now." Chambers paused, then his voice came back. "God, there's so many," he moaned.

She couldn't argue with that; this had to be the worst livestock escape she'd seen—worst she'd ever heard of.

"Progress?" She waited with bated breath as the seconds crawled by, then he finally came back on.

"At their current speed … shouldn't be more than a minute." Then his voice broke. "Are you sure this is a good idea?"

It was the only idea at the moment.

Seconds later, she crested the rise on the heels of the roiling herd and saw her deputy's lonely car splayed across the street. She hadn't thought this through. Lawns stretched to either side of the street; vast open yards with no obstructions. Still, it might work. The column of cattle hadn't strayed from the pavement as they moved inexorably toward the roadblock. It might just work. Hopefully.

"Errgghh, I don't know if I can do this!" Chambers' tone was anxiety laced with dread.

"Hold your position." She could almost picture his apprehension.

"Understood," the voice came back flat.

And to the kid's credit, he didn't run away or speed off as the herd closed. Then, moments before impact, two shots rang out and the torrent of cattle shifted, parting and flowing around the obstacle like a river around a rock. She drew to a stop in front of the deputy's vehicle, watching in chagrined resignation as their second effort failed miserably—the deputy's shots had only riled the cattle further, sending them surging away.

Perhaps it had been too much to hope for.

19

Hailey caught herself absentmindedly fiddling with one of the pearly snap buttons adorning her turquoise and black plaid shirt. Taking a trembling breath, she forced her wandering hand back down to her side, then ran her fingertips along the smooth cotton to either side of her stomach and around her waist to make sure the shirt was still tucked. Hailey took the opportunity to brush her hands along her hips, wiping away the traces of perspiration accumulating on her palms.

As another neighbor edged forward to express their sorrow and view the casket, she couldn't help but wonder if she shouldn't have dressed up more. Even in her best embroidered bootcut jeans and her freshly oiled Justin's, she couldn't help feeling shabby compared to most of her family. However, more than halfway through the visitation, it was a moot point.

Her eyes darted to her mom and dad again—it was so weird to think of Lexa as Mom, though nice—each of whom had dressed up for the occasion. More than she was, at least. Dad wore a nice pair of khaki slacks, a black dress shirt, and a vivid blue tie, matching his eyes. Lexa had on a simple, yet elegant, black dress, accentuating her slim physique. Hailey smiled at the sight of her twin brothers; the dark-haired boys each matched their father, right down to the pair of blue clip-on ties they couldn't stop messing with.

Her aunt and uncle stood across the way, working the room; Caleb in an expensive-looking charcoal suit, and Sierra in a strapless dress that, even nearing forty, showed off the lithe form her twin daughters had inherited. Chloe stayed in her mother's shadow, adorned in a similarly elegant, yet more substantial, dress. Only Zoe's band tee and garish plaid skirt threw off the elegant little family—when you factored in her vibrant hair, she looked a sight. The girl's parents had put up a token objection about the wardrobe choice, but Hailey could tell their hearts just weren't in it. Nor had they put up a fuss when Zoe had subsequently banished herself to a winged armchair in the corner of the room, nose in her phone like usual. At least that way, she wasn't drawing too much attention to herself.

For the last hour and a half, members of the town had been flooding into the small funeral home, representing all walks of life. From the local politicians, including the mayor, to rodeo clowns—who, according to her father, equated to the same thing—Hailey didn't think that was quite fair … to the rodeo clowns. There were ministers and mill workers, school officials as well as a network of farmers and ranchers her grampa had done business with; all seemed to be present. Not to mention the hordes of neighbors that had helped or been helped by him over the years.

However, neither the Sheriff nor the fire chief, an old friend of Grampa's, had shown up—which she thought was odd. When Rodger Sandrich turned up claiming to represent the sheriff's department, Hailey introduced him around as he made apologies for his boss's absence. "Unavoidable," he'd said. Uncle Caleb's expression made it clear he didn't think much of the excuse, but there was nothing anyone could do about it. And after giving his condolences, Rodger had retreated to a corner and seemed to take up station there. Hailey often caught herself letting her gaze drift over to the young man and couldn't help but feel a thrill when their eyes met.

At one point, when her father was otherwise engaged, Hailey received a poke to the ribs from a grinning Lexa. "Someone can't take their eyes off you." Hailey had returned a shy smile, though she reddened at the comment.

Other than that, and a few other inconsequential incidents, people flowed into the room, had a polite word, then trickled out to make room for the next wave of mourners.

So, Hailey was surprised when Rodger appeared at her elbow, his expression a grim mask.

"Hailey," Rodger murmured, then glanced at her dad and nodded. "I have to go. We're getting calls out of Cimarron Acres. It appears that some cattle have gotten loose and are tearing through the neighborhood."

"Are they ours?" Hailey asked, eyes widening.

"That's still unclear," Rodger said, shrugging. "Maybe?"

Caleb appeared at her elbow. "That's just great," he murmured.

At last, they agreed on something; that was all they needed right now. Had Greg left a gate open? She couldn't see him doing that. He'd always been dutiful enough in the past.

Hailey pushed the thought away. "How many? Do you know?"

Rodger shook his head and glanced at his watch. "Not yet. I just thought you might need to know."

Hailey turned to her father. "Dad, I better go. If they're ours …" she trailed off, shaking her head as she turned to leave. She could picture it now—cows steamrolling over lawns and gardens, trampling fences, generally being a nuisance—and occurring right after the fatal attack; they'd never live it down.

"Wait!" Lexa said. Hailey turned back, prepared to argue; couldn't they see this was important? But then her mom continued: "Your father will go with you. Help you out," Lexa offered, urging her dad ahead.

"Me too—I guess," Caleb said, rubbing his ribs where his wife had just elbowed him.

Hailey blinked at him, then nodded. "Yeah, okay."

"I'll help," Chloe offered, stepping forward.

But Caleb shook his head. "I don't think so, honey."

Chloe opened her mouth to object, but Dad lifted a hand.

"Caleb's right," he said, agreeing with his brother—another first—forestalling her protest. "The rest of you should hang around here until we get a handle on the situation."

As the others agreed, Chloe looked around at the stern faces, lip quivering, then dropped her shoulders and nodded.

Sheriff Johnson stood in front of her patrol car; a map spread out across the SUV's hood. After their second hurried attempt failed to turn the roving herd, she'd fallen back to the farm to coordinate the cleanup effort as well as get some much-needed answers about the cause of this situation. While she did, Johnson had tasked a couple of her deputies with trailing the cattle at a respectful distance; she didn't want to spur them into further chaos.

On the way to the farm, she'd received the devastating news of Deputy Hire's accident. Even now, off-duty deputies, paramedics, and firemen were flooding in. Flickering lights from multiple ambulances flanking the scene announced the severity of the situation. Hire was still in his cruiser; after the paramedics assessed the futility of his condition, they'd branched out to help those they could.

She glanced over a shoulder to see a gurney rattle by over the uneven gravel drive as paramedics wheeled a young man they'd found trampled beside an open gate. Perhaps it was fortunate the kid was unconscious; she wouldn't want to think about how that rumbling trip would've felt with his countless broken bones. Across the street, medics were wheeling Bethany's dad to the bus after plucking him out of a pool. They'd discovered the man draped over a pink foam noodle with a pair of broken arms. He might have drowned if it weren't for the pool toy left out by his heedless children.

And in the back of a nearby patrol car, Rockwell sat handcuffed, quietly getting a head wound tended in the middle of this chaos. When she'd pulled up minutes ago, the inebriated man had still been raving as he stumbled along, escorted by a pair of deputies. Loudly reminding them all in his slurred speech that he'd predicted this, told them the cattle were dangers to the community. It wasn't until he'd learned of Hire's fate that the man had finally fallen silent.

She sighed. At least now she had some answers. But there were many more problems that still needed solutions.

The fire chief appeared at her shoulder. In his late fifties, the man had decades of experience but still hadn't seen anything like this; he'd told her as much. At first, she was afraid he might try to prise control of the scene from her—part of her even wanted him to. But he hadn't so much as hinted at it, only offering the support of himself and his people until the crisis had passed.

She didn't know if she should be grateful for his confidence—or if the man was just unwilling to bear the responsibility. Either way, it didn't matter. She had a job to do.

"Here's what I'm thinking ..." Sheriff Johnson jabbed a finger on the map several inches away and sketched the outline of a new plan. For the first time, they wouldn't just be reacting to the situation.

The low growl of Grampa's 2500 reverberated through the cab as Hailey kept the new luxury pickup glued to Rodger's bumper. After cruising between the College, and the aptly named University Plaza, they whipped off Main Street. She barely touched the brakes as they raced north up University Drive, siren wailing and lights flashing.

If it hadn't been for the uncertainty awaiting them at the farm, she could have almost enjoyed the prospect of the police escort. She'd never had one before and she couldn't articulate the rush she was experiencing speeding through the packed streets—pedal to the metal—with absolutely no repercussions.

When they approached the southeast corner of Cimarron Acres, an anxious knot swelled in her gut; she was almost home. She tried not to imagine the scene she was hurtling toward. What had happened? Was anyone hurt? She couldn't help but hope it wasn't her cattle somewhere in there, wreaking havoc.

Before long they were closing on the intersection of Cracker and University, where University's four-lane hardtop ended, and County Road 15's dirt path continued north, bisecting their property. Once she followed Rodger around the corner, blowing through the light, the knot in Hailey's gut grew as a sea of flashing lights appeared a half mile on. What had happened?

Closer, she recognized a score of emergency vehicles idling at their property line. They were her cattle. But why now? What had happened? Where was Greg? One of the handful of ambulances sped away as they approached, and she could see people bustling around another as it was being loaded. Hailey couldn't begin to fathom the devastation she glimpsed.

Who was hurt? Greg?

As they neared, Rodger swerved off the blacktop, cutting through a break in the hedge wall lining their front yard. Hailey followed him, the truck's shocks barely registering the change in terrain as they tore across the yard. Her eyes fell upon one of the sheriff's vehicles; the evening sun beat down on it, highlighting the metal-flecked paint as a knot of paramedics clustered around the cruiser. Among the swarm, it had seemed like any other, but at this angle, she realized the hood was crumpled; the splash of crimson liquid across the obliterated windshield spoke volumes about the condition of the driver. *Oh God, oh God.*

"Good God," Caleb murmured from the seat behind her. "What happened here?"

As Rodger slid to a stop, Hailey stood on the brakes, the locked tires tearing divots from their pristine lawn. She couldn't think about that now. It didn't matter. Hailey spun the gear toggle around to P and bounded from the truck, not even bothering to shut off the engine.

Officers were crowded around the Sheriff's champagne and brown SUV, taking it in turns to glance at their comrade's mangled vehicle. Though a foot shorter than most, the Sheriff seemed to stand seven feet tall, barking orders, holding court— an unrolled map stretched across her hood.

As Rodger bolted over, the sheriff glanced up and made eye contact with Hailey, holding up a finger. Hailey stopped and nodded, then turned to scan the farm as Rodger's soft voice drifted over, his low dulcet tones incomprehensible.

Her eyes kept returning to the devastated police car.

A moment later, Rodger hustled back.

As the deputy rejoined them, Hailey's mouth opened, and she took a breath, ready to start a barrage of questions—she had plenty—but Caleb beat her to it.

"What's happened?" Caleb demanded.

"I'm not certain"—Rodger waved away Caleb's question, his focus not wavering from Hailey—"the sheriff needs you to do a quick count. We need to know how many animals we're looking at." Caleb didn't look pleased to be disregarded. But what could he do?

Hailey nodded, right to business; plenty of time for questions later. She dashed off—father in tow—to survey her herd.

20

Steven Jones was stoked; it hadn't even been a week since he'd gotten his license and he was ready to show off his new silver BMW. He rolled through a stop sign, barely glancing both ways, before turning onto the through street. Wider than the residential streets that fed into it, this section of road cut through the middle of the subdivision and only had a couple of four-way stops. It was why he'd picked it.

He let the needle drift above the 'recommended' 25 mph as he zipped through the neighborhood. His neighborhood. Surely the handful of cops he'd spotted whipping about wouldn't hassle him in his own neighborhood, and if they did, it was only money. Besides, with the lilting cry of distant sirens barely audible over the radio, they seemed to be a bit busy. What was that about? He shook his head, cranking the dial to drown out the racket as he accelerated. He glanced at the dashboard clock; if he didn't hurry, he'd be late.

He couldn't believe Taylor had said yes. The varsity basketballer was going to be a junior and had to be one of the hottest girls in the entire school—and she'd agreed to hang out with him. Not quite a sophomore himself, the newly minted sixteen-year-old, had doubted he'd have a chance with the upperclassman, but she'd said yes. Not only that, but she'd seemed enthusiastic when he'd told her about his sleek new BMW.

He glanced at the clock again; it wouldn't be too bad.

All of a sudden, a cow darted into the middle of the road. Steven jammed the brakes, but it wasn't good enough. As the airbag exploded in front of him, a ton of fresh beef rolled across the crumpling hood and over the splintering windshield, then the startled, ink-mottled cow launched overhead, its shocked face appearing briefly in the sunroof moments before the world went black.

A block away, Frank Carlyle had just pried up another hulk of sizzling ground beef, severing the tendrils of fat and grease from the stainless-steel grill, when the squeal of brakes and crunch of crumpling aluminum and steel carried through the quiet neighborhood. Glancing around, he let the thick hamburger patty slide off the spatula's blade, the raw meat hissing as it plopped onto the searing grill.

Where moments before, the yard had been filled with a din of overlapping voices and the hooting cries of splashing children, all around him, the knots of milling people froze, conversation dying. As he took in the concerned expressions blooming among his guests, he knew he had to do something—as a community leader; it was his duty to reassure them.

Besides, he'd arranged this cookout to bring the community together, and hopefully wrangle a few new investors. Cimarron Acres had been his baby, and it had exceeded his wildest expectations. For the last couple of years, people had flocked to the glamorous new development, withdrawing further from the nightmare of the big city. And it was only the beginning. He was set to break ground on Phase II early next spring. The quarter section of corn fields directly to the east (no reason to let the land just sit there unused) would soon become a hundred and sixty acres of new homes. And with Graham's untimely death, he had the inside track on more land across the way. He'd even invested in a steer for his kid in order to meet with one of

Graham's heirs, to feel him out. And from his initial, subtle inquiries, the man seemed primed to sell.

But that was for later. Right now, he had to calm these people. Leaving his fifteen-year-old in charge of the grill, he stepped out to soothe them. He couldn't very well get people to invest if they were distracted by some inconsequential accident.

"It's all right, folks," Frank soothed. "There's no need to be alarmed"—he waved at a couple of rambunctious teens tearing across the lawn. "We'll see what they have to say. I'm sure this will all be taken care of before …" He trailed off, as a low rumble finally caught his attention, and he found himself glancing up at the darkening gray skies. Was that thunder? There hadn't been any mention of rain in the forecast. That was all he needed, a thunderstorm on top of the wreck.

Instead of fading away, the rolling thunder only grew in intensity. Murmuring voices lifted around him as the earth trembled beneath his feet and windows rattled in their frames. The thunderous roar only grew, intermixed with the lowing of cattle. Frank's eyes widened. It almost sounded like—

About that time, the young men reached the fence line and flung the gate open. Half a second later, one of them spat out a loud curse, then a section of the custom privacy fence disintegrated in front of the stunned spectators. In that split second, the remnants of splintering wood cascaded over the kids, then they vanished beneath a wave of angry cattle.

For half a heartbeat, pandemonium was delayed as his guests tried to process what they were witnessing, then the frenzy began. A knot of people hovering around a table at the edge of the patio broke in panic. They collided with a plastic folding table, flipping it and incidentally sending an array of fixins' cascading across the patio. In their haste to flee, a couple of them tripped over the table itself; a few slipped on the scatter of toppings and condiment bottles; more simply trampled the heaps of buns, cheese, and potato chips strewn across the patio. A little ways away, the dessert table also toppled, and scores of desserts splattered across the ground only to be crushed underfoot by fleeing guests.

Yet their panic made little difference; Frank watched in awe as the wave of cattle crashed over them, making quick work of the minuscule gap they'd created, and soon the first wave of bodies had disappeared beneath the pounding hooves.

Among the clumps of lawn chairs dotting his expansive yard, panicked parents had risen and were shoving each other—and subsequently their neighbor's kids—aside in a desperate effort to reach their children. One dad flung his best friend's toddler aside in an attempt to reach his own. Several parents sprinted around Frank to the pool, plucking their children from the water as if bobbing for apples; though they shouldn't have—as, in the end, the pool proved to be one of the safer places. But how were they to know?

Before Frank's eyes, pandemonium reigned as the cattle seemed to strike out at anything that moved. In his paralyzed horror, he watched adults and children alike disappear beneath the rampaging beasts. His eyes jumped to his son, who stood in frozen terror next to the grill tucked beside the house, not moving an inch as the first wave of cattle reached him. The expensive grill slammed into his son, bulling him through the floor-to-ceiling windows lining the dining room as half-cooked meat and fragments of glass rained across the patio. The animal followed his son and the grill into the house.

The last he saw was his wife standing open-mouthed at the patio doors, red, tear-soaked eyes wide at the chaos, then he felt a tremendous impact, and everything went dark.

21

The Sheriff's radio squawked, the hissing static jerking Johnson's focus away, and she retreated a few steps. The information relayed through the transceiver merely exacerbated her pounding headache. More good news, on an already dismal day.

"… understood, Johnson out." *Great. Just great.* Yet another situation to handle.

This was a hell of a day … a hell of a week.

"Our rogue cattle have created more havoc …" Johnson said, sighing as she rejoined her deputies, briefly informing them of the cookout that had just been steamrolled. As she spoke, several of the ambulances peeled off from the periphery, lights strobing and sirens blaring; forcing her to nearly shout. "Calls coming in report multiple injuries, some serious." She paused, looking around, then indicated a few deputies at random: "You, you, and you escort the paramedics over there ASAP. We need to get a handle on this situation."

"Rules of engagement?" Stevens, a military vet, asked.

"Engagement? They're cows, not insurgents," Rodger cut in.

"They've killed people," the man said.

Rodger opened his mouth, with what would have surely been a witty rebuttal, but the Sheriff cut him off.

"Sandrich is right, they're animals. Scared animals. Valuable animals: these people's livelihood"—she motioned idly at the farm behind her. "By all means, defend yourself and others, but only shoot if it is absolutely necessary; don't kill them indiscriminately. The rest of you circle around to the staging point on the east side of Cimarron Acres." She clapped. "All right, people, let's get this mess cleaned up. Get to it." The shocked deputies murmured, peering around at each other for a long moment. "Go!" Sheriff Johnson barked, dismissing her people.

About that time, young Miss Graham and her father trotted back into sight.

As the troops fanned out, Johnson called, "Sandrich, hold here." The young man had shown great initiative by bringing the Grahams with him. Hell, she'd been so absorbed with working out the final details of her plan, it hadn't even occurred to her. He made a hell of a deputy.

Her eyes flicked to the ruined cruiser, and her chest tightened. She'd lost a man. She'd never lost someone under her before. Colleagues in the force, sure, but never someone under her command. She didn't know how to process this. Now, these cattle were rampaging through the neighborhood. Did this have to do with the other deaths? Could these cows be rabid?

She glanced over at the cause of this mess.

Mr. Rockwell sat hunched in the back of a patrol car, his head still swimming in his intoxication. Ashamed and stunned, he'd slipped into silence after learning of the deputy's demise— heartsick at the prospect and fearful of the implications. She knew he never meant for that to happen. But it didn't matter, he was responsible, no matter how indirectly, for the death of a man.

Forcibly shaking the thought from her mind, the sheriff flew to meet with the Grahams.

"Hailey." As her attention was snatched from the surrounding chaos, the girl started at the sound of her name. Johnson reached out, pumping her hand, while only giving the girl's father and uncle a perfunctory nod. "Sir." The niceties must be observed. But presently her attention shifted back to the young woman with laser focus. "According to Sandrich," she said, "you're the one to talk to about the operations."

"Y-yes, ma'am."

"Good. Here's the situation …" Johnson spent a minute laying out the broad strokes, giving her stunned audience the rundown on Rockwell's disastrously misguided attempt for retribution against their animals and Greg's injuries as the cattle escaped, then ended with the death of the deputy.

"Oh my God," Hailey's hand flew to her mouth, tears leaking from her eyes. "Is Greg going to be okay? His father—"

"He's been rushed to the emergency room," Johnson said, shaking her head. "His family is meeting him there. What I nee—"

"Surely, we can't be held responsible for all this," Caleb objected.

Michael Graham swatted his brother's arm. "Caleb, not the time."

"Your brother's right. Now isn't the time to place blame," Johnson dismissed his concerns. Caleb didn't seem mollified, but she bulled on, still addressing Hailey, "What I need from you is numbers."

Hailey nodded and relayed the results of her hurried tally. All told, there were a bit less than four dozen animals on the loose, including half a dozen young bulls. More than Johnson would have believed. Worse than she thought.

"What can we do to help?" the girl almost begged.

Johnson was about to tell them to stay back, but she realized they could be useful and slowly nodded her head; the more people helping to contain this mess, the better. Besides, their insight might prove useful. It couldn't hurt.

"I've gotten reports of a few strays loitering throughout Cimarron Acres. If you all could help us round them up, it would be a big help."

"Of course, Sheriff," Hailey agreed readily.

Johnson gave her a deep nod, then turned to Sandrich. "Stay with the Grahams, help them with whatever they need."

After the sheriff and her cadre of deputies vanished, Hailey went to work. Misgivings flashed through her mind as she sat in her grampa's office, fidgeting idly with a lasso and giving their closest neighbors a brief rundown of the situation. Before she had a chance to ask for assistance rounding up their wayward cattle, they'd offered their full support and promised to get a phone chain going.

Again, she was impressed with the generosity of her neighbors.

With that well in hand, she went to help her dad hook up the cattle trailer to Grampa's pickup. But when Hailey stepped outside, their ultralight stock trailer sat behind the truck, and her dad and Rodger already had everything secured. While the gleaming aluminum trailer wasn't their largest, measuring in at sixteen feet, it would be easier and quicker to navigate the neighborhood, besides it would hold quite a few of the wayward animals.

She was double-checking their work when Caleb slipped into the 2500 with a bundle. She didn't have the time or inclination to see what he thought he needed at this moment. After she was done, Hailey tossed her dad the keys. "You drive," she offered, then dashed to her old beat-up Dakota pickup. How would they pull this off?

The cow was standing on the edge of the road, gorging itself from the green on the curb strip when Hailey's Dakota swept in, whipping into the drive from one side as Rodger's patrol vehicle converged from the other, hopping the curb. The trucks converged at an angle, inches apart, forming a V that effectively blocked the errant cow's forward progress. As the distressed cow lowed in alarm and turned, Hailey Graham flew from the passenger door and, stepping on the rear tire, bounded into the Dakota's bed, just in time to see Caleb bring Grampa's 2500 into the gap behind the trucks, boxing in the frustrated animal.

While normally docile, cattle have been known to display sudden, seemingly unprovoked aggression, and after the events at the farm, Hailey didn't want to take any chances with her normally placid charges. She definitely didn't want to be gored by one of her ladies.

Hailey launched the rope; its loop soared across the gap and circled the bovine's large horn-laden head. Without even waiting to make sure, born from years of practice, Hailey whipped the lasso tight around the agitated animal's neck. The protesting cow bellowed in indignation, tugging against the snare. The coarse rope rasped against her gloved palms, producing a dull heat, making her wish she had somewhere to dally the rope. Luckily, the cow couldn't go far.

"Calm down, girl," Hailey cooed. "It's just me."

Wide black eyes locked on her, and like magic, either her soothing words or her presence seemed to calm the beast. Satisfied with its returned docility, Hailey coiled the rope to keep the line taut as she stepped over the tailgate, then hopped down to the asphalt.

Rodger appeared behind her. "Take this—" Hailey passed him the lead.

She kept a secure grip on the rope as she edged closer while scanning her lady for any sign of injury. The cow spun, keeping her in sight. When she was within an arm's length, she brought a hand up and used her teeth to peel off one of her gloves, then reached out—

"Hailey …" her dad warned.

"It's ok," she said. She could tell her dad wasn't comforted, but she couldn't deal with that now. Her palm rested on the big animal's head, and the cow relaxed, leaning into the caress. "Yeah, you know me"—Hailey stepped forward, her hand moving back and gently stroking the sweet spot on the animal's neck—"don't you girl." She kept a firm grip on the rope and her eye on the animal as she spoke to her uncle. "Caleb, pull the truck up a bit."

As the engine rumbled and the trailer rolled forward, the cow lowered her head and voiced a protest.

"Oh, I know, girl, I know; you're so scared. You don't know what's going on, do you?" Hailey soothed, continually running her fingers through the cow's coarse hair. "Dad, come around and open the gate," Hailey said. "Slowly."

Hailey kept a calming hand on the cow's neck as her dad skirted the trailer. Moments later, a *clang* rang from the disengaging locks, then the trailer door opened with a lingering *squeak*. The dewy-eyed bovine bellowed, tugging against the rope. *I need some WD-40.* Hailey gritted her teeth, but Rodger kept his hold on the lead.

"Oh, I know, girl. All those loud noises had you scared, huh?" Her eyes didn't stray from the cow as she kept up the soothing words, but she shifted her focus. "Rodger, go ahead and move toward the trailer."

Between the two of them, they turned the cow and steered her toward the trailer, as Hailey kept up her encouragements. "Come on, girl." The cow gave in to the pressure and allowed herself to be led by her human. "Come on; let's get you inside." Hooves clacked against the asphalt, then echoed off the metal ramp as Hailey led her into the rear of the trailer.

One down, Hailey thought, coiling the rope, *too many to go.*

22

While the Grahams were rounding up strays, the last few pieces of Sheriff Johnson's plan were falling into place. She'd learned from their past failures; she knew just where to set up their new blockade. University Avenue stretched over a small creek just on the north side of the stockyards, the wide, four-lane road tapering into the perfect choke point. The cattle wouldn't be able to just flow around this time.

A fire engine's powerful Cummins diesel growled as its front tire crawled over the curb, then inched closer to the concrete barrier running across the bridge. The massive gold-trimmed black fire engine lurched to a halt, blocking the sidewalk across the southern edge of the bridge, splaying at a sharp angle across a little more than half of the road. As the pair of firefighters secured the truck, a tractor-trailer roared to life behind them, and the massive vehicle crept out of the stockyard's parking lot. Angling toward the rear of the fire engine, it pulled its vast trailer across the gap and came to a stop within inches of the bumper, then the final piece, a throaty red and blue Peterbilt, fell into place.

Johnson waited a half mile north, standing among the sea of flashing lights, watching as the swell of beef surged ever closer. She couldn't help but wonder if they were prepared to face the oncoming storm. Despite having slowed a bit after annihilating the unwary cookout, the cattle still moved at a healthy clip as they rolled inexorably through the neighborhood, trampling anything unfortunate or stubborn enough to remain in their path. Though most residents had fled the streets, the curious still perched at windows and doorways as the bizarre parade wound through the neighborhood.

The herds' meandering course had led them down toward the southeast entrance of the subdivision, where Johnson had her people waiting behind a barricade arcing out across University Avenue. Emergency vehicles swept across the road, lined bumper to bumper, cutting off access to the north and east. And a line of vehicles sat idling on either side of the street, ready to escort the herd a half mile down the four-lane road and then turn them into the stockyards.

"Get ready!" Johnson called, turning to her deputies and inspecting them. Guns drawn; they stood safely behind the line of vehicles. They weren't taking any chances with the wayward cattle. Though she got a chorus of ascent, her heart still thundered. This was it. This was the moment of truth. Would her plan work? Or would they end up having to scramble to come up with a new strategy on the fly? Moments stretched and doubts bloomed as she waited with bated breath while the tide rolled ever forward, the rumbling clatter of hooves swelling in the evening air.

A wave of tension coursed through her deputies in the seconds before the animals arrived, but when the torrent of coal-smeared cattle poured from the subdivision, they behaved exactly as expected and the outside edge of the throng started pushing inward as they skirted the arc of emergency vehicles, miraculously turning the herd.

A sigh exploded from Johnson's lungs as the cattle flowed south, and the vehicles idling along the shoulders took off, flanking the animals. So far, so good, but it was too soon to celebrate. Just how much devastation had been left in their wake was unclear. That was for later.

As the roar of hoofbeats faded, one skittish young bull lagged behind, pacing back and forth, nosing curiously around the blockade and unnerving her flustered officers.

"Hold." Johnson held up a hand. She didn't want her deputies to cause the animal any unnecessary distress. *Let's see what he does.* Moments later, the bull seemed to realize he'd been left behind, and he dashed off after his fellows. Once he'd gone, the rest of her people clamored into their vehicles and took off in pursuit. The tail of emergency vehicles shadowed the tide of beef rolling relentlessly down University, bathing the herd in a wash of flickering color.

When the stream of cattle approached the barricade several minutes later, the massive black and gold fire engine loomed over them—an immovable, twenty-five-ton mass of gleaming aluminum. With no hope of pushing past, the herd shifted its course, skirting the edge of the blockade, passing the fire engine and the semi-trailer as they swept directly toward the stockyards, then poured across the parking lot. When the stream neared the main gates, a couple of the young bulls and a few of the more stubborn cows balked, turning aside and slipping among the cars—but they were the minority. Most of the herd obediently funneled into the sixteen-foot-wide main alley bisecting the yards.

The mournful cry of cattle reverberated across the grounds, intensifying as livestock already in residence—locked behind worn metal fencing, consigned for upcoming auctions—joined their voices to the newcomers as they flowed toward their destination. A handful of the enclosures toward the rear of the complex might have served, but only one of suitable size had enough space now; the rest were crowded, ready for the next day's auctions.

On the far side of the pen's entrance, a weather-beaten steel gate had been drawn across the alley to help turn the herd. A wrangler waited on horseback behind a rust-pocked barrier, watching the cattle surge forward. Once the cattle were within a few hundred feet, a pair of workmen opened the corral, swinging the heavy gate outward, folding it back until it was flush with the alley, then scrambled atop the battered white fence and straddled the rails to wait out the flood.

Holsteins trickled, then poured into the corral. Ink-blackened cattle mixed with a hodgepodge of crossbred beef: hints of black Angus, auburn Beefmaster, white-faced Hereford, and pale cream Charolais. The sudden influx of beef merged with the docile herd inside, agitating them, setting them to milling around the enclosure.

As the trailing edge of the herd drained into the stockyards at last, the main gates were closed to block off their retreat and those present gave a collective sigh of relief. It all seemed to be working; the cattle were now bottled up in the main alley and flowing steadily into the pen.

But the confused mass of beef inside the pen continued to churn, swirling around each other in an eddy of flesh as the two unfamiliar groups were thrust together, each trying to discover their place, all while their distressed chorus rose across the stockyards.

Then it all went wrong.

The roiling eddy of loudly protesting cows seethed around the pen faster and faster until a spout of beef surged away, sweeping for the exit. This sudden swell obstructed the enclosure's entrance, leaving the incoming animals little choice. The disgruntled brutes followed the current and were pushed directly into the worn gate blocking the alley. The thick latch holding the barrier in place proved no match for the tons of surging beef, and it buckled under the sudden pressure. The wrangler yanked on his reins and the horse cantered aside just before the gate folded in on itself, slamming into the side of the corral with an ear-piercing *clang*. The horse and rider huddled against the railed fence as the tide carried cattle toward the far end of the lot.

There was a swell of activity as panicked people tried to avert catastrophe, but there was nothing to be done. When the wave of beef rolled over the two gates at the end of the alley, the almighty wail of snapping chains and screeching metal echoed over the roar of hooves and a chorus of vocalizations, then cattle poured into the disused train yard out back.

That had failed spectacularly.

Not only had the Grahams' cattle gotten free again, but the others in the paddock too—nearly doubling the number of escaped cattle. Then, if that wasn't enough, inspired by the mass breakout, other animals attempted to break free. Metal clanged as livestock slammed against their gates. Quite a few of the battered enclosures crashed open and more animals escaped. Other gates held firm, so the inhabitants resorted to even more desperate measures to get out. Several tried to leap over their fences, and many succeeded, but others didn't—one unlucky bull failed to gain the proper clearance; when he dropped onto the steel rails, his immense weight warped the metal, and he rolled off, then plunged to the concrete below, landing badly; even over the roar of the animals, the snapping bones and pained bellows rang out across the yards.

Luckily, not all the animals that broke free were able to navigate the labyrinth of passages, leaving scores of angry cattle trapped within the side alleys, unable to join the mass exodus as chaos reigned in the stockyard.

23

Lexa didn't know what to do. A sea of red glowed ahead as drivers adjusted to the roadblock cutting off the northbound lanes of University. The police cruisers' strobing lights deepened congestion around an already busy intersection, suggesting it might take a while longer to contain the escaped cattle—and on a Friday evening. As impatient commuters trickled past, for the first time in her life she was thankful to be delayed in stop-and-go traffic. If the roads were this bad so far away from the chaos, what would it be like closer to home?

She glanced down at her phone again, then deposited it on the console as she looked around; she hadn't heard back from Michael or Hailey since the initial hurried call confirming their herd had gotten loose. Though she understood they were busy helping round up their wayward cattle, it would've been nice to get an update.

"Any word?" Sierra asked, breaking the heavy silence. Since they'd received news of the breakout, conversation in the vehicle had been eerily muted—save for her exhausted boys, happily distracted by Chloe, sitting on the floor between them, entertaining the four-year-olds. *What a good kid.*

Lexa glanced at her sister-in-law. "Nothing."

Her gaze drifted to the university's picturesque campus

sprawling out to the south. Vast edifices of stone rose around the idyllic central courtyard, giving the campus a traditional esthetic she'd expect to see among the oldest colleges along the east coast. Sporadic knots of students dotted the emerald lawns: some sat studying, while others hung out or played games. Say what you will about the small town, but the campus was impressive.

To the north, an enormous sign advertised the unimaginatively named University Plaza. The shopping center stretched a quarter mile, offering a range of options: everything from national and regional chain stores—including a supermarket, a big-box store, and a couple of trendy discount stores—to local businesses, such as Fair-Weather Leather Co. and Hoofer's Haven (shoe store).

"Can we hurry?" Zoe asked, huddled in the backseat, face washed in its ever-present blue glow. "My battery is running low."

"It could be a while before they get the mess cleaned up," Lexa said idly, still considering their options. It might not be wise to take them home—not yet, anyway. She didn't know the state of the place, nor did she want to deal with the questions involved if, God forbid, the dead deputy or his blood-soaked car were still present.

"Perhaps we should get something to eat?" Sierra suggested.

What a wonderful idea! Lexa waited a few more minutes until she reached a turn-in, then pulled behind a line of commuters at a local burger joint, Moue Chew—its logo, a pouting cow, shining in the dimming light.

At first, the churning mass of flesh was lost in the gloom of long shadows. As the roiling press of cattle streamed along the section of disused track in the alleyway, the thunderous clatter of hooves swelled, reverberating off the stone walls of the artificial canyon. The noise was an anomaly on a Friday evening; those few who confused it for a train could hardly be blamed, as the sound was oddly reminiscent of days past when the railroad was still in the business of ferrying countless tons of beef across the country.

Drivers were understandably startled when, what had moments before been an unrecognizable vague motion in the corner of their eyes, turned into a flood of cattle spewing from the alley. Brakes squealed and rubber burned as drivers swerved to avoid the tide of beef rolling over Main Street. While some were fortunate enough to miss the sudden influx, many others weren't so lucky.

One hefty roan cow had almost made it to the median when a silver luxury sedan struck it. The sudden impact and cry of brakes, along with the flying cow, shattered the cohesion of the blended herd, sending them fanning out across the road. Many more fenders were bent, not only from cars hitting cows, but also the reverse; many of the animals struck out at the bulky objects swarming around them, obstructing their path.

During a good run, Georgie's problems faded away, allowing her hyperactive mind to disconnect—status updates and notifications didn't exist. She could concentrate on the soft caress of a light breeze, on the air flowing through her lungs, on her muscles pulsating beneath her toned skin, and on the rhythmic throb of her heart.

She ran to calm her nerves; ran to work through her emotions, and at the moment, she had a lot to work through. Her roommate's grandfather had died a couple of nights ago, and when the call came—when her roommate was getting some of the worst news of her life—she'd been complaining about the late-night call. Georgie felt like a complete jerk. Worse, word had trickled down that Hailey had spent the entire night alone at the hospital. She wished she'd been there for her roommate, wished she'd known. No one deserved to go through something like that alone. Why hadn't she told her? She felt somewhat guilty for even considering it, but a situation that might have strengthened their bond had only widened the gulf between them.

Somehow, they'd gotten off on the wrong foot, and she couldn't help but feel it was largely her fault. She hadn't wanted that—Hailey seemed nice enough. They'd been having a pleasant conversation. All had been going well until she'd committed an 'unforgivable' blunder; Georgie had said her mom was her role model—a single mother juggling her career and kids—then made the further error of asking about Hailey's mom. Her roommate had just seemed to shut down, then made some excuse to leave and had been distant ever since. In the following weeks, she'd learned a bit about Hailey's background and understood her reaction. She'd hoped they could've repaired things, but they hadn't gotten around to it; they were both so busy, Georgie, with her athletics, and Hailey, with her farming.

As Georgie skirted the corner of Lincoln Hall, she slowed, noticing a commotion in the road. It took her a moment to fully comprehend the incredible sight, and she let herself flag to a stop, feet slapping against the ground. Nostrils flaring and chest heaving, beads of sweat trickled over her skin as she fought to catch her breath. She reached up to pluck an earbud out and the rumble of hooves replaced her pop tune as a roiling mass of beef streamed along the main road, weaving through the gridlock of vehicles. She'd never seen anything like it.

She didn't know how long she stood there frozen, gawking as animals surged past. After a bit, a wave of ink-blotted bovines—like a nightmarish living Rorschach spilling from the pages of *Fundamentals of Psychology*—changed course and poured onto the campus. Her eyes flew wide as the animals fanned out and people all around scrambled away.

She took several steps back, then spun and broke into a jog, eyes still locked over her shoulder. They were closing, and fast. She had to get inside. Her pace quickened, then she took a misstep and stumbled. She recovered quickly, but the cattle had gained.

Georgie thought about going for Murray Hall until the scaffolding along the front reminded her it was under renovation. Would it be unlocked? Could she take the risk? She decided not to chance it, continuing her pounding strides along the sidewalk, periodically shooting a panicked glance over her shoulder; each time, the cattle were a little closer. Her already racing heart hammered as she considered, then discounted several options: *too far, won't work, they're coming too fast.*

She was just about to make her break for Luing Hall when she glanced back and was shocked to see an irate bull—steam practically billowing from his ears—had closed to within a few meters. Oh God, she wasn't going to make it. Had he sped up, or was she flagging? It didn't matter.

Then she saw her chance; it was risky, but it just might work. She delayed cutting across the lawn for a few more meters as she approached the line of parked vehicles in front of Luing Hall. She could have sworn she felt the puff of the animal's hot breath across the back of her neck when she finally veered toward one of the parked cars. Georgie took two bounding steps, then reached out and planted a palm on the hood as she pulled her right leg and hip up, launching herself over the fender. Warm metal soaked through her thin, poly-elastane running shorts as her butt glided across the hood.

Before she'd made it much more than halfway, she heard an almighty rending crash, and the car lurched. Metal struck her hip hard, bouncing her several centimeters into the air. She sailed over the far fender and her shoes plowed into the concrete. She stumbled but, miraculously, she was able to keep her footing. Georgie didn't so much as glance back at the enraged animals as she tore across the yard. She couldn't. She didn't know what she'd do if her plan hadn't bought her enough time.

Somehow, Georgie made it to the entrance of the psychology building. She ripped the glass door open and bounded several steps inside. Only then did she think it was safe enough to peek behind her. Her heart skipped. The massive coal-blotted bull slammed into the closing glass door, shattering it into countless fragments. Georgie didn't stop, didn't hesitate, as she bolted across the foyer, then bounded up the stairs two at a time.

It wasn't until she'd reached the first landing and threw a quick look over her shoulder that she realized the bull hadn't followed. It stood at the base of the grand staircase, glaring up at her, huffing and snorting. Why wasn't it following? Was it the stairs? Could cows climb stairs? Truthfully, it didn't matter. Still, Georgie made a mental note to ask Hailey the next time she saw her as she continued her flight up the staircase.

Leaning against the headrest, Lexa waited in the drive-thru lane, gazing longingly at Prairie Dairy, the ice cream shoppe across the way, as she tried to ignore her sister-in-law's 'subtle' commentary about the importance of a college degree in today's job market. She had a craving for ice cream; perhaps she could treat the boys, and herself, after their dinner.

There was a loud screech off to the right. Her gaze flicked to the rear-view mirror and an odd movement caught her eye in the fading light. To her surprise, a trickle of cattle materialized in the road, weaving through the idling traffic. She turned in her seat to watch the spectacle in wide-eyed amazement. She gasped. How had their cattle gotten all the way down here?

"Moo Cow," Aiden and Alex chorused gleefully, clapping.

But no, they weren't all theirs; along with the occasional ink-spattered animal, there were others. A multitude of different breeds blended into the stream. She recognized some, but not many. Large, hornless black animals intermixed with brown, white, and auburn cows. There were mud-spattered dairy cows and some with hides of woven gold. And a couple had long horns stretching a meter to either side of their heads—those she recognized. Where had they all come from?

At first, the small stream of cattle seemed benign enough as they wove through the throng until one curious driver stepped out of his car to film the spectacle. The movement drew the ire of a particularly large blackish-brown bull, and the thing charged the filming man. He was able to dive back into his car a moment before the bull struck, ripping the door from its hinges.

And suddenly, just like that, the novelty of escaped cattle wore off. Vehicles peeled away, trying to flee; this only caused more chaos as bumpers crumpled and horns blared, then cattle fanned out, striking at noisy cars. The clash of crunching metal and plastic reverberated through the evening air. Pedestrians who'd been edging away fled in earnest toward the line of restaurants, capturing the attention of other animals, prompting them to charge. Never had she seen such aggravated destruction.

The stream of beef had turned into a flood by the time the first animal surged their way. Lexa sat in shocked silence as a brawny grayish-white bull charged past and bowled into the Taurus in front of them; cries echoed from inside the vehicle as the rear end was lifted from the ground and deposited a good six inches to the left. The bull ripped its horn from the crumpled mess that was the back quarter panel, then turned its attention to them. Lexa's heart froze in her chest as the animal eyed her. Too afraid to move. Afraid any movement would provoke the beast.

Then a commotion inside the burger joint snatched its attention; it turned, bellowing, and then it charged—straight through Moue Chew's plate-glass windows. People scrambled out of the way as it plowed through the lobby, leaving a wake of shattered and overturned furniture.

Then there was a loud *crunch*, and their vehicle rocked.

"Moo?"

The massive horned head of the coal-mottled animal peering through the window jolted Lexa into action; she reached for the gearshift, slammed the car into gear, and floored it, jumping the curb.

Hailey's murmured encouragements were laced with curses as they struggled to load another animal. Their efforts hadn't been progressing as well as she would have liked. This was only the third cow they'd come across—three out of nearly four dozen—and she was by far the most difficult. It was unlike her. Unlike any of them, really.

While Hailey huffed and grunted, trying to shove the stubborn cow forward—she'd already tried everything else—Rodger and her dad held fast to the animal's lead, trying to wrest her bulk toward the open door. They'd slipped the rope through a vent on the side of the trailer to help guide her, but it wasn't working. The bull-headed animal wasn't eager to follow their lead.

Hailey still couldn't believe this was happening.

Dad's cell blared in his pocket, startling the willful bovine, sending her surging into the trailer. Hailey quickly latched the gate as Dad stepped away, and the racket died.

After extracting the rope, she took in Rodger's exhausted face, giving him a labored smile. "Thank you for doing this," she said, wiping the sweat from her brow. "I don't know what's gotten into them."

He shrugged. "Just doing my job, ma'am," he said in an emphasized country drawl and tipped an imaginary hat.

Hailey rolled her eyes. "Still, it's a big help. I hate to be such an imposition."

"This isn't your fault … It was that idiot Rockwell, that put all of us in this position." His silly grin warmed. "Besides, I'm here with you, and there's nowhere I'd rather be."

"Really?" her heart swelled. Then she let a smile crawl across her face as she decided to shoot her shot. "I mean, it's not bad, but I can think of better places and *several* positions I'd enjoy more."

Rodger's mouth opened, but nothing came out. He just stood there. She could practically see the gears turning as he processed what she'd said. What was he thinking? Was he interested? Did he just blush, or was it the heat? It was hard to tell in the waning sunlight. Why wasn't he saying anything?

Before she could fully gauge his reaction, her dad appeared at their side, staring down at his phone, his face pale.

"Dad, what is it?" Hailey grabbed his arm.

"I just got a panicked call from Lexa. There are cattle at the shopping center … attacking everything that moves," he stammered as Rodger dashed over to his patrol car and climbed inside. "The kids were screaming in the background. I could barely hear her."

Lexa jumped another curb as she tossed her phone aside, then swerved into the straightaway. She sped up the row toward the line of shops, skirting an extended strip of emerald grass separating two lots. Eyes locked on her destination—the regional grocery chain: Cow Wow—she hadn't even noticed any movement to her right until a flash of dark brown darted out from the row of parked cars. It slammed into the front fender, lifting the passenger side, and tossing the vehicle a good foot to the left. When they landed, Lexa overcorrected, jumping the curb, and the vehicle careened down the sloped verge into the next parking lot. With the kids screaming in the back, the tires dropped off the opposite curb and the fender scraped the pavement. Lexa swerved again, trying to straighten up, sideswiping a parked car, renewing the screams from the kids and curses from Sierra as they whipped back and forth.

She searched for the animal in the rearview mirror, but it was nowhere to be found. All she saw was a compact behind her try the same maneuver over the strip of greenery, only to get stuck in the middle. She didn't even consider returning to help, not with her family in the car, and crazed cattle on the loose.

Her eyes traced the storefronts ahead, quickly weighing her options. And her gaze locked on a new target: Bullseye. The big-box store's glowing logo shone like a beacon in the dwindling light—two red rings circling an angry crimson eye.

She flew up the row, laying on the horn, trusting those pedestrians who remained to scurry out of her way. She whipped around the turn, narrowly missing another vehicle as she aimed for the front door. They screeched to a stop inches from the crimson bollards embedded into the concrete around the store's main entrance.

"Inside! Go," she screamed, ripping off her seatbelt and flinging her door open.

Lexa ripped the back door open to free the kids (child safety locks—if ever a thing defeated its purpose), then wrenched Aiden's seatbelt off.

As she hauled her whining boy from the car, she spotted Sierra ... halfway to the door—she'd left them. Chloe knelt beside Alex, tugging on the other boy's harness while Zoe scrambled over the back seat and crawled out of the rear door. As Zoe disappeared around the side, for a split second, Lexa thought she might follow her mother's example and abandon them, then the other door was wrenched open.

Chloe gave a whoop, and the harness detached, allowing Zoe to heave a pale-faced, whimpering four-year-old from his seat. Their gaze met for a moment over the roof and Zoe, cradling her cousin against her chest, gave Lexa a slight nod. Maybe Zoe wasn't so bad.

The crimson-shirted employee waiting at the open sliding doors barely reacted when Sierra pushed past him, his expression frozen in disbelief as he watched the utter devastation wreaked across the lot and in the street beyond. When they bustled up moments later, Lexa snatched his arm, squeezing tight and bringing him out of his stupor.

"Close the door!" she yelled.

"Huh?"

"Close the door," she said. "Lock it!" Didn't he see? If the automated doors weren't locked, they would open at any movement. Allow anything to get in.

But he didn't answer—his eyes left hers, snapping back to the parking lot, where others were fleeing from the deranged cattle; some for their cars, some for the storefronts, and some without any recognizable course.

"The others?" he objected numbly as she backed away.

As the guy dithered, a thirty-something blonde lady shot out from behind a dark sedan, angling for the door. He held out a hand and yelled for her to keep coming as Lexa backed into the store. With the swish of the interior sliding door, cool air enveloped her.

Her eyes were still locked on the man as he ignored her warning, stepping out and reaching for the woman—as if he could reach across the lot and pull her through the door, but she was still too far away. Then the man vanished—she might have caught a glimpse of flailing arms, but she wasn't sure. Where he had been standing just a moment before was a red roan bull, rearing its head and bellowing.

She just gaped as a gentle hand guided her away from the door and a small voice said, "Come on." She didn't know what else to do but follow.

A red-shirted employee shot up to the doors one after the other, and, standing on her tiptoes, flipped a switch to turn off the inner door's automated sensors. The young employee twirled back, a brown ponytail whipping across a round face awash in shock.

The girl—her nametag read Macie—stepped toward the crowd. "Everyone, back away from the entrance."

In a moment of clarity, Lexa tightened her arms around the squirming Aiden and glanced around the crowd fanned out in front of the doors, searching for the rest of her family. Chloe hovered at her elbow; Sierra loitered near the guest service bay, having somehow wormed her way behind the crowd; and Zoe was on the opposite side of the entry holding Alex's shoulder as he stood sniffling, rubbing his red eyes.

A relieved sigh exploded from her chest. They were all okay.

24

Guests and employees stood shoulder to shoulder, fanned out across the entry. Scattered among them were an assortment of people representing all walks of life: businesspeople, doctors, lawyers, factory workers, stay-at-home dads, and soccer moms. Compassionate, vain, rational, apathetic, modest, callous, ambitious, and impulsive … The responsible and the flighty, the sophisticated and the philistine, the rash and the cautious …

… and, of course, the fool …

"Look!" a middle-aged man cried, surging toward the doors, "They're gone."

The pronouncement sent a ripple through the crowd, and others joined him, gawking through the door. Twilight was finally falling across the parking lot, and bulbs flicked on, joining the wash of light flooding from the storefronts.

Among the sporadic bursts of conversation, some voices were clearer.

"Not all of them"—people pointed out several animals scattered throughout the parking lot.

"… it's close enough …"

"… I'm not going out there …"

"… we just have to be careful …"

"… let's get out of here …"

"… look, I'm parked right there. I can fit four people—"

"It'll be safer if everyone stays inside," Macie said, holding up her arms and raising her voice to be heard over the overlapping chatter.

"You can't keep us here," a woman said while shoving the emergency handle. A section of the sliding door broke out and swung open.

"Don't go out there!" Macie called. Her sentiment was repeated by a few others.

Despite their urging, the woman and several others surged through the open door, scrambling into the parking lot. Some of them even made it halfway across the crossing before the screaming started.

The people inside watched in horror as cattle charged from around a blind corner. The unlucky group scattered for cover, darting every which way to escape the rampaging beef. Some still made it to their cars, and engines roared to life. Others didn't and had to scramble for any place to hide. One person even turned back, managing to slip back inside before Macie was able to reset the door. Shaking her head and mumbling as she popped it back into place; several people distinctly heard the word, "idiots." No one contradicted her.

Then a stout reddish-brown bull strutted into view. The harsh florescent lights gleamed off a wide set of down-turned horns matching his white face, crest, and underline. Moments later, he tripped the outer door's sensors, and they slid open. The motion drew his attention, and he turned and charged. The muscular bull bounded through the entry—as expected, the sleek interior doors remained stubbornly shut; however, they had no chance of stopping such an enormous animal. He plowed into one side of the entrance, knocking both doors off their tracks while obliterating a side panel, causing the sheet of laminated glass to fold in on itself. As the door panels crumpled, glass draped across the entry, sending tiny shards raining over the sterile white tile.

The loitering crowd dispersed, scurrying every which way.

Some crossed the ring—a red-trimmed main pathway circling the store—breaking for the cavernous depths of the sales floor. Others darted through the coffee shop and hid in the employee's area. More flowed down the narrow corridor leading to the restrooms; ignoring the graphics posted on the doors and just packing into either room. The brawny white-faced bull, as if fascinated by the line of crimson baskets in the cart bay, plowed into them full tilt. One of the flying carts bowled into a group of fleeing guests, knocking them down, then clattered away.

Bellowing as the toppled guests helped each other limp away, the confused bull strutted around the entry, trampling what remained of the doors into a blanket of fine dust beneath its immense weight.

Even as the door disintegrated, Zoe was scooping her cousin into her arms and stumbling away. She ducked around the corner behind the closest shelves, an L-shaped aisle holding seasonal bargain items. But she wasn't the only one. Among those fleeing in all directions, a bearded, burly man crashed into her, sending her careening toward the shelves. Turning as she fell, Zoe protected the whining child cradled in her arms. Pain flared across her hip and back as she slammed into the shelves, then slid to the floor. Moments later, a wave of cheap items trickled off the shelves, raining around her. Luckily—for Alex, that is—she'd taken the brunt of the impact, or else he might have been crushed beneath her.

Even as the big guy fled, trampling her leg in his haste, she lost her grip on Alex, and he wriggled to the floor. Surprisingly, he didn't run. The wide-eyed boy just stood there gaping at her and the panicked crowd.

She shot to her feet, ignoring the pain flaring across her bruised shin as she scooped her little cousin back into her arms. Zoe dashed into the aisle, cradling her precious cargo. She hadn't taken more than two steps when another callous adult bowled into her. She was flung around, pinballing into someone else, but remarkably, she was able to stay on her feet. She didn't look at either of the jerks as she bulled on. Several more people, taking no consideration of her age or passenger, collided with her as she fled.

Then came a tremendous impact, and her world tipped to its side. Zoe was thrown aside, plowing through a cardboard display as she twisted to protect her cousin, before finally landing on a mattress of plush animals scattered across the floor: the same iridescent dragons, unicorns, griffins, and dinosaurs raining down around them.

She'd landed outside of the main thoroughfare, so no one else hit her as she struggled to her feet and led Alex toward the section of seasonal wear where they dove into a burrow of vibrant clothes.

As Zoe was minding her cousin and being knocked around in the process, her sister had her own burden. Young Chloe Graham had grabbed her struggling aunt, dragging her and her cargo—Aiden was firmly enfolded in his mother's arms—toward the maze of checkout lanes and then tugged them down, ducking into an alcove behind one of the registers.

The stout, white-faced bull plowed into the crimson carts again, scattering them before it turned and strutted along the aisle at the foot of the checkout lanes. Hooves clacked on the stark, gleaming tile as he plodded by. After it passed, a head poked up over the guest services counter, glancing around like a prairie dog searching for predators. Chloe recognized Macie, the employee who'd locked the doors, before she quickly disappeared. She also noticed the trail of crimson trickling down the side of the girl's terrified face.

With the animal's back to her, a thickset, middle-aged woman darted out of the bathroom hallway, foolishly making a break for the doors. She made it halfway to the entrance before another animal loped into the store, then another, then another. The woman darted backward, tripped over an overturned cart, and went sprawling on the floor. As she scrambled to get up, the newcomers spun, following the commotion, then she screamed.

This also attracted the original white-faced bull's attention, and it pounded across the store. As it passed the cart bay, Chloe tugged her aunt, and they scampered further away from the entrance, weaving between more checkout bays, peeking over the counters sporadically, to clock the cattle.

The employee, Macie, also took the opportunity and bounded over the counter, then fled across the aisle into a sea of childrenswear. About that time, a bone-chilling scream rang through the store as the large woman was thrown into a display of gourmet coffee.

The scream finally snapped Lexa out of her shock. "Stop that," she hissed, yanking herself free of Chloe's incessant tugging.

"Mommy, it hurts; it's too tight." Aiden's whimper filtered into her awareness as he struggled ineffectually in her tight embrace.

Lexa loosened her grip on the struggling boy, her eyes searching her niece. "Where's Alex?" She had to look for him. "Alex?" she called, popping up, only to be dragged down by her niece. She yanked away from the girl's grip again and tried to scamper back the way they'd come, through the rows of checkout lanes. To her annoyance, Chloe grabbed her again, this time much more firmly.

"Let me go," she said, tugging at the girl's grip. "I have to find Alex."

Chloe kept her voice low. "Aunt Lexa, stay down. They'll see you."

"Zoe has him," Lexa complained, but she stopped struggling. "I saw them duck off over there," she tried to patiently explain to the girl. "We have to get them!" Didn't she see that?

"We will! But we can't just go barging through. It's not safe. Just ... just a second." Lexa stopped struggling, but Chloe's grip didn't slacken as her eyes darted around. "You said they went that way?"

"Yeah," she sighed.

Chloe was quiet for a few moments, then she said, "Why don't we take the long way around? Across the aisle, then through Apparel. It should be safer." Lexa's eyes narrowed as she stared at her niece, then finally nodded. Chloe tugged at Lexa's arm again. "Come on, let's go while they're distracted." This time Lexa let herself be led.

They ducked beside a beverage display at the head of one lane and peeked around the endcap. As they did, another animal, a beefy golden-red bull, trotted into the wide main aisle, followed shortly by the stout, white-faced, auburn bull, then a massive ebony cow. Lexa's mind raced; she doubted they could get across the aisle without being seen. Even if they did, they would be too exposed in Childrenswear. It wouldn't work. She had to come up with a different plan. As she watched, the reddish-brown, white-faced bull squared up with a life-sized model of a white bull—two rings around its angry crimson eye—and charged. When the fiberglass-resin statue shattered, Lexa used the distraction.

"Come on," she said, tugging Chloe as they skirted past the final few checkout lanes.

Most guests she glimpsed were fading behind obstructions or into aisles, further away from the chaos, but one young mother used the distraction to drag her daughter across the aisle from Girlswear, into the checkout lanes. The woman's head shot up as Lexa pulled her niece and son around, into the first aisle of Pet Care. The young woman appeared to be looking for a chance to make a break for it. She couldn't have known the scope of the chaos outside. Lexa hid around the corner, peering through a display of plastic tubs filled with doggie snacks, considering whether or not to warn them when the strong black bovine turned and strutted their way. She couldn't risk it.

"Shouldn't we warn them?" Chloe asked.

Lexa shook her head. "We'll draw her attention right to us!"

"That one's a steer …"

"That doesn't matter." Of all the useless information … "Come on, Chloe." Lexa guided her niece a little way into the pet food aisle.

"Where are we going?"

"We have to figure out a way to get across, and"—Lexa lowered her squirming boy to the floor, but maintained a firm hold around his little wrist, careful not to squeeze too hard—"get to Alex and your sister. But we can't cross here, not with the cows so close. Maybe if we went over a few aisles? … If only I knew they were okay." Lexa cursed, stamping her foot. "I wish I had my phone."

Chloe stopped, eyes going wide as their gaze met.

"I left it in the car," Lexa explained, feeling the need to justify herself. "I didn't even think about …" Chloe just blinked at her. "What?"

"I have mine, Aunt Lexa," Chloe offered, digging for the device.

"You do?" Lexa blinked. She hadn't even considered it. "Of course, you do! Does Zoe?"

"When doesn't she?"

Touché.

25

Zoe fought down her panic as she huddled in the hollow of a circular clothing rack, hiding behind a wall of colorful fabric with a whimpering four-year-old hugged tight to her side. Luckily, the garments also obscured their view of the ongoing devastation reigning around them. She drew up her shirt, hissing at the massive bruise already blooming across her side, a large splotch of purple marring her alabaster skin. She couldn't believe that guy had just knocked her down, trampled her, then fled. Nor did she understand the callousness of the people scrambling around, knocking into each other.

Zoe let her shirt fall back into place and scanned her cousin yet again. Aside from the obvious wide anxious eyes, he seemed none the worse for wear. Their mad dash across the parking lot and being knocked around in the aisle hadn't left him harmed.

Zoe leaned forward and drew the curtain of clothes apart once again; somewhere beyond the wall of fabric, a phone called out in the mayhem, and more cattle trickled into the store. Why were they all coming in here? Herd mentality? Perhaps she should have listened more closely to Hailey. She shook her head; it didn't matter now.

With all these cows flowing into the store, they'd have to move soon. While keeping them hidden, their barrier of fabric wouldn't provide much protection from a tramping bull if it decided to come their way. None whatsoever.

The phone rang again. She blinked; that sounded almost like her phone. She reached back for the device. She could call her mom, her dad, or her aunt: find out what to do. Why hadn't she thought of it before?

Her hand groped the empty pocket. *Empty! Empty?!*

Her eyes scanned the floor around her; had she dropped it? Just her luck! She hadn't been further than a yard away from the thing in years, and now that she really needed it, it was missing. Her mind reeled as she fought for calm. Where was it? It must have fallen out of her pocket. That was the only explanation. But where? She tore the curtain of clothes aside and scanned the floor for her wayward device. And there, a dozen feet away, among the iridescent animals scattered around the gray woolen carpet, was her phone, the screen lit and pulsating.

Her mind whirred and her eyes flicked right and left as she scooted for the opening—could she make it?

"Where you goin?" a little voice squeaked. "Don't weave me."

"I'm not buddy," she assured, hugging her little cousin. "But I need my phone. I'll be right back."

"Oe, I'm scared," he whined.

"Me too, buddy. Me too. Just … just stay here." The boy whimpered, but nodded.

Just as Zoe dove through the wall of clothes, a white-belted black animal trotted into sight. Zoe pitched herself to one side, ducking behind another cascade of fabric. Leaning against the garment rack, her eyes sought her little cousin, his tear-streaked pale face barely visible through the curtain of clothing surrounding him. She smiled at him, a desperate attempt to calm him, though her own fear weighed on her.

She waited for the clopping hooves to fade a bit before she peeked around the draping, vibrant fabric. The 'Oreo' cow was distracted by a twenty-something in black leggings sprinting across the aisle. As it followed, Zoe took the opportunity. She bolted out, scrambling across the floor, and snatched up the phone. Already scuttling back to cover, her eyes locked on the animal chasing after the screaming woman as she went for the cash registers. Zoe whipped the phone up to her ear, pushing connect in one fluid motion.

"Hello?" she said in a low voice while she ripped her gaze from the scene and ducked back behind the rack of clothes.

"Zoe!" The familiar voice erupted in her ear.

"Aunt Lexa!"

"Mommy?" Alex asked, as his head poked out of their burrow.

Zoe waved for the boy to stay where he was as the voice continued. "Where are you? Are you okay? Where's Alex? Please tell me he's with you, and he's okay," Lexa said without pausing for breath.

"He's fine, Aunt Lexa," she whispered. "He's right here."

Hope blossomed on the little boy's face as he scurried out of his haven. "Mommy!" he cried. Way too loud. Zoe made a futile effort to shush the boy, looking over her shoulder to see if his outburst had alerted any of the rampaging beasts.

Alex ignored her frantic gestures and plopped into her lap, greedily peering into the screen. "Mommy? Mommy, are you daire? I can't see you."

"Yes, Alex, Mommy's here," she assured.

"Hush, Alex, not so loud," Zoe said.

"Where's Mommy? Why can't I see her?"

"Just a sec," Zoe tapped a button to activate the video option, then shot another fretful glance around the clothing rack.

"Mommy!" When she turned back, Aunt Lexa's tense face filled the screen. "Da mean cows are evweywhere. I'm scared."

"I know honey, I know."

"Where's Aiden? And Co'we?"

Lexa tilted the phone, bringing the two into view. "Aiden and Chloe are right here," she assured. "They're fine."

An anxious knot in Zoe's belly loosened. She hadn't realized she'd been so worried.

"Mommy, where are you?"

"We're in Pet Care."

Zoe glanced over that way. "Do you think we can—"

"No!" Lexa gasped. "No, don't try. Are you safe where you are?"

"Not really," Zoe said. "We're hidden, but it's not safe."

Lexa nodded on the screen. "Find someplace safe to hide … someplace secure and call me back."

"Where?"

"I don't know … maybe try the backrooms." She looked off screen and lowered her voice. "We'll make our way to you. It may take a bit. I think we'll have to take the long way around."

"Mommy, I miss you."

"I miss you too, baby," Lexa's face seemed pained. "Listen to Zoe … do what she says. She'll keep you safe. Thank you for grabbing him, Zoe. Keep my baby safe. And yourself."

Zoe nodded, "You too." The call disconnected, and her screen returned to the main menu. Zoe peered either way around the rack, then urged her cousin forward. "Back to our hiding place."

She kept watch as the boy darted over and dove into the mass of clothes. As Zoe crawled after her little cousin, she snatched a random stuffed animal on a whim—an iridescent purple and teal Narwhal that shifted to blue and pink in the light—and handed it to Alex.

"Keep him safe," she said. *And I'll **try** to keep you safe*. She didn't say.

The stuffed animal deformed in the four-year-old's grasp, yet, despite his new friend, Alex didn't appear mollified.

"I want my mommy!" he whined.

"Me too," she said. Zoe still couldn't believe her mom had just run off like that. Had she known they weren't behind her? She couldn't have; she wouldn't—

Zoe shook off the thought. Now wasn't the time. One thing was for sure: she wouldn't follow her mother's example.

"Come on, Alex; we have to move. We have to find a better place to hide." She took her cousin's hand and steered the boy further into the store.

Lexa let out a deep sigh; it helped to know Alex was safe. More than she'd dreamed it could. But she couldn't allow herself to get lost like that again. As impressed as she was by Chloe's cool demeanor in the crisis—taking control like that was something—she was the adult, and she had to act like it. She couldn't just react to the situation any longer, she had to actively plan their next moves. She was responsible, not only for her own children, but for her nieces as well. She had to be the strong one. And she wouldn't rest easy until her other baby was in her arms.

She took a few seconds to call her husband, updating him before they set off.

As Lexa led Chloe and Aiden to the end of the aisle, she took in her surroundings, scanning the shelves for anything that could prove useful. None of the colorful merchandise—be it the array of brand-name dog and cat food, or the wide range of canned and pouched meals—would have any effect against a fifteen-hundred to two-thousand-pound animal. Nor would the containers and packages of treats.

They turned the corner and paused, greeted by a scatter of shocked faces and the riot of garish color from useless products extending along the front aisle; more stuff than anyone could possibly use was packed along the wall and displayed on each endcap. She could see that some people had chanced the emergency exit—not knowing what fresh hell awaited them outside—others hunkered down along the aisle, hiding between the rows. She ignored the frightened customers and scanned the directories capping the aisles, none of which held much promise. Nor did the department signs dangling from the ceiling, proclaiming: Pet Care, Household, Beauty, or Health.

Lexa wondered how far they'd have to go before it would be safe to cross. If it would be safe to cross. Could she leave Aiden with Chloe while she searched for Zoe and Alex? The thought made her shudder, and she dismissed it out of hand. She couldn't let them out of her sight until this situation was under control. She couldn't help but wonder when that would be.

26

Sheriff Johnson relayed rapid-fire orders to everyone under her command as her small contingent of emergency vehicles fanned out across Main. Chaos greeted them. Traffic had come to a standstill, with many commuters cowering inside their vehicles while others fled the rambunctious bovines weaving through the sea of motionless cars.

However, none of that deterred the score of local farmers and ranchers accompanying her knot of deputies. They went right to work, spreading out and chasing the animals. Some cantered along on horseback, while others followed in pickups, pulling stock trailers. *Only in a small town,* Johnson marveled. It was inspiring. As soon as word had trickled down that they were steering the escaped cattle toward the stockyards, locals had filtered over with horses and trailers, volunteering their time and expertise to help.

Not far away, a young woman galloped after a hay-colored cow—the horse's shoes clip-clopping loudly against the pavement as the wind stirred her long chestnut hair, sending it swirling around her shoulders. She swung a lasso above her head as she expertly guided her bay mare after the fleeing animal. She let the rope fly across the gap, and it circled the wayward cow's neck. Once the cowgirl yanked the rope tight and wound it around the saddle horn, the animal was jerked around, creating an opening for her companion to trot up behind the animal and toss his lasso at the rear legs. As the slim young man tugged the rope and dallied it to his saddle, the ropes stretched the cow out at the head and the heels, pulling the animal off its feet. After the cow was on the ground, the young lady trotted up, leapt from her saddle, then bounded over and tied one of its front legs to the rear two. After that, the pair freed their ropes before mounting up and trotting off to find a new target, leaving the hapless animal where it lay for someone else to load.

Johnson pulled her gaze from the spectacle and instructed her officers to open the roadblock; they had to try to push as many of the motorists as they could up University Ave and out from underfoot. They needed to get this situation under control.

While her deputies jumped to follow her orders, she surveyed the surrounding chaos, unable to avoid considering the ramifications come the next election. Despite the dread that accompanied those thoughts, she was able to push them aside without much effort; she didn't have the time or the energy to worry about anything beyond tonight. And truthfully, at that moment, she couldn't bring herself to care; *que sera, sera*—what will be, will be.

It wasn't long before Johnson received word that her other units were arriving at their positions and setting up. After everything at the stockyards fell apart, she'd split her forces, sending some detouring through the neighborhoods to the east and others to the west. Very soon they'd have blockades erected on either side of this stretch of Main and be able to start cleaning up this mess. Despite all that, she had a sinking feeling that things would get worse before they got better.

How could things have gone so wrong?

On the campus across the way, a handful of brave fools were attempting to help wrangle the cattle, trying to corral a disgruntled reddish-brown animal on foot. The cow kept charging at the students, sending their little knot scattering out of the way. Johnson flagged down one of her deputies; she had to put a stop to that. Even though this was a rodeo town, she wasn't thrilled with the prospect of everyone thinking they could or should help out. That could just lead to more injuries. Before she could give any orders, a well-built young student dashed up to the irritated cow and pounced on it, grabbing its horns and wrestling it to the ground. She winced. Did he even know what he was doing?

It was about that time that members of the university's rodeo team pounded around the corner, mounted and ready, whirling lassos. She sighed; at least *they* were on horseback. They wore a mishmash of styles; some sporting cowboy hats or other western wear—several even wore protective helmets. One young woman seemed to be in a pair of blue sweatpants with a t-shirt proudly proclaiming the school's logo. Definitely not the usual western attire they were required to wear for competitions, but that didn't seem to matter as they charged into the fray.

In all the confusion, a cluster of thirty-odd, coal-smeared bovines escaped official notice. Continuing their unerring path south, they trotted along Fraternity Row, trampling the gorgeous landscaping. Brothers and Sisters huddled on porches or gazed from windows, watching in a mixture of amusement and annoyance as the herd traipsed across pristine lawns and through colorful gardens and blooming shrubbery. Many had their phones up, catching the madness in high definition, planning to share it later. Some few tried to call nine-one-one, only to find the switchboards jammed with incoming calls.

After the cattle had trotted out of sight, there was a rush to see who could upload their content first and come up with the most unique or cleverest captions. Many videos were uploaded, spread out across multiple platforms.

Elsewhere in the town, Dave yawned, blinking in the gloom as he stumbled down the small stairwell. Mr. Gleeson had called, reporting yet another alarm. They'd been plagued with false alarms for the past couple of weeks, and he was just about tired of it. He'd been working part time at Mr. Gleeson's antique shop for a while now, supplementing his income as he went to college; so, when the old man offered him an apartment above the store for a reasonable rate, he'd jumped at the chance. He hadn't seen any downsides; it had felt like a godsend.

However, in the weeks that followed, Gleeson had been gradually slipping extra responsibilities to the young man. It started with little things: asking him to run down and check this or that, or asking if he minded waking up early to sign for a delivery. Dave grunted, shaking his head; it was feeling like Mr. Gleeson was treating him more and more like a servant: calling him up whenever their alarm malfunctioned, which was a lot these days. Why the old man wouldn't just get a new alarm system, he didn't understand.

Dave sighed as he padded to the bottom of the stairs into the darkness of the store's backroom, then he heard the commotion. A rattling crash broke the silence. He froze, goosebumps spilling over him. What was that? Was someone in the store? Was this more than a false alarm? He blinked away his remaining weariness. It wasn't easy. He'd been up late last night playing a video game—grinding the MMO's newest dungeon— and crashed right after class. He hadn't expected to be disturbed. But if he thought about it, it was par for the course.

He crept around the corner, fighting to see through the gloom when a police car whooshed past. Blue and red lights glinted off a cascade of glass shards strewn in front of the shattered front door. However, the flashing lights revealed something even more ominous. It took him a moment to fully comprehend what he saw silhouetted in the pulsing light. After the patrol car passed, the antique shop fell back into gloom, but the shape remained. His mind reeled, struggling to find some rational explanation for the massive figure. He idly wondered if it was some new acquisition. Had Gleeson bought a sign or a statue?

But then the thing moved.

The massive horned shape turned, brushing against a display of turn-of-the-century China. Antique dinnerware crashed to the floor, the racket startling the bull, causing it to lurch aside. Wood splintered as the animal bulled through an ornate display case, sending its contents spilling to the floor. But it didn't stop there. When it turned, its flank clipped the edge of another case, and glass splintered. The bull spun again and lowered its head, preparing to charge the row of glass-fronted cases.

God, that would be catastrophic.

Dave darted forward and cursed at the bull, successfully catching its attention. Perhaps too successfully—the animal snorted as it lurched around, sending more valuable knickknacks spilling to the floor. With the animal's angry gaze locked on him, Dave had a moment to regret his rash intrusion before the bull charged.

The animal's bulk tore through every obstacle with hardly any effort. Wood splintered and glass shattered as the bull shoved through display cases, tables, and shelves. Antique wooden chairs were smashed to kindling and bookcases toppled, sending a cascade of rare books spilling to the floor to be trampled under the two-thousand-pound animal's hooves.

Dave turned and sprinted through the backroom, retreating to the stairs, all while the animal bulled through everything in its path. He rounded the corner, then bounded up the stairs two at a time. He'd paused halfway up the staircase, fighting to catch his breath when the animal stampeded into sight. To his shock and dismay, the bull didn't stop—didn't even pause—as it rounded the corner. The two-thousand-pound animal slammed into the banister on its wide turn, snapping the metal supports, before continuing, charging up the stairs.

What—how—why? The thoughts flitted through his head too quickly to snatch any as he bounded up the stairs. Dave made it to the top floor and raced for his open door at the end of the hallway. As he darted into his apartment, he slammed the door, then waited, edging away from the entrance. Glancing around, he kept backing through his modest studio apartment as he took in the small kitchen area, a sink cluttered with plates; the old, broken couch in front of a 4K TV; and the narrow full-sized bed sitting beside his desk; there was nowhere to hide.

Panic rose as the bounding steps closed and the door exploded, the thin membrane of composite wood doing nothing to delay the bull. As fragments of the splintering door flew into the room, Dave turned and grabbed the first thing he could (his ridiculously expensive new laptop) and swung it toward the locked window. The impact shattered the window, and incidentally the laptop—but that made no matter. He took a second to drag the remains of the device, with its dangling monitor, along the jamb to knock out any lingering shards of glass, then dove out of the window moments before the bull caught up.

Dave landed on an awning running along the front of the building and scuttled away as the bull poked its head from the open window and gave out an angry bellow.

"What the ..."

27

Sierra Graham hunkered behind the counter, huddled as tightly into a corner of the guest services bay as she could manage. Tears trickled down her cheeks, and she couldn't stop shaking as she fought to curb her overwhelming panic. How could this have happened? Why did it have to be these horrendous, hulking beasts?

Bovinophobia, they called it: the fear of cows. For years, she'd been ashamed of the phobia, even thought it was silly at times. Not anymore. She was transported back to that nightmarish day all those years ago. She'd been excited to visit the farm. What first-grader wouldn't be? She'd always loved cows—always pointed them out on road trips—so, when she'd had a chance, she'd run out to greet the docile, lumbering animals. But it had all gone wrong.

She shivered, still remembering the excitement as the curious cows pressed forward to meet their young visitor. They were so much bigger in the flesh than they'd appeared from the safety of a vehicle. The excitement drained in a moment, only to be replaced by spiking anxiety, then outright fear, as the walls of flesh closed in around her. Though the cattle hadn't harmed her—had actually bounded away when she'd screamed—it had taken hours to calm her down, and she'd never looked at the large animals the same.

Then she'd gone and married the son of a dairy farmer. Of all the crazy things … Visiting her in-law's farm had always been a chore, but the animals had been safe behind sturdy fences, and she'd never had to interact with them. Every time she'd visited, she'd fought down her own fear and anxiety—battled not to pass on her phobias to her girls so the twins could have a relationship with their grandparents.

Where were her daughters? Why hadn't they come for her?

Sierra took a deep, quavering breath, drawing in on herself.

She was alone now. Had she always been alone? No, there'd been that young employee—the one who'd been urging her to flee into the store (as if that would happen—as if she would venture out from her hiding place). Where had the girl gone? Oh, right—she'd long since fled. But that was alright, Sierra didn't know her; the girl wasn't important.

Another of the massive animals trod past, hooves clacking against the tile, and Sierra cowered lower, curling tighter into the corner, her panic-filled mind still reeling from the unexpected onslaught of frenzied cattle. Never had she heard of anything like it. The cattle were flooding the streets, not just the streets, but the store. When she'd heard about the mass escape, she'd hoped that little brat, Hailey, would realize it was best to sell, get rid of the horrid beasts, but she hadn't expected this. Were they after her? Did they know what she'd done, what she'd helped to do? Surely, they couldn't; they were just dumb beasts. God's gift to man for meat, milk, and labor.

This couldn't be happening. No way was this happening. Yet the screams and crashes around her seemed to belie that assertion.

Alice huddled behind a wall of greeting cards, peering through a gap in the shelves as the parade of animals drew inexorably closer. She would need to move soon—if she was going to. She eyed either end of the greeting card aisle as she weighed her options. She could either charge across the aisle, toward the exits up front—in full view of the animals—or fade back toward the rear of the building, hidden from the aggressive livestock.

When she put it like that, the choice seemed obvious.

Alice let out a breath and lurched back, hip-checking her forgotten cart. Before she could snatch it, she watched in horror as the cart sailed across the thin aisle and slammed into the next row with a resounding *clang*. An avalanche of useless card stock cascaded from the shelves as she whipped back around and saw an enormous, scruffy, white-faced beast glaring balefully at her. She had but a moment to think before the nearly two-thousand-pound animal charged. Alice dashed toward the far end of the row. She'd only taken a handful of steps before the shelves behind her exploded. She threw a glance over her shoulder, yet she didn't slow as a storm of confetti fluttered around the irate bull—a colorful flurry of wasted birthday wishes, congratulations, and condolences.

Alice reached out for the upright at the end of the row and swung herself around the corner. As she dashed along, she glanced over as the bull plowed through the next shelf of greeting cards, then a third. She paused briefly when the bull's shaggy white face and large downturned horns appeared through the splintering peg board halfway down the aisle, knocking loose a couple of shelves and spilling a wave of themed napkins, paper plates, and party favors to the floor, but quickly shrugged off the sight and darted between the cross aisles, leaving the ill-tempered brute fighting to free itself, bellowing as it knocked more shelves loose and obliterated swaths of composite wood.

Across the store, Zoe and Alex hunkered down next to a selection of licensed retro tees, waiting for the right moment. The girl could hear the chaos around her; the clacking hoofbeats of strutting cattle nearby set her on edge. They hadn't been harassed as they'd followed the divider wall, leapfrogging from cover to cover, one garment rack to the next, one display to the next. And now they needed to skirt around the wall and sneak into Footwear, but they were too close to the main aisle for her liking and the table displays lining the strip of white-tiled floor wouldn't provide much cover. She took a deep breath as she reminded herself there was no hurry. No reason to rush; no reason to put themselves in danger.

Across the wide aisle, people had hidden themselves among masses of colorful clothing. She caught snatches of motion as they peeked out from behind garment racks and displays. Some brave fools wormed their way slowly toward the entrance, while others (considerably wiser) trickled toward the rear, but more stayed where they were, frozen in fear.

She glanced at her little companion. "Be ready."

"Okay," he murmured.

His iridescent stuffed animal shimmered in the store's harsh light. "You like your Narwhal?" she asked idly, trying to distract the boy.

"Yeah," Alex murmured. The single gold-trimmed ivory horn folded against his cheek as he tightened his grip on the toy.

"What's his name?" she asked.

"Narby."

"Narby, huh? I like that—"

Zoe raised a finger to her lips as the clack of hooves thudded closer. She ducked further into the folds of fabric advertising ancient video games and TV shows as a pair of animals trotted by—an extremely muscular pearl-colored cow and a wide ivory steer that had swaths of color smeared along its sides: brindled with hints of cinnamon, mahogany, and chocolate. Despite the sheer terror of the moment, she took a second to appreciate the natural beauty of the mottled pigmentation.

Then, there was a sudden clatter and a curse across the aisle, followed shortly by the crash of shattered glass and the crack of splintering wood as display cases were overturned and trampled by charging cattle. People broke, fleeing in every direction as the pair toppled carousels and displays, trashing decorative jewelry and handbags under their hooves.

Several customers flowed past, making a break for the front of the store and the exit as the cattle were distracted. But that wasn't Zoe's goal. She grabbed Alex's hand, intent on using the commotion for the opportunity it was.

"Come on!" She whisked her cousin around the corner and ducked among rows of shoes, fading back into the maze of shelves as, across the aisle, panicked screams and cries of alarm still rang out in the midst of the destruction.

Lexa led Aiden and Chloe around the wall of pain medication, then bolted for cover, huddling behind an endcap. In front of them stood the abandoned pharmacy—closed and shuttered for the night. Her eyes were drawn to the rolling shutters as they moved to the next row, then the next. She couldn't help but imagine what a wonderful hiding place it would make. The pharmacy might be the safest place in the store. Could they get in? Perhaps they could return once they'd reunited with Zoe and Alex.

In fact—

Lexa glanced down at her son; the four-year-old was struggling to keep up. And Chloe, she'd lapsed into an uncharacteristic silence. Though she was loath to part with them, it might be safer for the two to hole up in the pharmacy. She considered it; considered leaving them with an employee so that she'd be free to rush across the store to the others.

However, as they rounded the corner at the far side of the pharmacy, a scruffy, balding man emerged into an alcove just beyond the cross aisle. Thin boxes overflowed from his arms, spilling onto the tiled floor as he jerked to a stop. Lexa threw an arm in front of her niece, tightening her grip around Aiden's wrist. Though he wore red, he was definitely not an employee. The boxes of prescription medication tumbling to the floor, along with the momentary look of shock playing across his masked features, told her all she needed to know about the man's motives.

Wide eyes narrowed as he glanced around and shuffled over to a cart to deposit the armload of medication. Tucked in the recess, he was hidden from everywhere but the corridor where they stood. His eyes took her in, then her little boy, and spent way too long scanning Chloe. Lexa's heart raced as the man stared at them. Blindly stumbling upon a crime could prove disastrous.

"What do you want?" he said in a deep, gruff voice.

Lexa pointed down the cross aisle. "By."

The man leered at them, his eyes crinkling and his mask twitching, then he jerked his head to the side. "I'm not stopping you."

Lexa glared at the man for a moment, before urging a petrified Chloe to move on. She followed on Chloe's heels as they slipped past the man. He didn't move, nor take his eyes off them until they left his sightline. As much as it pained her to do so, Lexa left the man to his crime. It was none of their business. They had much more important matters to attend to.

"Mommy, is dat man sick?"

"Yes, honey, I think he is."

28

Z oe and Alex crept along the row of footwear until they came to another gulf of gleaming white tile. Huddling against a shelf, Zoe glanced around the corner just as a horned, muddy-red monstrosity turned off the main aisle. Its long, droopy ears; a prominent flap of loose skin running below its neck; and other things jiggled as the humped beast ambled their way.

She snatched Alex and backtracked, hiding in a gap between the shelves of footwear moments before it passed.

"I want my mommy," Alex whined. Zoe understood; she wanted hers too.

Once the clacking hooves tramped past, Zoe took the chance and dragged little Alex from their hiding spot. Holding her cousin's hand tight, she hunkered against a rack of shoes, teetering at the precipice between carpet and tile. She glanced left, following the stout animal as it lumbered away, then right, to search for any oncoming cattle.

The coast was clear, as long as the wall of beef didn't turn back. Her chest tightened as she squeezed Alex's tiny hand and took the chance to sprint across the aisle. The few steps across the gulf of tile seemed to take forever, and then they were diving behind a rack of sports bras. She sighed deeply, peering at the hefty muddy brown animal as it continued along the aisle, oblivious of their flight.

Then Alex's hand slipped from hers and, before she knew what he was up to, he'd darted back into the aisle. She gaped in stunned silence at the running boy for a moment, then launched herself after him. What the hell was he doing?

As she bounded across the aisle, the boy ducked down between the shoe racks and grabbed his sparkling stuffed animal off the coarse carpet. She caught up to him a moment later and snatched her cousin up, then whirled around and glanced toward the retreating bull, praying it wouldn't turn. However, as she pivoted, her sneaker let out an ungodly screech, and she froze. Why did she have to wear them to the viewing? Though, on reflection, dress shoes or heels would have been worse.

As she idly contemplated her footwear choices, the beast stopped, its skin wobbling as it started to turn. Zoe sucked in a breath, remaining frozen, perched on the edge of the aisle, afraid any further movement would draw the beast's eye that much quicker.

Hours passed in the second it took the animal's horned head to come around. For a split second, its eye seemed to widen. Had it seen them? Would it charge? Did they stand a chance? Then it came to a stop, lowered its head, and charged into Baby/Toddler. Screams shattered the silence as the animal plowed through racks and tables. Zoe used the distraction, sprinting back across the aisle into Activewear. She ducked back behind the rack of sports bras and glared at the petrified boy on her lap.

"What were you doing?" she asked breathlessly. "What were you thinking?"

"I wost Norby." Tears leaked down the boy's face. "He's my sponsibeewity. I haff to keep him safe."

Damn. She sighed, letting her shoulders slump. He was right; she had told him to keep the toy safe, but she hadn't meant … but how was he to know?

"You can't run away from me like that," Zoe gently chided, hugging her cousin.

"Cause I'm your sponsibeewity?" he asked.

"Yes, you're my responsibility," she agreed, wiping the tears away.

"Promise me you won't run off like that again."

He looked down. "I pwomise."

Lexa edged back to the corner and peered around. They'd just darted across the southwestern edge of the wide main aisle ringing the store. A pair of dreaded bovines still wandered aimlessly ten to fifteen rows away. However, it seemed neither the white-faced rusty bull nor the proud golden-red bull had noticed them.

She let out a long breath, drew back around the corner, and rested her head against a sign, considering her options as she idly gazed across to the rows of grocery aisles. She caught the mixture of relieved and incredulous looks from curious people peering around displays and corners. They probably thought she was crazy, dragging a couple of kids—one a four-year-old boy—deeper into the store. She couldn't blame them. But she didn't have the luxury of just sitting back, hiding among the stands of fresh fruit and vegetables or along the back aisle of meat and cheese. She had to somehow find her other baby boy.

Once her ragged breathing steadied and her heart had eased to a more manageable level, she brushed off the accusing stares and started to lead her charges along the row of food storage containers.

Then a loud voice broke the eerie silence dominating the store. "They're gone …" For half a heartbeat the words hung in the air, and she could almost swear there was a massive sigh of relief audible in the surrounding silence even as she tensed. That wasn't right. They weren't gone. She'd just seen them not a minute before, strutting along the main aisle. And now this person was saying they'd gone? *How reckless. How dangerous.* Then the voice resumed. "… the parking lot is clear!" The voice echoed in the stillness. "They've moved on!"

Oh.

"He's right, they're gone," a feminine voice rejoiced.

There was a moment of silence following the revelation, then chaos reigned in the store again. People flowed out of the woodwork to join the mass exodus heading for the emergency exits. Lexa drew her party to a stop, hugging the wall of Tupperware as people scrambled past.

As was inevitable, it was only seconds before the sudden wave of movement and sound caught the cattle's attention. The already frenzied crowd went crazy as the animals pounded toward them, screams erupting as they charged into the fray of scrambling bodies, then came the cries of pain and wails of agony.

The hysterical crowd swarming for the emergency exits lost all sense of decorum, and people collided, slamming into and knocking each other over as the cattle bulled through the crowd. People took no consideration as they shoved their neighbors aside. One towering, well-dressed man was knocked into a mountainous display of energy drinks; the cliff of aluminum crumbled, toppling to the floor. Blue and chrome cans rolled, fizzing across the tile as the red logo spun around and around. People tumbled over the scattering cans, sprawling over each other, then shoving one another aside as they fought to regain their feet.

Lexa gaped openmouthed at the chaos until she was blindsided. The sudden impact ripped her charges from her grasp, throwing her to the floor and snapping her teeth shut. Her jaw ached as she looked around for the source of the collision. What had hit her? A fastidious-looking woman in her mid-forties, apathetic or oblivious to her carelessness, fought to regain her feet, tripping over Chloe, who'd been knocked aside and lay sprawled in the center of the aisle several feet away.

Her wide-eyed niece looked around at the mass of feet plummeting to the tiled floor as she tried to scoot out of the way. A moment later, there was a loud *crack*, and a scream escaped Chloe's lips as a large foot fell upon her outstretched hand. Chloe moaned, snatching the limb back and cradling it protectively against herself as she rolled over and curled into a fetal position.

Lexa took a moment to find her son, the only one who hadn't been knocked down by the collision, and tucked him into a gap in the bottom shelf between the megapacks of reusable containers. "Stay here for Mommy." He nodded through his tears before she scrambled toward her niece.

As she was crawling closer, an enormous blue-trimmed, black sneaker came swinging out of nowhere, connecting with the side of Lexa's head. Stars exploded across her vision, then fizzled away nearly as quickly. Fighting the sudden wave of vertigo, she forced herself to inch toward her niece.

The same person who'd kicked Lexa in the head tripped over Chloe's prone form and tumbled to the tiled floor with a *smack*. The compact man kicked out at the cowering young girl, cursing her for being underfoot, but luckily, he was too far away and didn't strike her in his anger.

Lexa scrabbled the last few feet to her niece and grabbed Chloe, who tensed in her grip, then started struggling—likely afraid she was being attacked again—as Lexa pulled her against the shelves.

"Chloe, it's me," she soothed, "it's Lexa."

Chloe calmed as Lexa hunched over her, using her own body to protect the slender girl. A few more guests scurried past, then Lexa lifted her niece into a sitting position. Silver-blonde hair hung across her face—a portrait of panic and pain—as she gazed wide eyed at her aunt, cradling her right arm against her chest. The pinky and ring finger of her right hand had already started to swell, and the skin was a kaleidoscope of color as the bruising deepened.

"Let me see." Chloe relaxed her grip on the extremity and looked around, peering over Lexa's shoulders. "That doesn't look too bad," Lexa lied, hoping to calm the girl.

"W-where's Aiden?"

"Oh, he's right over th—" Lexa's voice failed as her eyes fell upon the empty spot where she'd stashed her son.

Chloe watched as Lexa sprang to her feet, seeming to forget

about her injured hand, as she raced back up to the head of the row, scanning each of the grocery aisles along the way for her wayward child. She dashed out into the middle of the wide main aisle, glancing around, ignoring the bulls ransacking the produce aisle across the way.

Pain numbed Chloe's mind as she struggled to her feet, cradling her broken hand as her aunt doubled back, trotting toward her.

"I don't know where he went," Lexa fairly shouted. "He was right there. I only took my eyes off him for a moment."

"Shh! Shh! Not so loud," Chloe hissed, glancing down the produce aisle as she held out a palm to stop her aunt's frenzied babbling. "We'll find him. He couldn't have gone far."

Her aunt paced to the end of the row, checking each grocery aisle as she went, then glanced down the cross aisle that ran along the far side of Kitchenware. She ran a hand through her hair—the shiny, black strands sliding between honey-beige fingers—as she took a step back and spun to scan the rows of snack foods packed along either side of the opposite aisle, then dashed to the other side of the divider wall and looked down the next cross aisle.

When Chloe limped over, Lexa grabbed her arms. "We have to find him." Her voice had lost some of the volume, but none of the stress.

"We will, we will."

Pained dark eyes gazed into hers for a moment, then Lexa nodded.

"I'll search Kitchenware, you check"—she waved vaguely at the dividing row—"the next department ..." Lexa didn't wait for an acknowledgment before turning and striding away, glancing down each row as she went.

Chloe limped toward Storage Solutions, still cradling her hand as she took in the various fabric hampers and baskets, a wash of muted colors displayed along the outer row. There was no sign of Aiden. The cross aisle extended nearly halfway across the store, giving her a clear view all the way over to Childrenswear where she could make out the boy's graphic tees advertising this and that: whether it be a character, show, or movie. Various products lay scattered over the tile, but no little boys.

The first aisle held a variety of molded plastic and wicker baskets on one side, and plastic storage towers on the other. She saw no hint of him among them. "Aiden," she said as loud as she dared. She didn't want to draw the attention of the bulls. Cliffs of plastic loomed to either side of the second aisle: rows of large storage bins, tubs, and containers, housed one inside of another with the lids stacked on top. The massive tubs continued along the next aisle, accompanied by scores of smaller containers. And the next held boxes of particle board shelves and organizers.

Chloe was about to start for the next aisle when a stack of red, white, and blue plastic cups tumbled to the floor on the far side of the wide aisle at the end of the row. Her breath caught, sure a bull was about to charge around the corner and mow her down. After a few seconds, no bull had materialized.

Could it be ...? Chloe edged up the aisle, hugging the right side, her lungs burning as she continued to hold her breath; she couldn't be too loud—didn't dare draw its notice—but she had to find out.

A slight movement drew her attention, then her little cousin's straight black hair came into focus, peeking out above a table laden with patriotic merchandise. The oxygen-depleted air escaped from her lungs, and she took in a fresh breath as she stepped forward. Chloe paused and looked back. "Lexa!" she called, not much louder than a stage whisper. Chloe glanced down the row and saw the boy peeking out from behind the table.

"Co'we?" came Aiden's little voice.

She couldn't leave him hanging; she threw off her caution and called, "Aunt Lexa."

Moments later, she heard the staccato *click-click-click* of Lexa's footsteps as the woman crossed over from Kitchenware and dashed into view, stopping halfway across the aisle when she caught sight of Chloe and turned toward the girl, hope and fear amplified in her frantic expression.

Chloe pointed down the aisle to the child as she announced, "I found him."

"Mommy?"

Her aunt bustled past, relief flooding her face. Chloe followed, limping and cradling her injured arm as she watched the tearful reunion; Lexa drew her son into her arms and gave him a big squeeze. When Chloe staggered up, Lexa lifted her head and thanked her, then really seemed to take in her injuries for the first time. Her aunt's eyes flicked to the cradled arm, then to her awkward shuffling gait. Her eyes widened, and a hand flew to her mouth.

"I'm so sorry … I didn't even think …"

Chloe waved off her aunt's concern, despite the intense pain.

"No. No, I'm so sorry," Lexa said, sweeping the decorative dinnerware off the edge of one of the tables, letting it shatter against the tile floor. "Sit down. I'll see what I can do." Lexa turned, then spun back, pointing at little Aiden. "And you, mister, don't even think about leaving Chloe's side."

The little boy hunched his shoulders, nodding as Chloe wrapped her good arm around him. "Don't worry Lexa, I have him."

Lexa returned moments later with an armload of supplies, but her eyes were locked on a spot behind them. Chloe followed her gaze, glancing over a shoulder at the crimson double doors standing half open at the far end of the aisle.

"I think I know where we're going next," Lexa said, then set about dressing Chloe's wounds.

29

Moments after the anxious call from Hailey's stepmom, Rodger was on the radio, apprising the sheriff of the situation. Though he hadn't been seeking explicit permission to assist Hailey and her family, the sheriff had still given it. All hands were needed; the switchboards were flooded with calls, and everyone was busy trying to wrangle the cattle along Main Street.

They'd abandoned Graham's 2500 and the stock trailer, with the meager handful of stray cattle they'd been able to round up, and Hailey had joined him in his patrol car while her dad and uncle followed, clinging to his bumper. Her Dakota gleamed in the rearview mirror, flickering red, blue, and purple in the deepening gloom. The siren's banshee wail accompanied them as they rocketed down University. They'd breezed past the chaos at the stockyards, only catching hints of the desperate struggle inside as people scrambled to regain order. It would still be hours before they got everything sorted out.

As he came up on the shopping center, they were greeted by a stream of cars pouring from the lot. He slowed, pressing a button to alternate his siren—*woop-woop*. While the traffic pulled aside, attempting to make room for him, the turn-in was still a mass of congestion. He'd never slip through.

Instead, Rodger created his own route. Slowing even more, he aimed for a section of two or three vacant parking spaces in front of a fast-food restaurant sitting on the south side of the entrance—one of many eateries along the street front. The cruiser bounced over the curb and across the sidewalk, flinging its occupants back and forth. They landed with a huff. Thank God for seat belts. Behind them, Hailey's old Dakota followed, heaving off the ground, shooting sparks as something on the undercarriage scraped against the curb and a lone hubcap launched across the lot, disappearing into the gloom. Her little truck wasn't made for that.

As Rodger skirted a restaurant famous for its roast beef, he took in the chaos inside. Sheets of plate glass once ornamenting the building were now a sea of glinting shards scattered along the sidewalk and across the lobby. Inside, an agitated mud-spattered bovine strutted around, scattering the lightweight aluminum chairs and shoving tables aside. What guests that hadn't fled huddled behind the counter with the employees.

Rodger applied pressure to the brakes, about to render assistance before he recalled his mission. He glanced over at the passenger seat; Hailey's pallid face was a mask of worry. On the way down, they'd heard from Hailey's stepmom again and learned the cattle had swept into Bullseye. Instead, Rodger called the situation in as he continued around the side of the fast-food joint, then launched his cruiser over another curb and across the island. He landed a moment before a lone car whipped past and he was forced to swerve—where had they come from? As if the flickering lights and wailing siren weren't enough. His hand shot out and alternated the siren again before he accelerated, arcing through the empty outer edges of the vast lot.

Lexa led her charges through the dismally utilitarian storage space running along the side of the store. She'd never really put much thought into what the stockrooms of one of these megastores would look like; but if she had, she wouldn't have been too far off. Dim halogens flickered and buzzed overhead, barely illuminating row after row of steel-reinforced plywood shelves lining the far wall, packed with mostly useless items.

When they'd first entered the stockrooms, Lexa had hoped to find something useful, anything. She'd seen old episodes of MacGyver and knew some of the myriad cleaning products they'd passed could be mixed into any number of chemicals, but she'd never excelled at chemistry, nor had she gotten around to reading *The Anarchist Cookbook.* After checking the first several shelves thoroughly, she'd resigned herself to merely glancing down each row as they'd passed—so far, the best she'd come across was a kid's baseball bat.

She glanced back at her niece, making eye contact with the limping girl. Chloe held the bat in her uninjured hand—it wasn't much of a deterrent, but it seemed to make her feel safer. She wasn't looking too good. Lexa had used some patriotic towels to make a crude sling for her arm, but her niece's hand looked terrible. While she was putting on a brave face, Lexa could tell every step pained her—there wasn't much she could do about that. Once her husband and daughter arrived (what was taking them so long?) and they found Zoe and Alex, they'd be able to take care of Chloe.

They came to a crimson door leading into the next section and Lexa reached out, shoving the door open. Then she froze. A blonde cow stood with its back to them, in the middle of the aisle ahead. She sucked in a short breath as her mind whirred. What could she do? How had it gotten back here? She'd just about decided to retreat and was bringing her foot back when the door finished its arc and slammed into the far wall. The resounding *clack* echoed through the chamber, startling the animal and eliciting a deep low.

No time for thought. No time to consider. Lexa grabbed the kids—eyes locked on the turning beast—and tugged them ahead into the nearest alcove. Had they made it in time? Had it seen them? She didn't think so, but she couldn't be sure. How good was their vision? She wished she'd paid better attention when her daughter was going on about the animals.

Lexa led Chloe and Aiden halfway along the aisle before

pulling them down behind a product-laden metal cart. As the trio huddled behind the crimson cart, she edged an eye around the mound of cardboard, watching, waiting while the clattering hoofbeats approached. They listened as the *clack, clack, clack* of the hardened keratinous hooves drew near. She ducked back, glancing over at her charges, and held up a finger; they nodded—Aiden's eyes wide in terror, Chloe's pallid face a mask of pain and panic. Holding her breath, she waited, eyes clenched as the plodding hoofbeats grew louder, then paused at the head of the aisle. Anxiety filled her chest, and she braced for the inevitable attack, but it was only moments later that the footsteps passed by.

It was another minute before she allowed herself to move. She slipped off her shoes, then edged to the end of the row and peered around the corner. The massive fair-haired shape was on the other side of the open crimson door, plodding along the way they'd come. She gave it another half minute as the beast continued, periodically pausing to sniff or prod one of the rows, then darted across the aisle and eased the door shut.

When Rodger neared Bullseye, their progress was reduced to a crawl, but the lights and siren did their job, cutting a path through the people milling about the parking lot. He stood on the brake as they overtook the family's dark blue SUV, Hailey flinging open the door and hopping out before he came to a stop.

"Hailey, hold up," he ordered as he bounded out of the cruiser. "We can't just go rushing in there." His words froze her in her tracks, but from her expression, she was none too thrilled. Rodger released the twelve gauge from its center console mount, eyeing it for a moment, then peering into the broken glass doors, and deeper as if seeing through the walls.

"Rodger, my family's in there." Pointing wildly toward the store, Hailey's voice carried over the screech of worn brakes rising from her Dakota as her dad slewed to one side behind them.

"All the more reason to be prepared. Come on," he said, circling to the rear. "Now!" he called when she hesitated.

She huffed, but followed him.

Rodger flung the SUV's rear door up, then laid the shotgun on the lip of the trunk and dove for the gun vault.

"What are we waiting for?" Caleb growled as he and Hailey's dad joined them at the cruiser. "Chloe's safe in the stockrooms with Lexa and one of the twins, but I still haven't heard from Sierra, and now Zoe isn't answering her phone."

"Hold on a second," Rodger grunted as he ripped one of the gun vault's drawers open. It could be dangerous to bring too much firepower. And more dangerous to abstain.

"We don't have time. We have to …" Caleb trailed off as Rodger's AR-15 appeared. "Ohh … be right back." His eyes followed the man for a moment as he jogged back toward the Dakota, but he didn't have time to figure out what Hailey's uncle was up to.

Rodger laid the rifle beside the shotgun, then dug out several magazines and a couple of boxes of double-aught buckshot, stacking them next to their respective weapons, then pulled out a tactical belt and a vest. Rodger eyed the firearms lying side by side on the lip of the trunk for a moment before scanning Hailey and her dad.

He passed the belt to Hailey—its twin ammo pouches might come in handy—then nudged the shotgun toward her. "You take the Remington. I've seen you shoot." She nodded and wrapped the belt around her waist. "Careful, it's loaded." She looked at him, raising an eyebrow as the buckle clasped together with a pronounced *click*, a wry smirk spreading across her pretty face. Perhaps that had been unnecessary. He smiled and shrugged in apology.

After that, Hailey grabbed a box of shells, and, as she stuffed them into an ammo pouch, Rodger claimed the tactical vest and slipped it over his rumpled uniform. He was snugging spare magazines in the vest's pockets when Caleb trotted back over with an old lever-action rifle.

"I brought this … I almost forgot."

Rodger winced; he didn't like the idea of firearms in untrained hands. "Let me see it." Caleb dutifully handed him the rifle, and Rodger looked it over; Graham kept his firearms in excellent condition. He couldn't see a reason not to let the man carry it, besides they might need the firepower. "Fine …"—he handed the weapon back—"but you stay at the rear. Only use it as a last resort."

After Caleb nodded, Rodger scanned his companions, eyeing each in turn. The brothers were stained with sweat, in disheveled slacks and dress shirts. Though Hailey's jeans and plaid shirt were rumpled and stained, she was as stunning as always, looking badass, sporting his police-issue Remington twelve gauge.

"Stay behind me and remember, the building isn't cleared. Watch your firing lines—there could be people anywhere inside."

He waited for nods before taking off.

30

Forgoing caution, Rodger set a fast pace as they dashed to the entrance, barely pausing for the automated outer doors to slide open before rushing through the vestibule, then toward the crumpled glass doors. Fragments of glass disintegrated beneath their feet as Hailey followed on his heels through the inner door and slowed. She barely noticed his quick sweep of the entry; her gaze was locked on the destruction. She took in the shimmering fragments of glass strewn across the floor, the scatter of toppled carts, and the swaths of darkening crimson splashed across the white tile. Were her cattle responsible for this?

A sudden noise to the right drew Hailey's attention. Her head whipped around and she scanned the debris peppering the coffee bar's tiled floors: scores of crushed, matte white paper cups, a blend of gourmet coffee grounds spilling from torn bags, and a body. Hailey's eyes had locked on the unfortunate soul—a plump, middle-aged lady—when an enormous pale shape surged from a recessed section in the shop's corner.

The blood-spattered white bull looked like a macabre Jackson Pollock—crimson on cream—as it snorted and tossed its head, confronting the fresh intruders in its domain. She swung the shotgun around, backpedaling as she took a split second to scan the area behind her target; and it was lucky she did. Pale faces had been peering out from behind the counter, riveted by the new commotion until they saw her gun's barrel sweeping toward them. Heads disappeared, and people screamed. That didn't help—*when had screaming ever helped?* She pushed the thought aside. There were more important things to occupy her mind.

That the massive animal—easily two-thousand pounds—was polled held no comfort; an animal of that size could merely bull right over them. Horns or not.

And it was an imminent threat; it only took a split second to recognize the signs—it was about to charge. She didn't have time to weigh the pros and cons. She didn't even have time to call out, barely had time to move as the animal bellowed and lowered its head. She continued edging backward as her gun finished its arc. The moment her firing line was clear, she yanked the trigger.

Unfortunately, her first shot went wide, and colorless pockmarks bloomed across the red walls as buckshot ripped into the sheetrock. The bull roared and lunged. She backpedaled two more steps as she racked the weapon, allowed a split second to steady herself, took a breath—held it—then shot again. The bull's bellow mixed with the roar of the shotgun as the stream of metal pellets hurtled from the weapon. Continuing to backpedal, she chambered another shell, then the bull took one more step and collapsed.

For the next few seconds, only the poor animal's labored breathing broke up the stillness, then the dam broke; a dozen people scrambled from behind the coffee shop's bar and out of its backroom. The trickle became a flood as people poured out from the restrooms and surged across the aisles. Several thanked Rodger or her before they escaped into the deepening twilight.

Caleb held his breath as he scanned the faces flowing around him, barely listening while Rodger dealt with a barrage of questions from the roiling crowd while assuring them that help was on the way. As the crowd thinned, worry built in his heart.

He'd still seen no sign of his wife. Where could Sierra be? Why hadn't he been able to get ahold of her?

And she wasn't the only one he couldn't reach. Why had Zoe stopped answering? What did that mean? It seemed his obstinate daughter hadn't been without her phone since she'd gotten the thing; now, when he needed her, she wasn't answering? Last he'd heard, she was nearing the stockrooms at the rear of the store. She'd wanted to head up front to join him when she learned he was close, but he'd insisted she continue to the backrooms. He couldn't help but wonder if he'd done the right thing. If anything happened to his baby girls …

No, he shook his head. His girls and his wife would be fine. They had to be. He pulled out his phone and tried Sierra again. A loud ringtone erupted on the other side of the cart bay, behind a counter labeled Guest Services. His wife's ringtone.

"Sierra," he called, rushing to the secluded space. "Sierra!" He peered over the divider wall, saw her, then dashed around the corner and through a set of swinging doors. She'd wedged herself into a corner of Guest Services, half hidden behind a stack of open-boxed items. "Sierra," Caleb pushed the rubbish aside and crouched by his wife, shaking her shoulder. "Sierra, honey, are you alright?"

She looked up. "Caleb? Caleb, is that really you?" Her eyes teared up as she fell into his arms. "Oh, it was awful. They were everywhere," she whined. "Are they gone? I just couldn't …" His wife stiffened when Hailey peered over the counter. "You! This is your fault. Why did you have to keep those brutish animals?"

His niece's already pale face drained of color at the venomous words.

"Honey, now isn't the time for recriminations," Caleb said, cradling her as he pulled her to her feet.

"But it is … it is her fault—"

He stroked her hair. "Come on, we've got to get to the girls."

His wife's eyes widened, and her confusion melted away. "The girls! Oh my God, where are they? Are they okay?"

"They're fine …" He continued stroking her hair as he

assured her Chloe and Zoe were okay—hoping it was true. He was having a hard time reconciling the bundle of anxiety in his arms with his strong, resilient wife. Was it the cows? He'd known she had an aversion to cattle, had noticed the apprehension swelling whenever she was around them, but he had no idea it was this bad—

"Hailey!" An unfamiliar voice drew everyone's attention. A red-shirted young woman emerged from a section of girls' clothing, glancing both ways before darting across the main aisle. "Hailey! Oh, thank God, you're here." He didn't recognize her right away—the stream of crimson oozing down the side of her cheek didn't help—but he'd seen those familiar features not long ago: those large eyes, that round face. She clearly worked here; her shirt told him that much. But he couldn't …

Then it hit him. "Cassie?" Caleb asked, confused by the teenager's presence.

"Kaycee, actually," she corrected.

His eyes flicked to her name tag, which read Macie now.

"Right, sorry," He blinked at her. "You work here? I thought you worked at the feed store—"

"Young miss," Michael said, cutting off their immensely important conversation. "We could use your help. My wife and sons are somewhere in the building. Could you help us find them?"

"I-I dunno." Her eyes flitted to the desperate faces, then to the armed deputy who was prudently scanning the store for any sign of danger. She turned to Hailey. "Your—?"

"My mom and brothers. Twins."

"The cute little Asian boys," she said, nodding.

"You've seen them?" Michael asked.

Kaycee bit her lip but continued nodding. "I'll come, as long as I can stay between them." She pointed at Rodger and Hailey.

"What's the quickest way to the stockrooms?" Michael asked.

"Through softlines"—Kaycee pointed straight back through the sea of childrenswear, and Michael took off. The rest of them had no choice but to follow.

Rifle at the ready, Rodger crept through the middle of softlines as the employee had called it. A divider wall draped with vibrant clothes ran the length of Childrenswear to one side, effectively covering their flank. It was the other side that concerned him. The racks of clothes blocked his sightlines more than he would have liked. There were plenty of blind corners where cattle could pop up without warning. This wouldn't have been the route he would have chosen; he'd have much preferred taking one of the wide main aisles.

Rodger glanced back at Hailey's dad, wishing the man would have waited. But no, Michael had rushed ahead, leaving no time for discussion; he wouldn't be deterred. Not that he blamed the man. Not with his family in danger. They'd raced after him; it was that or let him go by himself, and he doubted that would have gone over well with Hailey. Even though they caught up quickly—just inside of Girlswear—it was all the deputy could do to slow him down and convince Michael to let him take the lead. After that, he'd assigned Hailey to cover their rear as they edged through Childrenswear—girls, then boys.

Rodger took it slow; much slower than Michael would have liked, as he continually reminded him. But they were already taking enough chances—the stakes were already too high. It wouldn't help anyone if they blundered into the path of a rampaging bull.

What a mess this day had turned out to be. And it wasn't over yet. He'd called for backup as soon as he'd seen the scope of the destruction in the store, but it still might take a bit; most of his comrades were spread out, still trying to get a handle on the chaos sweeping across their—once idyllic—small town.

The nerve-racking journey through Childrenswear couldn't have taken more than a couple of minutes, but it felt much longer. When they approached the wide, tiled aisle on the other side of boys' clothing, Rodger paused, glancing around. A wide swath of destruction ran through the middle of the baby and toddler section ahead: tables overturned, shelves dashed to pieces, and clothing racks shattered. Not to mention the mass of pastel fabric strewn across the floor. However, there was no sign of the animal that had torn through the space.

To the left was a clear view all the way over to the grocery aisles; numerous items lay scattered across the tiled floor, and a large black beast was currently tussling with a gray linen sofa—the frame shattering as he watched. And to his right, two large animals stood among the broken heaps of particle board and warped metal that had made up some of the displays in women's clothing.

Neither the black bovine down the way nor the two critiquing the modern trends in women's fashion appeared to be an immediate threat to anyone. He couldn't just kill them indiscriminately, could he? No. He couldn't. Besides, there could still be people around—all it took was one stray bullet—he wouldn't risk it unless it was an emergency.

He glanced back at the faces of those following him, reading the reluctance on some and the impatience on others. He nodded, then dashed across the aisle and slipped between the remaining racks of tiny outfits. They were almost there. The toddler's section wasn't very wide; he crossed it in seconds, then slipped between a divider full of strollers and the wall of diapers as the flooring morphed back into gleaming white tile. Finally, he would have clear lines of sight—

He'd just started to bring his rifle back up when the cross aisle came into view, and he froze, face to face with a well-built russet bull a little more than a yard away. He felt the air leave him as he stared into the enormous beast's piercing black eyes. The barrel was still pointed down around the animal's knees; he didn't have a clean shot. All he could hope to do was wing the massive animal—but that wouldn't be enough to stop it. Not from this distance.

He inched the barrel up as fast as he dared while they stood there, staring at each other. Hours passed—or was it seconds?—before he sensed his companions drifting closer, then an ear-splitting scream erupted from one of the women. Rodger hunched his shoulders at the ungodly wail, cowering as he jerked the weapon up, keeping his aim locked on the enormous bull. But it didn't matter; even as he was preparing to shoot, the thing started, letting off a peeved snort as it lurched back, then turned. Before it strutted off, it tossed a final disdainful look over its shoulder and snorted again.

Hailey materialized at his right shoulder; weapon locked on the retreating brown bull. The air exploded from Rodger's lungs, and he took in a deep breath as he lowered his barrel and glanced at her, then around at the crowd behind them. Hailey's dad stood with an arm flung out in front of his brother and his sister-in-law as the young employee cowered behind him, peering around his shoulder—Caleb himself held his rifle down to the side and was cradling his pale-faced, hyperventilating wife.

Rodger glanced back at Hailey and whispered, "Why didn't he attack?"

Hailey sighed and shook her head. "Could be the weapons. Could be our number"—she glanced back at Sierra and smirked—"or, it could have been that impressive bloodcurdling scream."

For Rodger's money, it was the scream. He shrugged it off, then started to pick their way back to the stockrooms. Only a little bit longer.

31

Lexa crept up to the next aisle and peered around the corner. This new room was much larger—positively cavernous— the rows of storage lining the side wall stopped at the wide cross aisle, only to be replaced on the other side by much longer rows that stretched dozens of feet back to the far wall. While the possibility of finding something useful among the array of products increased exponentially, so did the danger.

She let her eyes trace the cliffs of particleboard and steel shelves ahead, until they fell upon another crimson door, left slightly ajar at the end of the long row. They were getting closer, but that only seemed to increase her anxiety. She hovered there, straining to hear the slightest indication of movement. Cattle could be tucked in any of the more than two dozen aisles—they were wide enough. And if one popped out, there wouldn't be much time to hide.

She'd been moving much slower after coming across that last cow, fighting her growing apprehension. Why was it back here? The beast's sudden appearance had heightened an already unnerving atmosphere, and she hadn't been able to extinguish her worries. Would Zoe and Alex be safe? Why couldn't she get ahold of them? Had Zoe's battery finally run out? The girl had said it was running low. She'd insisted her husband and daughter go after Zoe and Alex first. Even now, they were somewhere in the store, working their way toward the stockrooms. They just had to find each other.

With effort, Lexa shunted the concerns aside. She sighed. There was nothing for it; they couldn't stay here—she had to get to her other baby—nor could they retreat. Not when an animal lay waiting for them along the path they'd taken.

Retreating to the backrooms had seemed like such a good idea after Aiden's little disappearing act—he would get a stern talking to about running off—and Chloe's injury. Lexa had plumb run out of patience for any more surprises out front. Now, she was wondering if the stockrooms hadn't been another big mistake. It seemed like mistakes were all she was making as of late. Would they have been safer if they'd stayed in their car? The way the cattle were pushing the vehicles around, it had seemed perfectly reasonable to flee into one of the stores—who would have thought the livestock would follow them inside?

Zoe sat with Alex at the back of an aisle, huddled in a pool of shadow on the raw cement floor. One of the overhead lights was offset, expending most of its illumination on the shelves above, leaving only a diffuse scatter of light that cast the row in perpetual gloom. It was a stark contrast to the gleaming showroom out front, but it would fit her needs perfectly until her dad came.

Unfortunately, she didn't know when that would be; her phone was missing again. Zoe couldn't believe it—she could have hit herself. For the life of her, she couldn't figure out when or how she'd lost it. They'd been about to dash across the aisle to Menswear when her dad called, letting her know he was almost there and asking if she'd seen her mom—what had happened to her? Zoe had offered to meet him up front; anxious to fall into her dad's arms. She'd been almost taken aback when he'd snapped at her: "No!" he'd said, "No, it's not safe. Continue on to the storerooms." She'd done as he'd asked—ordered.

It was only after she'd found a good hiding spot that she'd gone to call him—tell him they were safe—and found the phone missing. She'd backtracked, creeping to the head of the aisle (much to Alex's consternation), and scanned the bare concrete floor leading to the crimson double doors. There'd been no sign of the thing, and she wasn't about to return to the showroom floor. So, she'd given it up and pulled a crimson cart across the head of their aisle, then dragged her little cousin to the end of the row, where they'd hunkered down, wedging themselves behind a foldout metal ladder, snug in between two of the utilitarian shelving units.

The minutes stretched as she waited for rescue. Why was it taking so long?

A loud bang reverberated from the enclosed space, stripping her breath and causing her to jump. Moments of panic crawled by, then came the sweetest sound she'd ever heard. "Zoe!" Her name! And not just from her dad. No, it was a chorus of voices, all calling her name.

She let in a shaky breath and responded, "Back here."

Footsteps echoed off the bare concrete as the group approached. After rising, she dashed towards the ladder and slammed into it. It was stuck, locked in place across the aisle. She'd hoped it would prevent any cattle from following her in, yet now it was impeding her own escape.

"Zoe, where are you?" Her dad asked.

"Back here. The ladder's stuck"—she shoved the offending contraption and it let out a loud *clang* but didn't budge—"I can't get by."

A police officer—the same deputy who'd had eyes for her cousin at the viewing—dashed in front of the row and peered down. A second later, her dad appeared, shoving the cart aside. She caught the worry melting from his face a moment before her mom, and then Alex's dad shoved into view.

"Daddieee!" Alex yelled jubilantly, then banged against the ladder.

Zoe grimaced apologetically at them all, a prisoner behind aluminum bars.

A small figure shoved between her parents and uncle. "Move aside … I've got this." For a moment, she thought it was Hailey. But the crimson-shirted teen—an employee—couldn't have been much older than her. She trotted over and lifted a catch with her toe, then the ladder folded up, twisting aside.

"Daddieee!" Alex yelled again, darting to his dad as she rushed to hers.

Zoe fell into her parent's embrace. Tears in her eyes, she asked, "What took you so long? Where were you?" She soaked in their comforting assurances, then sniffed. "Where's Aunt Lexa? Where's Chloe and Aiden?"

"They're our next stop," they assured.

When Rodger bulled into the next section, he flung the red door aside and it slammed into a shelf with a *crack*. Hailey winced; if they hadn't known they were coming before, they knew now. She banished the thought as she followed on his heels and took in the room.

Towering shelves loomed over them to either side of the aisle, tightly packed with an abundance of useless items. She only afforded the merchandise a glance. To the left, flat screens stretched up toward the ceiling, shelf after shelf of TVs lining the wall; some ridiculous sizes—who needed a seventy-five-inch television? On the opposite row, harsh light bathed scores of large colorful boxes; within a couple of seconds, she spotted everything from bookshelves to baby cribs wedged among the steel-reinforced shelves. Then her gaze moved beyond the cross row and traced either side of the aisle all the way across to the far wall. The pallets of soft drinks, mounds of toilet paper, and stacks of diapers lining the shelves further on failed to make a lasting impression.

"Hang back while we clear the room," Rodger said.

Glancing back, she could sense her dad's reluctance, but he held back, Alex cradled in his arms. Her eyes drifted to Zoe, standing with her parents—she couldn't begin to articulate the relief she felt at having found both Alex and Zoe safe and sound—then to young Kaycee hovering off to the side, weary of intruding on the family, yet unwilling to stray too far. She barely had a moment to consider it before Rodger set off.

Hailey followed as he skirted the shelves along the end of the row, pausing at the next aisle, then the next as they worked their way to the rear of the store while scanning each row for any threat. Nothing. She glimpsed ramparts of chrome-trimmed grills, box fans, and inflatable swimming pools along the shelves, but no cattle.

As they approached the final row, her eyes strayed to the massive cardboard compactor sitting along the right-hand side of the north wall and idly wondered how many boxes that large green monster swallowed every day. Then they rounded the corner, and the loading bay came into view on the far side of an expanse of bare concrete. Her gaze traced the open rolling door—a gaping maw in the darkness, letting the warm night air drift into the building—then slid over to the cluttered mess that was Receiving: cardboard boxes were heaped atop lines of crimson carts flanking either side of a worn conveyor. The entire north wall was strewn with half-full pallets holding tons of boxes waiting to be sorted.

But none of that mattered for long; a movement across the room snatched her undivided attention.

All thoughts of cover and caution fled from Hailey as she spotted Lexa, Aiden, and Chloe edging along the aisle halfway across the room. It was her mom. Lexa scooped Aiden into her arms and dashed forward. As Hailey rushed to meet them—shotgun dangling uselessly to one side—she might have vaguely heard Rodger's voice admonishing her for failing to clear the room. But it didn't matter; it was her mom.

"Mom!" The look on Lexa's face at that tremendously important little word, the love that swelled within her eyes, nearly broke Hailey's heart. How could she have spent all these years despising this woman? What was wrong with her?

32

Rodger couldn't do much more than take a cursory scan of the room as he followed close on Hailey's heels. His eyes searched for any hint of movement among the shadowed rows and alcoves. If it were up to him, they'd have taken it nice and slow, thoroughly scanned the room before dashing into the center; but Hailey wasn't even responding to his words. *Civilians.* He shook his head but didn't put up much of a fight when a smirk threatened to crawl across his face.

Within moments, the two women met in the middle of a cross aisle, Hailey crashing into her stepmother's arms and enveloping the woman and her little brother in a mighty hug. The enthusiasm of Hailey's reunion with her stepmom was surprising—he'd never gotten the impression either of them really liked each other.

Rodger tore his gaze from the reunion and scanned the length of the aisle, stopping on the crimson double doors leading to ... *what is that?* Rodger craned his neck. *Electronics? Yeah, looks like it.* After making sure the aisle was clear, Rodger stepped away, letting his eyes roam across the rest of the cavernous room, seeking out any movement among the shadows along the north wall on the far side of the conveyor. When Hailey's aunt and uncle rushed past him, his gaze followed for a second as they reunited with their daughter. He couldn't help but notice the pain etched into the young blonde's face. He'd head over and administer first aid in a moment; after he finished clearing the room. His eyes flicked back to the lines of six-wheeled hand trucks—also known as U-boats—where had he heard that? The rounded handles on either side of the metal frame made it look like a U (hence the name). Some of the crimson carts had a shelf across the middle and some didn't, but most were stacked high with cardboard boxes.

His eyes strayed out into the gloom of the open loading bay. Why was the door open?

When Hailey and her stepmother peeled apart, the movement drew his attention, and he watched as they rushed back over to reunite with Hailey's dad and other little brother, who was struggling in his father's arms, calling for his mother.

Rodger finally lowered his rifle, giving the room one more look. Still seeing no threats (no cattle), he turned and took a step toward Hailey's cousin—he couldn't remember her name; he'd have to remedy that. He hoped to spend more time with the family.

He'd only taken a couple of steps when the double doors from Electronics banged open, startling their little group. Rodger brought his rifle up as he whipped around toward the threat, only to be confronted with a gray-faced thirty-something in a crimson polo. The man—he had to be an employee; probably a manager—slid to a stop as he recognized the barrel of a rifle pointing at his chest. The man's eyes widened, a mixture of fear and confusion. Rodger quickly shifted the barrel aside and moved toward the man, holding out a palm.

"W-what? No," the man said, his breath coming in ragged gasps. "Wh-why?" His brow crinkled, and then he shot a look over his shoulder.

"It's okay, sir." The man didn't seem to hear him. His eyes jumped to all the people standing around the storeroom, then back.

In the silence, a small voice drifted over, "That's Steve, he's an assistant manager."

Rodger glanced back and saw the young employee; apparently speaking to no one in particular—what was her name? It ended in …cie. Stacy? Gracie? Lacey?

Rodger shook his head and returned his attention to the man as he stepped forward. He needed to calm him. "Steve," Rodger said. The manager's gaze whipped back over and focused on him. "I'm a dep—"

"No," Steve blurted. "Y-you're not supposed to be here." He shot another look over his shoulder. "Wha-what are you doing here?"

Why did he keep sending glances over his shoulder?

"It's okay, we're not—" he never got to finish.

The manager interrupted. "No! No, you don't understand. They're headed this way."

"Who—?" A jerk of his head stopped Rodger in his tracks. *Oh.* Rodger's blood went cold.

Then he saw a hint of movement through an oval window in the crimson door. Unsettled murmurs rose behind him as Rodger brought his rifle back up, frantically waving for the man to move away from the door. Steve had only taken a few steps when the double doors exploded open, tossed from their hinges.

In that instant, Rodger was forced to do some quick thinking. The man was in his line of fire, but he was also in the path of the rampaging bulls. He could step aside to get a bead on the incoming cattle, but even if his rifle had a full auto setting—it didn't—he wouldn't be able to stop the stampede before it reached the man. Steve was as good as dead unless—

Rodger released his rifle, letting it fall aside to catch on its sling, as he lunged forward to meet the fleeing manager. He slammed into the man, shoving him into the nearest aisle as screams erupted behind him. He was able to push Steve out of the way and the man toppled into a pallet of paper towels.

Rodger wasn't so lucky. Pain bloomed across his ribs as a massive white shape slammed into him. Gravity switched off and he lurched to the side, thrown across the aisle. When the deputy crashed into the shelving unit's steel frame, there was a mighty *crack*, and agony flared across his forearm. Then gravity returned, and the floor came up to meet him and darkness followed.

Chaos reigned as the cattle swarmed through the doors. All around Hailey, people, her family, scrambled. It was hard to recall exactly what happened in those next seconds. She'd glanced back toward her family and caught sight of young Kaycee snatching one of her brothers, then yelling something at her parents. Apparently, they were moved by her words, or else the theft of their child, because they turned to follow. Movement across the aisle proved to be one of her cousins, Zoe, scrambling behind her parents. Chloe, on the other hand, was shaking her head as she backed away. Her skin seemed ghastly pale in the harsh light.

She'd shouted something to the girl—she couldn't recall what.

Hailey was still rooted to the spot when Rodger snapped into action. She watched in awe as he shoved the manager out of the way. Then, in growing dread as he was hit by the pale bull and launched across the aisle. His impact with the opposite shelf was accompanied by a resounding *crack*, then he fell. But he didn't get back up, didn't move.

Rodger. Hailey gasped. Rodger just lay there on the ground as a big white bull approached. Those viciously sharp horns were inching ever closer to the unmoving deputy—looming over him. Was he unconscious—dead? She shuddered as she pushed the thought away. No time for that.

Either way, Rodger's peril snapped her out of her shock.

She had to get to him—she had to hurry—but with the cattle flooding into the stockroom, streaming down the aisle, she couldn't take a direct route. So, she created her own. Hailey bounded forward and jabbed her shotgun's barrel between several boxes packed on the shelf, then let it roar. Blotches of crimson bloomed on the pale animal's chest and side, and it jerked away, roaring in agony. Hailey didn't stop. She racked another shell, then sent another spray of lead into the looming bull, then another. She didn't stop firing until the thing collapsed in the middle of the aisle, luckily not on Rodger.

She didn't know how many rounds she'd fired, didn't concern herself with it at the moment; Rodger still hadn't moved.

Hailey shoved a hand into the gap between blackened and torn cardboard and raked the boxes aside, sending them tumbling across the floor. She took a moment to glance back; her dad was safe, peering out from behind the compactor, worry etched on his face—*clever hiding spot.* Across the aisle, her uncle seemed to be holding his own as he protected his family; his gun cracked as fast as he could cock the lever and fire.

Seeing her family was safe was all it took.

Hailey dove into the space she'd just cleared, shoving the remaining stock aside as she wormed her way toward her fallen friend—hopefully, he was interested in being more than a friend. Or had she read that wrong? In the seconds it took to shimmy through the shelf, she was able to get a clearer picture of her uncle's undisciplined fire. While he'd been able to strike a few unlucky animals, most of the projectiles were pinging off the shelves and sending sparks flying from the steel frames. Despite his abysmal aim, his wild fire seemed to be keeping most of the rampaging animals away from him and his family.

Ignoring her uncle's terrible aim, she continued crawling, shoving the remaining boxes aside. They went cascading over the side, into the aisle beyond—hopefully, nothing too heavy would land on Rodger. Hailey slithered over the edge and tumbled out into the aisle. She brought her gun up and blasted another curious bovine as it edged closer. While she didn't bring it down, the deep-red splotches blooming across its flank were enough to deter the creature. Keeping the barrel aimed at the oncoming herd, she scrambled over to Rodger's prone form.

Hailey didn't have time to check Rodger's wounds. She had to get him out of the middle of the aisle before the cattle's attention returned to them. Hailey shuffled over and kicked at a stack of boxes piled along the bare concrete floor—whatever was in them was smashed as the boxes deformed—and she was able to clear a spot under the shelf. Hailey snatched the side of Rodger's tactical vest and pulled him into the hole she made. Her hand came away stained red. God, how badly was he hurt? She couldn't think about that. She settled on a knee and brought her barrel up, taking a bead on the rampaging cattle as they surged past.

Mercifully, the animals' attention hadn't returned to them; they seemed to have other concerns at the moment. A pained bellow echoed through the room and one of the cattle went down. Her eyes flew to her uncle; he'd finally gotten one. But instead of a look of triumph, fear clouded the man's face. Dropping the colorful steer only seemed to anger the others, and they lost their hesitance. He'd drawn the ire of one particularly large animal; it charged—moments later they met, then her uncle disappeared and his rifle clattered across the raw cement.

When the screaming began, Chloe had edged away from the commotion and, incidentally, her family—who'd dashed over and ducked behind the nearest shelf.

Not again! Where had all these cows come from? Why were they here now?

She flinched, eye twitching, as her dad started shooting, the—*crack, crack, crack*—of the old rifle mixed with the pained bellows, grunts, and roars. At first, it seemed her father's shots were enough of a deterrent to keep the cattle away from their side of the room.

They flowed past, some continuing outside, bounding out of the open loading bay door, while others broke for the opposite side of the aisle where the employee had pulled her little cousins, aunt, and uncle behind a massive bit of machinery. Unfortunately, she couldn't make it over there—not with the cattle between them.

The roar of Hailey's shotgun snatched her attention. She was shooting between the boxes; cardboard disintegrated and the bull that had thrown Rodger bellowed, then went down. She hoped Rodger would be okay. The next moment, her cousin dove into a gap she'd cleared on the shelf. Maybe she could do that. Chloe glanced across the aisle. Her mom cowered behind her dad, but her expression had gone beyond fear; it seemed as if terror was hewn into her features. Her sister was still huddled behind her parents, but Zoe was waving at her. Motioning for her to come over, mouthing words that were lost in the thunder of crashing hooves and the crack of gunshots. Still, Chloe edged backwards; she couldn't bring herself to do anything else. She just kept falling back.

Then came a pained bellow, and the smack of meat hitting the concrete. Chloe followed the sound and saw a multi-colored animal writhing on the floor; then came a roar and a blaze of brown fur and her dad was knocked aside. Her eyes widened as his rifle tumbled across the bare concrete floor. But it was the massive ebony animal coming her way that broke her paralysis.

Chloe whirled and bolted, fleeing from the charging slab of beef. She took a couple of bounding steps toward the cluttered receiving station, then squeezed and scrambled between and over the line of thin handcarts, sending stacks of cardboard boxes tumbling to the floor. She managed to clamber atop the conveyor right before the massive animal struck. The huge black bull slammed into the line of handcarts, some were knocked aside while others warped beneath its weight, all while more cardboard boxes spilled across the floor and were crushed under hoof.

Her thin dress provided little protection from the metal rollers digging into her skin, but she paid the discomfort no mind as the animal lunged at her repeatedly. Metal clanged as the beast drove the carts into the conveyor's metal frame again and again. A gap opened as handcarts continued to bend and warp or were pushed away under the assault. It wouldn't be long before the bull created enough space to get at her.

Chloe kicked at the conveyor, pushing herself along the rollers. When her dress caught along the frame, she didn't pause. She just pushed that much harder to get away from the raging bull. A rip in her dress was nothing, no matter how expensive it'd been.

But her effort was for naught, as the animal only followed, moving a few carts down, then trying to push its way toward her. Its previous efforts had opened gaps in the line of handcarts, so the bull's head wedged itself uncomfortably close on the first try. Chloe pushed herself a few feet further on, but the bull just followed, slamming into a new section of carts and wedging itself even closer to her.

Oh, God. Oh, God.

Then came the most welcome sight ever.

She'd been so focused on the rampaging bull in front of her—the tunnel vision so complete—it took her a moment to recognize a rifle barrel slipping in from the side. A second later, there was a resounding *crack*, and then the massive ebony bull crumpled to the floor. Oh, thank God. Someone had come to save her. Chloe's eyes whipped over to her savior, and her mouth fell open. She stared, dumbstruck, at the person holding the rifle.

Zoe! Her sister Zoe. Zoe, the adamantly vocal vegan, held the smoking rifle. The expression etched on her sister's face was familiar, but the disgusted look—the look she normally reserved for all those she held in contempt for not accepting her worldview—wasn't aimed at Chloe, but at the bull.

"Y-you," Chloe stuttered, "you shot it."

Zoe's gaze traveled to her, losing its disgust, morphing into—was that concern?

"You shot it?"

"Yeah?" Zoe's brows knit as if she hadn't a clue what Chloe was on about—

"But … You shot an animal … You killed an animal, for me?"

"Of course I did, you doof," Zoe rolled her eyes. "You're my sister. I love you."

Chloe opened her mouth, but she couldn't think of anything to say to that, so her jaw just bobbed a few times.

"Close your mouth. You look like a fish." Zoe mimicked a fish gulping air. Yep, there was her sister. But Chloe couldn't help seeing the relief in Zoe's eyes and the smile creeping across the side of her face. "You're just lucky it wasn't that one," her sister pointed to the dead animal in the aisle. The white steer had an assortment of rich mottled browns smeared in a triangular shape across its side. "I liked that one."

Again, Chloe didn't know what to think. Was she serious?

Then Zoe's smirk deepened, and she held out a hand.

After a final loud crack, the last bull collapsed to the floor. Michael peered out of his hiding spot to make sure the others had all fled through the open loading bay, then Kaycee slipped out from behind him and darted to the large rolling door. With the push of a button, the door came rattling down and Michael finally felt it was safe enough to slip out from behind the massive compactor.

Several animals lay about on the floor, dead or dying. But they weren't important.

"Hailey!" he shouted. It had been a while since he'd seen or heard from his daughter. What if …

"Yeah!" Her face appeared in a gap in the shelving. "Dad, I'm alright … but Rodger's hurt. He's bleeding pretty bad." She ducked back down, and Michael heard the squelch of a radio, then his daughter's voice returned. "Officer down! Officer in need of assistance at …"

He let the words drift past him as he rushed out into the open expanse of concrete, taking in the rest of his family. Lexa and the boys had followed him out, but were still right beside the compactor, ready to slip behind it at a moment's notice. Zoe was helping Chloe, lending her a hand as the blonde shoved out from between the row of twisted hand trucks. A bull lay at their feet, and it was Zoe holding the rifle. Okay, he'd have to revisit that one later.

"Are you two, okay?" he asked, pointing at the girls. They nodded and assured him they were. From the look of his young niece, he had his doubts, but he pushed them aside. Despite the pained grimace and noticeable limp, she was on her feet. Across from them, his brother wasn't so lucky. Caleb lay on the floor, moaning as Sierra fussed over him. Michael paced over. "Caleb, are you alright?"

His brother groaned, but he lifted his head and nodded. "I think I broke some ribs."

Sierra pushed his shoulder. "Lay back down," she chided. "You could have internal bleeding." She turned to Michael. "I'll feel much better once we get him checked out."

As Michael nodded, the manager slipped out of an aisle looking toward Hailey and Rodger. "I'll get a first-aid kit," he said.

"What was that?" Michael asked as he darted past. "Where did they come from?"

The man paused, reluctance flooding his features. "I was trying to get them out of the building."

"You led them back here? Why would you do that?"

"… there wasn't supposed to be anyone in here. I checked." Steve stayed for a second longer, then bolted back to meet Kaycee, who'd grabbed a pair of first-aid kits from the back wall. He took one and dashed back toward Hailey and Rodger. Michael let the man go—there'd be plenty of time to discuss it later—and followed Kaycee to his brother's side, joining his nieces.

It wasn't long before they heard the cry of an ambulance approaching from behind the loading bay.

Epilogue

Sheriff Johnson let out a sigh of relief. State police were flooding into their small town at last. With them and the scores of locals who'd shown up to assist, they were finally getting a handle on this thing. The locals had sure stepped up. To the west the cattle had been rounded up in the town square—even now the cowfolk were keeping them corralled as they whittled away at their number, slowly loading them in stock trailers. On the east side of town, the cows had been herded up and driven into the college stadium—she could just imagine the angry calls she'd get for that. And south of Main, they were using a water retention park.

What a mess. There were several casualties, including Hire, and scores of other injuries. Word had come down that Sandrich had been injured as he'd helped the Grahams reconnect. He and Caleb Graham were both stable and on their way to the hospital. If she'd realized the situation in Bullseye had devolved so much, she would have sent more deputies to assist. And there were at least a dozen other businesses that had been struck by the cattle: shops, restaurants, and even an antique store—it was a disaster zone. She couldn't picture the sheer scope of the destruction; the cost had to be in the millions.

And they still hadn't gotten everything in hand. A new

situation had come to her attention, so she'd left the operation at University and Main in the capable hands of Baines and recruited some residents, a few of her deputies, and a score of state police to follow her. Social media had been inundated with posts about their town and the 'Great Escape', which was how she found out about the scores of cattle that had slipped through their cordon, bulling south through the college campus, then along fraternity row. From the video, it appeared to be mostly black and white cows; Holsteins; Cracker Farm cattle, the Grahams' cattle. What was up with them? They seemed to be sticking together for the most part, which was good.

And they weren't being subtle. There'd been reports of cattle running along a road south of the campus. Calls of cows tearing through the elementary grounds—further south. Cattle crossing the road at Randall—south again. It didn't take a genius to recognize the pattern, so she had her little force shoot straight down University. They'd eventually catch up with the herd and cut them off.

As they closed in on the high school, they received another call reporting that the cattle were tramping through the school's campus. She racked her brain, trying to figure out what was going on. Were they going somewhere?

When her contingent finally caught up, they cut through the high school parking lot, approaching without lights or sirens—no need to spook the animals. A single row of massive LEDs lit their path to the far side of the lot where the ag barn shone like a beacon in the night. The herd crowded around an open rolling door to one side of the barn. The harsh light bathing the cattle near the structure diminished further out until the outer edges of milling animals were almost lost in the gloom.

Her people fanned out in front of the barn, crawling to a stop before they got too close.

Creak—Snap.

Johnson paused. What was that? It was hard to make out in the surrounding clamor. She tried to push past the chorus of lowing cattle; beyond the clanking and squealing of opening doors as stock trailers were hurriedly unloaded; and through the neighing of horses as they were led out and saddled. And there it was, the curious sound—metal clanging against metal. Then there came another creak and a snap. And the lowing increased.

What were they doing?

She pushed the thought aside, and had started to relay instructions when another loud crack echoed through the night. Something tickled in the back of her mind, but she dismissed it and focused on the troops.

The riders were mounting up and spreading out, cantering slowly around the edge of the milling herd. Luckily, the cattle hadn't moved. They were still preoccupied with something in or around the ag barn. She couldn't help but wonder what.

In the several minutes it took for everyone to get into place, there were several more bursts of cracking metal. She paid them no mind, deciding to let the cattle do what they wanted until it was time. Finally, the last person took his position—he'd had to take a circuitous route on his way to the practice field's main gate. As soon as the gate creaked open, the wranglers went to work. At first, the herd paid the mounted riders no mind. Standing resolutely in place as the cowfolk tried to steer them away. There was one final *creak—snap*, then the herd let themselves be slowly driven away from the barn.

She didn't notice at first, but after a moment, she caught hints of smaller animals hidden among the herd as they allowed themselves to be steered toward the field. Calves. And not just Holstein calves, but a blend of different breeds as well.

"Well, I'll be …"

Jamison Roberts

A fan of horror, Jamison Roberts particularly enjoys the monster movie, the creature feature. In Horns, his most recent foray into writing, Jamison shares his love of the genre with this parody of Sharksploitation films and novels. Prepare for Cowsploitation.

A proud member of the Cherokee Nation, Jamison is a native of Tulsa, OK, and attended Tulsa Community College, where he studied videography, photography, and graphic design.

JamisonRobertsBooks.com